HEART MEN
a novel

In Liberia, the saying goes, 'If you go swimming alone in the night, a [1]jinna could catch you, [2]mahmie watta could catch you, and a heart man could catch you. But only with the heart man, and this has been true all over Liberia, death is certain'.

1   A sinister spirit
2   An evil mermaid

Also by Ophelia S. Lewis

2014 - Dead Gods (HM2)
2013 - **Good Manner Alphabets (*how to be a super polite kid*)
2012 - Montserrado Stories
2011 - The Dowry of Virgins & Other Stories
2009 - **A is For Africa
2009 - **The Good Manners Alphabet Book
2007 - Journeys (a collection of poems)
2004 - My Dear Liberia—Recollections

**CHILDREN'S BOOK

Readers of this book are encouraged to contact the author with comments; email *(ophie2020@yahoo.com)* personal website: (*www.ophelialewis.com*), twitter (*@ophie2020*), facebook (*www.facebook.com/ophelia.lewis*)

Village Tales Publishing provides traditional publishing services and turnkey services to individuals that seek to successfully self-publish and promote their books. We handle all aspects of publishing—editing, design, production, marketing and order fulfillment.

Please visit our website: www.villagetalespublishing.com

HEART MEN
A NOVEL

OPHELIA S. LEWIS

VILLAGE TALES PUBLISHING

NORCROSS, GEORGIA

ISBN:978-0-9753609-6-5
Library of Congress Control Number: 2010943342
Available from Amazon.com and other retail outlets

Available in eBook
eISBN: 978-0-9753609-9-6
Available on Kindle and other devices

Printed in the United States of America

Dedication

In my brother's memory
Jenkins N. Lewis, Jr.

Acknowledgement

To the Almighty God, whom I give all the glory! I thank God for giving me unbelievable strength to do what seem impossible.

This novel was a challenge to write, as writing is challenging for me. However, I'd like to thank the people who helped make it possible.

My mother, Jeanette Lewis-Harding, thanks for your immeasurable love that has always steered me towards a better direction. I am grateful for your support; the best siblings on earth—Aaron, Marie, Veronica, [Jenkins], Joann, Derick and Akitee—thanks for always carrying me on your shoulders…what a journey, guys!

Nadia Assaf-Cole, my best friend, thanks for everything through the years; Donald and Mariah Ross, I will forever be grateful for your love and support. You have a special place in my heart.

Alex, Benealda, Dannie [Daniel & Mary], Derek, Dre, Duke [Elijah], Emmi, Farah, Kaela, Kevin, Kia, Kiema, Lemriel [Logan], Mahdia [Brandon & Ethan], Malik, Manseen, Mylaeka, Nebe [Camyrn, Kai, Christian, Kayden & Cobi], Nostelda [Emmet & Aostelda], Pia, Razaq, Sydni and Tara [Ryan], I love your enthusiasm.

Pastor M.I. Harding, Helena "Mama" Yancy, Nazira Dendy, and Delores Maxwell, I am grateful for your love and support; you've always come through when there's a need; the crew at Bella Beau Marketing & Publicity, LLC,—Aostelda, Benealda, Iesha, Lemriel, and Manseen—you guys are the best. Thanks for a job well done. Portia Langley, thanks for working magic with your camera.

Prelude

August 2010
CRIMINAL INVESTIGATION DIVISION (INTERROGATION ROOM)
MONROVIA, LIBERIA

"THE man was screaming as we chased him from the road, and then towards the beach. He was strong and in great shape, but he was beginning to get tired. As he ran, he continued to yell, 'Somebody please help me!' He knew we were going to kill him."

Charles Sarpo spoke directly into the micro recorder set before him, without a trace of remorse. He paused and looked up at the CID officer, his mind running a mile a minute, waiting for the go-ahead to continue his confession. The officer hit the pause button.

"Quite frankly, I think the government should kill all of you and let God sort out the innocent ones," he snarled. He then pushed 'record' and ordered Sarpo to continue.

Sarpo hesitated, knowing this was a mine field where he had no choice but to tread. It had turned out to be a very rough night.

"We were not far behind now, chasing him, until he could go no further," Sarpo continued, hesitantly. "He looked over his right shoulder, clearly frightened, that's when Duo Boley grabbed him and knocked him to the ground.

"Johnny continued to yell. 'Stop yelling and we will not kill you,' Boley lied to keep him quiet. It was pitch-dark, but I could see tears roll down his face. I felt sorry for him…he had seen my face and I could not let him go. That would present a terrible problem for us. You see, I knew Johnny was new in the area. I was told he had just come to Monrovia from the country. I told the medicine woman that he was strong, he had a good body and I knew that he always walked by the beach on certain days, a shortcut home. Based on my description, Ma Wonde told me Johnny was perfect for what she needed."

Sarpo paused.

"Go on," the officer snarled.

"I hit him with a hard blow to his head and his eyes rolled back," Sarpo continued, showing Johnny's head tilting backwards. "As Johnny lay dying, he was asking, 'Why are you killing me? Aaaaah my people, I got children. My wife is waiting for me at my home. They are all waiting for me.' I could feel his strength leaking away, even as he was pleading. Then Boley swung his cutlass high and chopped down, as if he was in the thickest jungle bush, as if he was cutting a tree with a single stroke, clean and hard. Blood splattered on us as the man's flesh and bone parted. Johnny's blood was quickly soaked up by the sand, leaving dark red stains.

"Do we have to clean it up?" I asked Boley. He shook his head, 'no' and assured me the ocean water would wash it away.

"I stripped off Johnny's clothes. Duo Boley was the one that did the butchering while I held the flashlight, removing certain parts and telling me to place those parts in special containers."

****

In Liberia, the saying goes, 'if you go swimming alone in the night, a jinna can catch you, mahmie watta can catch you, and a heart man can catch you. But only with the heart man, and this has been true all over Liberia, is death definite'.

Monday morning headline read:

RITUAL KILLING?
MAN FOUND DEAD ON SUGAR BEACH
CID INVESTIGATING

The article in the Liberian Journal Constitution left no doubt that it was a case of ritual murder. The coroner report made clear the raw, violent, and animalistic murder of the body found, missing some parts such as the skin around his eyes, pieces of flesh from behind both ears, and portions of his nose. The report also stated the deceased was missing his heart, both of his kidneys and his male sexual organ. Every local newspaper reported that ritual killings were happening in all regions of the country again.

Ritual murders had been reported each decade in Liberia, but it was in 1979 when the last ritual murderers were executed by hanging. After that, reports had yet to cover the discovery of bodies. The arrest of a few suspects occurred, although trials of the accused never came about, until the disappearance and discovery of Johnny Bono's body in 2010.

Since the end of the civil war, change is the reason for the openness in the Liberian press and the new Justice Ministry; there is no wonder. One explanation for the freedom of expression and of the press that characterizes these days is the World Wide Web—the internet.

The new Justice Ministry had established a system for both investigations and prosecutions of so called Serious Crimes, crimes defined as crimes against humanity, ritualistic torture, murder and sexual offenses, especially against women. Investigative power was allocated to the Serious Crimes Investigation Unit, the SCIU, made up of the CID and the MPD, who were under the supervision and direction of the Office of the Attorney General. To make things as easy as possible, the SCIU was given access to expertise and foreign resources to perform their job satisfactorily. After an arrest, the defendant is charged and brought into the court system at the Temple of Justice to have his or her case heard. A judge, ten jurors, three alternate jurors, the prosecutor, witnesses, the defendant, and his lawyer plead their cases.

Transparency had also been in place, for change sake, so those cases the criminal justice system tried were open to the public. In other words, those who did not believe change had come to Liberia had no excuse not to attend in order to get an idea of how things were proceeding these days in court. If the defendant is convicted, he or she goes into the corrections system—prison or capital punishment.

Liberia had not abandoned capital punishment, so the death penalty, groaning under the weight of change, was still carried out by hanging.

Chapter One

GIA was wearing a short black patent-trimmed cutout dress, soft and rich in hue. She looked fabulous as she walked through the crowded party in a pair of Jimmy Choo Gilbert pumps. She noticed this amazing man looking at her from the other side of the room. Their eyes met for a brief instance, but not to look too forward, she turned away. Every few minutes, they caught each other's gaze and each look was different from the last. First, it was playful, and then, intervolve; finally sultry and seductive.

Now, he could not keep his eyes off her. She was far too mysterious, far too beautiful. He raised his eyebrow and gestured as if to say, 'May I join you?' He continued to look at her and this time, she smiled. RJ could not breathe, he could not speak; he could hardly stand. Suddenly his soul came alive. His heart was racing and his voice inside him was shouting, 'If you do nothing else in your life, don't let this magnificent woman, this soft tender miracle, slip through your fingers'.

"I want you to meet somebody," Osei's voice startled him.

"What…," RJ said, absentmindedly. In that brief moment of distraction, he had lost sight of her. "What did you say?"

"I'd like you to meet somebody," Osei repeated, handing RJ the glass of wine. "They are out of red, so I brought you white."

"White is good, thanks," RJ murmured and took a sip. "Damn, where did she go?"

"Where did who go? Boy, are you out of it this evening," Osei laughed. "What's going on? This is a Christmas party...we are here to relax and have fun. Please...don't tell me you're on a case."

"No, I'm not. I thought that I saw somebody I knew," he lied.

RJ continued to comb the crowd hoping to find her.

"What was it? Yes, I almost forgot. I want you to meet somebody," Osei said again, then signaled that RJ follow him.

They wind their way through the crowd recognizing familiar faces and expressing holiday greetings to people they knew and perfect strangers alike. Then RJ spotted her.

"That's her," he said to Osei.

Osei stopped to look.

"That's her over there... the woman in the black dress," RJ carefully pointed without drawing attention. "Man, is she wearing that dress!"

"Can you believe it? That's who I want you to meet," Osei said and chuckled. "Come on, you'll like this one."

They hurried their steps to the two women standing.

"Gia," Osei called softly.

When she turned and faced them, RJ's heart nearly stopped. He was right, she was strikingly beautiful. Shoulder length brunette hair, hazel-green eyes and wearing red lipstick like a super model on the front cover of Sports Illustrated Swimsuit Edition. The dress was a size ten, Versace, a modern design in fine Italian wool with patent leather details and a dramatic cutout back giving it a sense of gracefulness; just the right elegance for the evening.

"RJ, I'd like you to meet Gianina Ricciola," Osei made the introduction.

Gia held out her hand.

"Miss Ricciola," RJ greeted, stressing the 'miss'.

"Miss," Gia also stressed, and then said in Italian, "L'anima, ha fortunatamente spesso un interpretatore...un interpretatore unconscious, ma ancora sincero...negli occhi."

"Whatever you just said, sounds lovely...but not as lovely as you look," RJ charmed. "Now tell me, what did you just say to me?"

Gia smiled.

"The soul, fortunately, has an interpreter, often an unconscious, but still a truthful interpreter... in the eyes," she translated without a hint of accent. "You may call me, Gia, for short. Everybody does."

"Gia... what a lovely name," RJ charmed. "I'm RJ... everybody calls me RJ."

Everybody chuckled.

"And you are?" Osei asked the woman standing with Gia.

"Paola," she introduced herself with a strong Italian accent, and then added, "Would you please excuse me. I better find my husband and join him. Gia, please, call me tomorrow and we can finish the conversation," she winked and walked away.

"And, I better find my beautiful wife, Ama," Osei joked with a thicker-than-usual British accent. "You two chat while I find Ama," he said and walked away.

Gia wasted no time continuing their conversation. "Your parents gave you the name RJ, or is that an initial?"

"It's Robert Jenkins Douglas, the third," RJ said, sounding diplomatic. "But, I like RJ instead. It gives me my own identity."

"Your father must be an important man."

"No, not really... he used to be; now he's retired."

"From...?"

"You ask a lot of questions," RJ joked. "Don't tell me...you are a journalist."

"No," she said and smiled.

"A lawyer?"

"Nope... now, you have one last guess."

"I got it... CIA?"

They both laughed.

"No, I'm not CIA, although I would make a good agent, my mother would agree. I am a psychologist."

"A psychologist... I must admit, I don't know the difference between Psychology and Psychiatry. Is there a difference?"

"In fact, there is. A psychologist trains in social... developmental... learning, and biological basis for human behavior. A Psychiatrist, on the other hand, goes to four year medical school like all physicians do after graduating from college. I'm into counseling… now, enough about me, what about you?"

"I'm a lawyer," RJ said, "a poor man's lawyer."

Gia had always put up a wall when dealing with men socially, especially the handsome ones. RJ was an eyepopper—ooowee-handsome, with a sculpted physique of an NFL wide receiver—6-2, 215 lb. He looked like the fine guy at the office that every woman secretly has a crush on. That night he had made it over her forbidden wall; he had gotten inside her defenses. Maybe it was the fact that besides his good looks and sensibility, there was a sense of innocence about him. Or maybe it was how he was formal with her, old fashion in the best sense of the word. There was something nicely mysterious about him, something under the surface that pulled at her.

For the better part of the evening they talked about careers, family and the simple things they each liked. Dr. Gianina Ricciola was born in Veracruz, Mexico, raised in California, and had moved to Atlanta after her fellowship at Stanford University School of Medicine in 2006. She had completed her Ph.D. training in Counseling psychology at Stanford the year before. Gia spoke fluent Spanish and Italian, having a Mexican mother and an Italian father. Her only sibling, a brother five years younger, was the midfielder for FC Barcelona soccer team in Spain. RJ had not heard of Dante Ricciola until now, he had more interest in American football, having played in college. Besides, George Weah, the only famous soccer star he knew, had long since retired.

If at all they had anything in common, it was having parents from different countries, both parents in their early sixties, both healthy and trying gamely to enjoy forced retirement. RJ's younger sister, Mellody, was a medical doctor in Rhode Island. His Liberian father, a retired senator, American mother, a volunteer social worker, and Razaq, his fifteen-year-old adopted brother lived in Liberia, where they called home. Throughout high school RJ and his sister lived with Mrs. Douglas' mother in Georgia and went home, to Liberia, every summer. While Mellody attended college and medical school in Rhode Island, RJ stayed in Georgia on a football scholarship at UGA. He had received both his undergraduate degree, a B.B.A. Management in 2000 and his law degree, Juris Doctor, in 2004 from the University of Georgia, graduating Cum laude. He was a strong supporter of women's rights and equality. RJ was happy at Crane & Morton, a small husband and wife law firm with four other lawyers and three staff members, including the owners that were ready to help people in diverse legal matters. He took on two pro bono cases a year for indigent clients.

After that night, they exchanged phone calls over the next couple of weeks. Four calls turned into six, six into eight, but neither of them were really counting, nothing as rational as that. The two needed the thrill of seeing each other again, but time would not permit. Paola had Gia's calendar maxed out the entire month. Once, she had time to squeeze RJ in for coffee, but had to cancel because of walk-ins. RJ understood without a fuss. Then when she finally had time, RJ was in court all day. Gia understood. Their separate careers would have no chance of coming between them, it seemed, putting each other first. Gia liked that. But after her long inward crave, she could not stop thinking about him.

"Paola, please, no appointments this Monday after twelve," Gia said to her best friend who was also her office manager. It was more of a demand than a request.

Then she texted RJ to tell him that she was free the entire afternoon on Monday. He texted back he couldn't wait to see her and was eager to look into her hazel-green eyes again.

When he reached Gia's office at noon on Monday, the receptionist behind the desk froze him with surprise. He recognized Paola from the party although it was for a brief moment when they met.

"I'll get her for you," Paola said, smiling. She picked up her receiver and buzzed. "RJ is here," she said, as if she was talking about a long-lost friend, and hung up. "She'll be right out," she winked.

"Thanks," RJ said and added, "It's good seeing you again."

Moments later, Gia came walking through the door.

"So, you're here," she said, seemingly excited. "Don't get the wrong impression… I'm not too busy that I cannot have coffee."

"I bought you something," RJ said and reached into his pocket. He blushed as he took a little stuffed animal out of his jacket pocket and handed it to her.

It was a beanie baby bear, one Gia had not seen before. Her eyes widened as she looked at the name tag, Flaky.

"Happy holidays 2007, to my Gia, from her RJ," she read out loud what RJ had written. "The blue one is impossible to get," Gia whispered, looking pleased. She knew immediately that he had done something special for her.

RJ had remembered from their conversations that night, Gia loves bears and somehow he'd found one she did not have. Most men would bring roses on the first date; RJ brought something she actually likes. Gia looked at the beanie baby and felt her heart melt inside her. She became even more attracted to him.

"I'm ready," she said. Then she instructed Paola to close early, she wouldn't be back the rest of the day.

They walked toward his car, and RJ followed her to the passenger side, opened the door and guarded her by the hand as she got in. He made sure she was safe, shut the door and then got in on the driver side.

"What do you feel like having, honey," he asked.

"What we're having is at my place," Gia said, "If you don't mind."

"Sure... I don't mind at all," RJ said. He had been caught off guard. Was this a good idea? Did it matter? Maybe not, he thought. "Where is your place?"

"1855 Piedmont Avenue, Atlanta."

He made the entry in his GPS before taking off, following every detail of direction offered by the sexy female voice, ending in front of the gated community surrounded in casual elegance. Gia told him the code to enter the gate and then showed him where to park. He got out, opened her door, and freed the way so she led. As they passed through the charming European-style courtyard, he noticed how reminiscent it was of the Old South hospitality. And, he sighed from the moment they stepped through the inviting double French doors into the marbled grand lobby.

"Impressive... yes?" Gia said, reading his expression correctly.

"Yes," he said. "You live here?"

"It's not mine. Dante is hardly here, rather than get a place, I use his. He comes to Atlanta, maybe twice a year, just to visit. We fly down to Florida to see our parents and then he's off to Europe again."

The elevator took them to the tenth floor. RJ stepped into the apartment, his eyes surveying the place. In the living room window, downtown Atlanta was framed like a massive billboard. He took off his jacket and draped it over a chair.

"May I use your rest room? I need to wash my hands."

"Straight ahead, through that door," Gia directed.

Dante had quite a pad in Atlanta. The alabaster white walls offered a sunny atmosphere, high ceilings and large glass windows offering natural light and views. It had a special place with the section of the kitchen, small balcony with views of the city, fine accessories and lighting styles that went with the rest of the apartment. The bathroom had an airy grace of modern Italian design with a contemporized style. The small dining room let out a genuine feeling of warmth, elegant, but not too serious. There were small decorative items that cheered up the place and brought a plus of Italian originality. The set included an oval table with elegant matching chairs.

He returned to find Gia wearing an apron. She was cooking. She had also livened up the atmosphere with Andrea Bocelli's Dare to Live, coming through the Bose speakers.

"If you've never had Italian food, you're in for a treat," she said handing him the glass of red wine. "Or, if you don't like Italian food, I'm about to change that."

"I love food, period… and I'd like to help," he offered.

Gia looked surprised. She took off her apron and tossed it to him. "Here, I'd rather wear the mess."

He caught the thing, without spilling his drink. "I still have it," he said, referring to his college days of playing ball.

"Baseball?" She asked.

"Football… wide receiver."

There was a feeling of comfort and contentment attached to the food they were preparing. Gia had planned this time to study RJ, instead of gaining immediate trust. He fitted too well in her defenses. He had more kitchen skills than most men, thanks to his grandmother. Women found it romantic and RJ was happy to do boyfriend things. He was actually helpful, more than Gia thought he would be. RJ quickly overtook any task seemingly dangerous for her, like taking the garlic bread out of the oven, draining the hot water off the pasta, opening cans; every opportunity to get near her. The smell of garlic bread was wafting through the apartment. Soon everything was ready and the two lovebirds set the table together. Gia lit some candles to set the mood.

They started with antipasto, some minestrone soup, veal, garlic bread and marinated vegetables. For dessert, Gia had prepared some formaggio and frutta.

"Everything is just… wonderful," RJ commented with a smile.

"Thanks to you," Gia replied. "I love good food, good wine and good company. That's the best way to catch up with the important people in your life."

RJ liked hearing that.

"I don't mind being spoiled like this," he admitted.

"That makes the two of us," she whispered, staring at his face.

After they had coffee, to top off the evening, Gia washed the dishes and RJ dried them. When he checked his timepiece, it was eight-fifteen already.

"Thanks for a wonderful evening," he said, reaching for her hand. "We both have a full day tomorrow... I'd better take you to get your car."

"I like this," she whispered, and landed a series of tender little kisses on his cheek. "I really like this."

"So do I."

"I'm serious," she said, leaning on his shoulder. "What happens now?"

RJ looked at her, "I don't want you out of my sight," he replied. "I don't want to be separated from you, ever."

Gia smiled. Clearly, she had found amusement in his words. His presence in her life would add a perfect ratio to her career. Everything had gone prefect. She was enthralled. There was a second date, and a third date, each with a surprise, each with the help of Paola.

Chapter Two

RJ met Gia's parents sooner than expected, she was eager to show off her open-minded parents. Elodea Ricciola hugged him, surprisingly, before Gia could finish the introduction. She was so much like Gia; friendly, open and more beautiful than she came across in the pictures.

"Hi Mom," RJ greeted, "I'm happy to finally meet you in person."

"Él me llamó, mamá. Él me cae bien," she said in Spanish.

"She liked the way you called her, 'Mom,'" Gia translated.

RJ blushed.

Valentino Ricciola was the same. RJ got the feeling he was very Italian; strong with family morals, respectful, and very protective.

When they got to the Ricciola's home, Elodea had prepared an exquisite Italian dinner; stuffed Chicken Marsala, Pasta e Fagioli, Caesar salad and Chardonnay for wine. Elodea's Zeppoli blew him away. For dessert, they had soft, traditional Italian doughnuts dusted with powdered sugar, and chocolate sauce for dipping. RJ soon realized where Gia had gotten her skills in wine and dining. Before taking a place at the table, he sat Gia; pulling her chair out, making sure she was comfortable. Elodea watched it all from the kitchen.

"Él es un buen hombre, Gianina," she said in Spanish, and placed a platter of antipasto and cheeses on the table.

"My mother thinks you're a prince," Gia translated, and added, "English, Ma… please, speak English."

RJ had even suggested sleeping in the guest bedroom, alone, the entire weekend, which he did. Valentino and Elodea Ricciola got to know him over Friday dinner and just about everything about his family. On Saturday, while Gia and Elodea were out shopping, RJ and Valentino sat in the den and watched recorded soccer matches, mostly Dante's games in the European league. Talking to Valentino was easy and the conversation drifted from current affairs to sports to business and his hopes for their daughter's future. RJ liked him. He could see how Gia's family was close knit, like his. He attended church with the family on Sunday morning and he and Gia flew back to Atlanta Sunday evening.

For the next eighteen months, every dawn Gia awaited RJ's first kisses that took the morning out of her eyes. Most Sunday mornings he would walk into the bedroom with a breakfast tray for the two, with fresh-squeezed orange juice, toast and coffee, creamed with coffee-mate hazelnut liquid creamer. Gia was finicky about her coffee, he'd quickly learned. They ate breakfast and watched the news program called, *This Week on ABC with Christiana Amanpour.*

Now RJ's mind was on marriage, settling down. Gia was the right woman, the perfect woman. He wanted her as his wife, not just as his girlfriend. He got up the courage, caught an early flight to Florida, and asked Valentino to please meet him at the IHOP near their home. After telling him how much he'd admired the man, he confessed the real reason for his travel. He'd come to ask Valentino Ricciola for permission to marry his daughter.

"Have you asked Gia?" Valentino asked.

"No, Sir," RJ answered. "I need your permission, first."

Valentino considered it only for a brief moment.

"You take good care of my daughter… and not just in front of me," he said. "Robert, you've shown me that you are just that man. Yes, you have my blessing."

No one calls him Robert, and RJ didn't mind it now.

"Thank you, Sir," RJ said, and shook his hand. "I love Gia and I plan on spending the rest of my life with her. Now, I hope she agrees."

They both laughed, knowing Gia. She was strong and independent; never afraid to be on her own and had the propensity for instinct like no other.

****

RJ drove straight to the Cassava Patch Restaurant from the airport. He got there in a hurry and brought Osei up to speed, brother to brother, on the details of his meeting with Valentino.

"I'm going to ask her to marry me tonight," he said to Osei, beaming.

"What?"

"Yeah, she has made me ready… no, I am ready," he corrected.

"You used to run from commitment like it was a viral disease," Osei joked.

"That was after Juanita Sherman and I broke up and before Gia," RJ said. "You said it, man. You told me that I would like this one, those were your exact words. Remember? The night you introduced us… even if you hadn't, I would have introduced myself. It's funny the way the whole thing happened. Our eyes met, I thought I had lost her, and then when I saw her, you were taking me to her to make the introduction. I swear, Osei, we were meant to be together. She is perfect for me… and I make her happy."

Beautiful tears welled up in RJ's eyes. The hard-hitting lawyer had stood up in court against some of the toughest bastards in Atlanta and he had finally put Juanita Sherman in the past. But until that moment, expressing his true feelings for Gia, Osei had never seen RJ cry.

"I feel you, my brother," Osei said. "When Gia has your attention, not even a bomb can distract you."

"Dammit, if it isn't the truth," RJ said, smiling. "I'm so happy that she loves me."

"Honest… I've never seen you so complete. So tell me, is Ms. Sherman in the past?" Osei said.

"At the bottom of the past," RJ said, making a cross signal over his heart.

Then he pulled out the ring. A Tiffany novo, brilliant cushion cut creation with spirit, fire and style.

"Wow! That's a pretty baby," Osei said, looking at the ring. "How much did that cost you?"

"For my Gia, she's worth every penny," RJ said and kissed the 1.5 carat platinum ring. "Isn't she beautiful?" he added, and put the ring back in his jacket pocket.

"How much?" Osei insisted.

RJ shook his head and walked away, laughing.

He got in the car, and before turning on the engine, dialed Mellody's number.

"Hey, Mel… I need your help."

"My help… this must be about Gia," she guessed correctly.

"You know your brother so well…," he laughed. "I'm going to ask her to marry me. How do I pop the question?"

"Just ask her," Mel said, only teasing.

"You know, it should be better than that."

"I know, just teasing," she said. "That's wonderful, RJ, she's a good woman. I would marry her if you let me."

"Down, Mel… down," he joked.

They both laughed.

"Whatever you do, please don't go on your knee… that is soooo outdated," Mel said, still laughing.

"I thought that was romantic."

"It's not," she said quickly. "I have an idea."

"I'm listening."

After a brief pause, Mel said, still laughing, "Give her a foot massage and place the ring on her baby toe."

RJ was quiet for a moment, actually considering it.

"I like that," he said.

"Are you serious? I was only kidding."

"But, I like it," he said and hung up.

✦✦✦✦

Flowing along with I-85 traffic, RJ felt his spirits rise dramatically. The pleasant sensation inside made him smile to himself. Approaching the subdivision, he noticed the opened garage and

Gia's car was parked. She must have just gotten home, he thought. She usually leaves the garage open when she is sure it won't be long before he comes home. He was right. She'd gotten home about twenty minutes ago and knew he would be home soon.

"Hey," she greeted him at the door with a kiss, wearing only his pajamas top. "How was your day?"

"Good," he said. "What about yours?"

"As good as any day… we're having leftovers tonight honey," she said right away, almost apologizing. "Hope you don't mind. Mama's tired tonight."

"That's fine, baby, and if you don't feel like having the same thing, I can make dinner."

"No, I'd rather you not. We've got a bit of everything," she said opening the refrigerator as he had followed her into the kitchen. "Beef stew, chicken breast, lasagna… what would you like?"

"It doesn't matter, baby, anything," he said, "whatever you have."

"How about some lasagna? I can make us salad to go with it."

"That sounds terrific," he said and kissed her again. "I'll wash up while you heat up."

Gia pulled out a head of lettuce and tomato from the bottom drawer of the fridge and rinsed them under the faucet. She diced the tomatoes and the lettuce, added both to a wooden bowl, and then topped off the salad with olives and set it on the table.

"Ranch or Italian dressing?" she called out, as she scooped out generous portions of lasagna onto two plates and popped the first into the microwave.

"Italian," he yelled from the bathroom.

Moments later, RJ and Gia were sitting at the table with their plates before them, the lasagna was steaming. He opened a bottle of white zinfandel and poured two glasses, humming her song, *Forever, Forever*, by Keiko Matsui.

"How about me giving you a foot massage when we finish dinner?" he offered.

Gia wore a curious expression. "A foot massage?" she asked, realizing he was singing her favorite song.

"Well… yeah," he said, smiling. "You said you're tired… and maybe that will help you sleep."

"Okay," she agreed, so willingly.

As they ate, neither RJ nor Gia said much of anything, each wondering what the other was thinking. Only the sounds that were coming from their forks as they hit the plates, gave the atmosphere life. Then again, sometimes after a long day of dealing with work, a little peace and quiet time is appreciated.

After dinner, RJ cleaned up and did the dishes, insisting Gia's daily chore was over from the time she'd prepared dinner.

"Ready for your massage?" he asked, walking into the bedroom.

He sat at the foot of the bed and found the tube of lotion Gia had put there. After squirting a good amount in his hand and rubbing them together, he began by stroking the top of her foot, moving in the direction from toe to ankle. He stroked the sole of her foot, first gently, then applying a little more pressure.

"This is better than I thought it would be," she confessed.

"I haven't gotten to the best part yet," he said, smiling.

He made circular motions with his fingers over the sole of her foot and stopped, as he could tell from her facial expression, she was enjoying it.

"Baby, why did you stop… I was enjoying that."

"I stopped because… because I need to ask you this," he said. And then slipping the ring on her baby toe, he said, "Will you marry me?"

The metal felt cold against her skin and it tickled a little. She sat up and looked at her toe.

"Is that what I think it is?" she asked, laughing lightly.

"Yes," he nodded.

"Baby, you really want us to get married?"

"Please say, 'yes'.

Gia sighed. "This is so romantic, but I cannot help it, the psychology in me…."

"Say, 'yes."

"Baby, are you sure?"

"Yes, yes…."

"Because you see, every day I talk to people at work and many of my clients find themselves in situations where their lives are ruined because their partner invites other people into what should be sacred."

"I know, honey," he said, "I'm not one of your clients. I want to be your husband… *your* husband… nobody else's."

"And you do know that in any marriage, there's room for only two people," she said, stressing the word 'two' and holding out two fingers. "Is that the marriage you're inviting me into?"

"Yes," he said and shouted, "Yes! Yes!"

"Well, then… Counselor Douglas, that ring belongs on my finger, not on my toe," she laughed. "Yes, my love, I would love to be your wife."

RJ wanted an echo of his enthusiasm, and got just that. She leaned in and kissed him as he placed the ring on her finger. There was a deeper passion to her kiss, more vibrant. He kissed her neck and shoulders and felt the warmth of her breath in his ear. Then he slid his hand under the pajamas top and pulled it off, she was naked beneath the shirt. The sensation of her skin against his was like fire, and they began to make love. RJ whispered to her how much he loved her.

They made love a second time and when Gia finally fell asleep, he found himself staring at her. Everything about her was exquisitely peaceful.

Chapter Three

THEY were inseparable for months, until Gia had to visit her parents in Florida and RJ had to attend a funeral. Gia had not seen them since Christmas when she and RJ were there for the holiday, now summer was here already. Come rain or shine, he was going to attend Brook Hicks' funeral, the twenty-one year old college student whose missing body had been found in her boyfriend's apartment. He had taken on the case as his second pro bono for the year.

Twenty-eight young adults, mostly teenagers, were streaming past RJ toward the back of the church. They had just finished Leonard Cohen's Hallelujah Lyrics, their tribute to Brooke Hicks. KD Lang had brought spirit to the 2010 Winter Olympics in Vancouver, Canada when she sang it a few months ago. Such an emotional song, so beautiful, everyone in church felt what the children had sung. And, what they believed, quite fitting for young Brooke's funeral.

As the pastor raised himself to begin the eulogy, his eyes fell on an incredible sight. A burst of sunray rained through the church's beautiful stained-glass window, the illustration of Christ's blessing over a child at Capernaum. Everyone at the service noticed it. There was never any doubt, the presence of God was celebrating Brooke's home-going as well. There was some crying, and then, the sound of Brooke's mother whimpering. RJ felt his heart sink as his eyes came to rest on the grieving mother. He had never felt anything so sad and so senseless.

Brooke was the first in her family to go to college, on an academic scholarship at Emory University. Her mother had raised Brooke and six other siblings on her own, on a minimum wage nurse's aid job. While Brooke was focused, the boyfriend was living his life with no care or purpose; staying out late, sleeping in, and still hustling his old parents to pay for his living expenses. While she zigged, he zagged. The sad thing about it was, she was too concerned about his feelings if she left him. Since they met she'd completed high school, tossed her cap into the air at commencement, gotten into college on a full scholarship, and found work as an undergraduate lab assistant; all on her own, while nothing was changing on his end.

Two weeks ago, the Atlanta Police had found her hanging in the closet in her boyfriend's apartment, an electric cord tightly wound around her neck. At first, the police assumed it was a suicide because there were no abrasions or defensive wounds found on her body. The next day however, during the autopsy, a flaky residue was found packed under her nails. It turned out to be human skin with microscopic specks of dried blood. The poor girl had been desperately digging into someone, someone she knew; her boyfriend. She had not hung herself after all, she had been lynched.

✦✦✦✦

Gia was due home from Florida early Sunday evening. RJ finally flung himself out of bed at six-thirty, took a long hot shower and put on a pair of cherry silk boxers; one Gia had given him for Valentine. He'd missed her so much that he stuck his feet into her slippers, slippers that were made to look like cocker spaniel heads. Dopey eyes staring up, pink tongues lolling, and floppy ears. He sat on the couch, turned the TV to CBS 60-minutes, and waited for her to come home. Close to the end of the program, he heard the garage door open. Moments later, the car engine went dead and the door slammed.

Gia looked nothing short of terrific as she opened the front door and walked in from her trip. She was wearing a dusty lavender habotai silk shirt and a pair of faded jeans. Her hair was tied back in a brooch, with a few loose curls dangling down her cheeks. Her eyes were dazzling and looked pleased to see him. He felt the same way. RJ rushed to her, kissed her and ran out to the car to get her bags. She had made it to the shower by the time he was back.

"It's really fun to watch!" Gia said as she came through the bathroom door walking toward the bed.

"What is?" he asked.

"Mom's new addition," she replied, while taking off her pink satin top. She draped it over the stool at the foot of the bed. "Dad bought her two new fish...kissing gourami. He had to because my mother is still in mourning for the ones he accidentally killed. In two years she had grown them to around a foot in her 100 gallon tank and he accidentally fed them the wrong food. They are amazing. One is pink, the other green. She named the pink one Smoochy because of her big kissy lips and the green one, which I think is the guy, Mr. Posy."

"Mr. who?" RJ said, laughing, lifting the covers for her to join him.

"Don't ask," she said and slipped into bed, her eyes surveying his mood.

"That's why I love your mother...she reminds me of mine," he joked.

"Can I finish telling my story before you go on worshipping our mothers?"

"Sure, honey," he kissed her forehead. "Go on."

"It is not so strange for two people to fall over each other at first sight," Gia continued. "You feel so close, as if you've known each other for a longtime. Like us, when we first met."

"I thought we were talking about fish?"

"I am," she playfully elbowed him. "I was comparing my feelings to Mom's fish, the kissing gourami. Did you know that if one of them dies, the other dies too? They refuse to eat and they dry up from malnutrition. That's how much I love you honey...I might just dry up if you left me alone."

"Oh honey, I'm not going anywhere. I would never let you dry up," he whispered. "You see that ring," he pointed at the engagement ring, "I know what I want…I'm just waiting for you to pick out a date. You are the only one who really understands me, baby. I love you with my life."

"I did not get a call from you today, and you knew I was traveling back home," she said, trying not to sound as if complaining. "I know you went to that young lady's funeral."

"Brooke Hicks."

"Brooke's funeral," Gia corrected, knowing how passionate her man was about his clients.

"I'm so sorry honey," he said, and made a needy face.

"Apology not accepted," she teased, rolling her eyes, but then smiling.

RJ smiled.

"Oh, baby," she whispered, cupping his face in her hands. "You are too emotional…sometimes I think you get too close to your clients."

She brushed a kiss against his cheeks, then his eyes and lips. RJ pulled her toward him. Her mouth felt soft and warm, and tasted delicious. Gia began kissing him hard. His hand traveled under the covers and reached for her breasts. Every nerve in his body grew excited and on edge. She had very soft skin, very nice breasts. Gia kissed his chest and ran her tongue across, licking the edge of his nipple. Then she poked at the waistband of his cherry silk boxer. Without losing his spot, RJ pulled them off, then her panties. Gia kissed his lips again and rolled on her back, her long hair falling over the pillow.

"I love you, baby," he whispered, his lips touching against her cheek, then her lips. He moved between her legs until he was finally inside her and it felt good.

Most times their lovemaking is like slow dancing with perfect rhythm. Tonight, it went up a few notches. They moved against each other, into each other and made love just like the first time; like two people who could not get enough of each other, who had not been with anyone for a longtime. It was sweaty and frantic. They came about the same time, looking into each other's eyes.

Then RJ collapsed onto Gia, his body damp with perspiration. "Oh, honey, I love you so much," he said exhaling, and then rolling onto his back.

"Baby, you don't even give a girl time to breathe," she sucked in her breath. "I like it."

They coiled in each other's arms and stay entwined and exhausted until sleep took over.

Chapter Four

THE barefoot boys playing soccer on the beach were too involved in their game to notice the dark bloodstain in the sand where two large rocks were placed as goalposts. At some point during the game, the ball was kicked out of bound, into a nearby bush. There was no hurry in finding it; the game was still scoreless even after twenty minutes of playing. The youngest player, about eleven, was ordered to get the ball. With a stick, he mapped his way into the underbrush and instead of the ball, found the horribly mutilated body of an adult man.

"What are you doing?" shouted the other boys. "Hurry and bring the ball!"

He stood frozen. The rest of his friends soon joined him to get the ball and get back to the game.

The body was on its back with the head turned to his left shoulder. His arms were by the side of his body as if they had fallen there. Both palms upwards, the fingers slightly bent. His left leg extended in a line with his body and his abdomen was exposed. His right leg was bent at the thigh and knee, and his throat cut across. Intestines were drawn out to a large extent and placed over his right shoulder—they were smeared over with some feces. A piece of about two feet was detached from the body and placed between his body and left arm, apparently by design. The lobe and auricle of his right ear were cut through, at an angle.

His face was greatly mutilated. There was a cut, about a quarter of an inch, through the lower left eyelid, dividing the structures completely through. There was a scratch through the skin on the left upper eyelid, near to the angle of the nose. His right eyelid was cut through to about half an inch. There was a deep cut over the bridge of the nose, extending from the left border of the nasal bone down near the angle of the jaw, on the right side of the cheek. This cut went into the bone and divided all the structures of the cheek except the mucous membrane of the mouth. The tip of the nose was detached, by a slanting cut, from the bottom of the nasal bone to where the wings of the nose join on to the face. A cut from this divided the upper lip and extended through the substance of the gum over the right upper side tooth. There was also a cut on the right angle of the mouth. The cut extended an inch and a half, parallel with the lower lip. On each side of his cheek, there was a cut which peeled up the skin, forming a triangular flap about an inch and a half.

Within twenty minutes, officers from the Monrovia Police Department had gotten to the scene, geared with latex gloves, evidence bags, tape and markers, and a Canon PowerShot camera. About fifteen less important police officers had already been deployed all over the beach, like survey engineers. They were taking notes, making measurements, bagging any and everything that looked like evidence. The police chief was late four hours in getting there, because he'd been away investigating another ritual killing in Maryland County. He got all over the officers when he arrived.

"If I find anyone holding important evidence, they will be look-ing for a new job!" he was raising his voice, making sure he got the point across. "This is part of the SCIU now. I'm not going to lose valuable information… no, not on my watch!"

To his credit, the chief of police, Aaron Dolo, was frustrated himself because a wave of ritual killings had started all over again, since the civil war ended.

"Nobody understands a goddamn thing!" he continued yelling at his officers. "Change does not mean anything to these murderers."

His men ran around collecting and bagging everything in sight, shoes, pieces of items, and taking pictures. The initial few shots taken by the officer were well-composed photos, close-ups and wide-angle shots. The photographer's instincts were pretty good, such that the sight of the crime scene left everyone feeling a little sick.

Chief Dolo met with his superiors the following week, assuring them he was sure there was struggle, and believed it was the act of more than one person. The throat had been so instantly severed that no noise could have been produced and he did not expect much blood to have been found on the persons who had inflicted the wounds. The perpetrators must have had considerable knowledge of the position of the organs in the abdominal cavity and the way of removing them. It required a great deal of medical knowledge to have removed the kidney and heart and to know where it was placed. He could not assign any reason for the parts being taken, though some of the parts removed could be of use for juju, if not, then for professional purpose. Dolo had his men working day and night on the Johnny Bono case.

✳✳✳✳

Three weeks marking the day of the body's discovery, The Liberian Journal Constitution headline read:

VICTIM IDENTIFIED
JOHNNY BONO WAS RITUALLY MURDERED
BIG NAMES INVOLVED

The paper named Charles Sarpo, an ex-child soldier, who'd made a silly confession to his girlfriend that he had slaughtered a man for one thousand US dollars, cash. The Bono investigation was the topic of discussion in the entire country, mainly in Monrovia. Sarpo's girlfriend needed to be important, so she told a friend about her boyfriend's recent activities and that friend told another friend, until the gossip reached the ears of an ununiformed police officer.

In his preliminary testimonies, Charles Sarpo confessed that he and a male nurse, Duo Boley kidnapped and killed Johnny Bono on the suggestion of Wonde Gedeh, the medicine woman. Chief

Dolo was determined to arrest not only those who directly carried out the criminal act, but those who ordered it as well. Evidence was gathered also against higher ranking suspects, Tamba Nah Wumah, the Mayor of Monrovia and Robert Jenkins Douglas II, a retired senator. To the Chief's credit, soon the "masterminds" behind the atrocity now sat side by side with the least rank suspects.

Four weeks later, The Liberian Journal Constitution new headline read:

FIVE SUSPECTS HELD FOR RITUAL MURDER:
Senator Robert J. Douglas II,
Mayor Tamba Nah Wumah, Duo Boley,
Charles Sarpo and Madam Wonde Gedeh

Chapter Five

THE evening was spent quietly, with just the radio on ELWA station, playing classic gospel music. Mellody was at John F. Kennedy Medical hospital doing another late shift and did not think she would be home until about noon the following day. A little passed ten, Senator Douglas had just joined Katharine in their bedroom, and had no sooner fallen off to sleep, when they heard a banging sound on the front door; loud banging, persistent noise. Katharine jumped out of her sleep, her heart was thundering inside her chest. The headlines had sent them days of warning that the senator was a suspect; now trouble had made it to the home.

Senator Douglas got up. Katharine got out of bed. While she hurriedly put on a housedress, the senator went to see the caller or callers. He looked out the large living room window and saw red flashing lights, it was the police. Katharine stood behind as he went to turn the lock. Instantly, the front door flung open, and about a dozen police officers and a CID investigator rushed in with their guns drawn.

"Oh, my God," Katharine screeched, her eyes fastened on their weapons.

Two officers barged passed her, as they were searching for Senator Douglas.

"What are you doing at my house? This is insane!" the senator shouted. "Do you know who I am? Do you idiots have any idea what I can do to you?"

"Senator Robert Douglas, you are under arrest for the murder of Johnny Bono," the CID investigator read the warrant. "Your partners have all been arrested," he shouted, and then he forced the senator's hands behind his back and roughly handcuffed him, making no effort to be gentle at this point.

Senator Douglas's legs were shaky and he almost fell, but the arresting officer held him up easily with one hand. He was fuming mad, with the humiliating feeling he had been made a fool of.

"Now move," the officer ordered.

People were starting to file outdoors on the sidewalks, even at this time of night. Razaq ran out of his room, then into the living room. He stood horrified as the officer marched the senator through the door, then to the police van, and drove him straight to the Monrovia Central Prison.

The senator was thrust into the interrogation room and shoved in a chair. One officer sat in a chair across from him and another stood by him, after slamming the file on the table. The sitting officer asked questions, posing a series of them, one after another, about the victim, the crime, and other suspects while the standing officer manhandled the senator. This went on for two hours, but resulted without a confession. They were more determined to make him talk.

Terrified and disgusted, but trying not to show it, Senator Douglas asked for some water. His mouth was dry and he was thirsty beyond belief. Instead, the questions kept coming at him. They wanted him to talk, tell them about how he had helped plan the killing.

Suddenly, with one hand, the standing officer yanked the senator to his feet, pulling his arm hard, as if he was trying to tear it from its socket. Senator Douglas yelled as violent pain shot up his arm. He shoved the officer back, instinctively, putting some space between him and the officer.

"That was stupid!" the officer yelled into his face. Then he leveled the stun gun in his hand at the senator's chest and shot him.

Senator Douglas tried to keep standing, willed to stay up, but his body didn't oblige; he slumped to the floor.

"The old man wants to fight!" the officer yelled. And then he raised his boot and began kicking at him. A tooth spun in slow motion, across the cement floor. It took the senator a moment to realize that it was his tooth. He tasted blood and felt his lips swelling.

"You think about that, old man!" the sitting officer yelled and stood up.

After that, both officers walked out of the room, leaving Senator Douglas on the filthy, cold cement floor. They had given him some time to think things over.

Three hours later, maybe more, Senator Douglas was still lying on the floor when the door opened and the officers walked in.

"Get up!" one officer shouted.

Senator Douglas remained on the floor.

"Few minutes ago you wanted to fight me, now you're too old to get up?" The officer yanked the senator by the sore arm, and pulled him to stand. "If you want to be rough, than I will be rough; but if you want to cooperate, I will be gentle. Do you understand?"

Senator Douglas nodded, 'yes'.

"Now, sit down," the officer ordered.

Senator Douglas sat, lowering his eyes.

"If you don't want to talk, it's okay," the same officer that sat before him said and resumed the position. "You don't have to say squat! Your friends have all confessed, each person has mentioned your name, that makes you part of it. We know that you all have killed in the past. You have cut open many people, not only Johnny Bono; removing their hearts, kidneys, lungs…you are a Heart Man," he pointed, "Juju medicine is your trademark, we know that. You've even stolen the poor man's nuts! This time, you all have been caught. Douglas," he said loudly, frowning, issuing a baleful stare, "I swear on my mother's life, you are not going to get away with this one."

After that, Senator Douglas asked for nothing else, not water, not food, not even for his lawyer.

The officer wrote in his note, the motivation for the murder has been described as ritualistic murder, blood lust, money lust and juju.

Chapter Six

THERE was heavy traffic on 285 East and more on the approach on I-85 North that crazy evening. Gia's eyes twitched as she got off Spaghetti Junction on to I-85. She was heading to the Cassava Patch, the famous West African restaurant-bar in Norcross to meet RJ. He loved their relationship the way it was, secure, exciting and always fun. They had become one of those sickening best-friend couple, the let's die at the same moment, Romeo and Juliet, soul mates. They were so much in love.

Just about every Friday night RJ and Gia met at Osei Agyeman's club, the Cassava Patch. He and Osei had become best friends in college. The roomies had a cute oddness about them; one being a Ghanaian kid with a British accent and the other, a Liberian kid with an American accent. Osei was devoted to his family, wife, Ama and their seven-year old son, Michael and he genuinely liked his music. He'd married Ama right out of college and the two started the restaurant, adding a bar area so Osei could continue playing with his band.

That Friday was no exception, and by seven-thirty RJ was sitting at the bar, watching the band set up, and waiting for Gia. Suddenly, Osei remembered the good news he had to share with RJ and walked over to his table. He was about to brag about the two bottles of Gulder Beer he'd just purchased from a cousin who had returned from Ghana, when Gia walked in.

"Tell me later," RJ patted Osei's back and walked away, then toward the door smiling, obviously feeling better as soon as he saw her.

Gia had always had that effect on him since their meeting. She was wearing red lipstick and had put on a new perfume, he discovered as he took her into his arms.

"It's about time you got here," RJ said. "I've missed you."

"Then hold me, hug me, kiss me," she teased, and then she added, "traffic on 285."

Osei, the band members and a few customers were watching them, and most were smiling. How could they not? Osei was glad to see his brother happy again. They were heading for their favorite seat near the stage, when RJ's phone buzzed. He glanced at it on the fourth ring.

"It's Mel," he said to Gia. "She's in Liberia."

Gia nodded, acknowledging she already knew Mellody was there.

"Hello," RJ answered, and walked outside to get away from the band's loud warm up noise.

"RJ...Oh...RJ...you have to hear this!" Mellody was crying.

"Mel, what's wrong?"

"It's Daddy...they've arrested him," she sobbed.

"What?" He looked at his timepiece, it read eight o'clock. He counted five hours ahead; it was one in the morning in Liberia. "Mel...what are you saying. Stop crying, honey, and talk to me. Where's Mom?"

"She's here with me. She's okay and Razaq is okay. They arrested Daddy while I was at work and took him to jail. They wouldn't let me see him or talk to him...they wouldn't let Mom either."

"Why? Did they tell you why he was arrested?" RJ lowered his voice.

Mellody was quiet.

"Hello. Mel...can you hear me?"

"I'm here," she said. There was a pause, and then she said, "Murder."

"What?"

"Ritualistic murder," she said and broke down crying.

"Sweet Jesus," RJ whispered. "Mel, are you sure?"

"RJ, he's in jail," she said, coldly.

"We're at the Cassava Patch. Let me call you when I get home," he said and shut his phone.

Gia had walked outside to find RJ about the same time he was making his way back in.

"Is everything okay, honey," Gia said, reaching him.

"No," he said, obviously nervous.

Gia frowned, sensing something was not right.

"You're trembling," she said, "what's wrong?"

"Gia, baby, something bad has happened," he said, glumly.

He had never called her by name since they met. He started to say something else, but hesitated.

"What's wrong?" Gia asked again.

RJ clued her in about the horrible news from Liberia.

"Oh, my God!" she sighed. "I think we should go home. Osei can do without us tonight, c'mon baby, let's go home."

"Let me talk to him," he said and went to find Osei.

Osei noticed RJ walking toward him and stopped plucking his bass guitar when he approached the stage.

"Osei, we've got to run," RJ whispered, sounding serious.

Osei gave him a disgruntled look. "Why?"

"Can't talk right now, but I'll call you later…maybe tomorrow morning," he said.

Akin to the sound of his voice, RJ's face seemed troubling.

"Call me later," Osei said and flashed a smile of understanding.

Chapter Seven

THE night before his trip to Liberia, RJ could feel Gia watching him as he packed his suitcase. He also did the same thing when she packed to leave without him on her trips. She leaned her five-foot- seven-inch body against the doorway to their bedroom, arms folded across her chest, a frown tugging on her face. She hated the thought of their being apart, especially not knowing for how long. Gia didn't say anything, just stood there as RJ filled the suitcase with mostly summer clothes and a few dressy outfits.

"Baby, you know I have to go and see how things are first," he said. "I hate this too."

"I already miss you," she murmured.

He stared at her with a grin and a twinkle in his eyes.

"Oh, oh, I know that look," she said.

"What look?"

"The one that says you want a going away present."

Gia thought for a moment before flashing a grin of her own. She slowly walked up to him, purposely stopping just inches from his body. She was wearing only her bra and panties.

Leaning in, she whispered in his ear, "From me to you."

There wasn't much to unwrap, but RJ took his time anyway. He gently kissed her neck, then her shoulders, his lip tracing an imaginative line downward to the perfect curves of her perky breasts.

There, he lingered. One hand stroking her arm; the other reaching around to remove her bra. Gia shivered, her body tinkling. He knelt and kissed her stomach, his tongue lightly drawing circles around her bellybutton. Then with his thumb resting on each side of her hips, he began to roll down her panties, charting the progress with kiss after kiss after kiss.

"That's very nice," she moaned.

Now it was her turn. She began to quickly, but sensually, undress his tall muscular frame standing before her. They stood still for a few seconds, perfectly naked, gazing at each other. Then, RJ gave her a quick playful shove and she fell backward onto the bed. He was fully aroused. She looked like an enormous sunflower on the bed, willingly lying there and ready. They made the most of what would be their last night together for a while.

✦✦✦✦

Early that morning, Gia cooked scrambled eggs, toast, and bacon for breakfast. They purposefully tried to engage in other discussions, as if grasping for normalcy. RJ would only mention that it was best not to share the news with Gia's parents until he'd gotten full details. She agreed.

They skipped lunch.

The late fall sky was graying steadily as they pulled into Harts-field-Jackson airport. Gia swiped at her eyes as she pulled to a stop at Delta terminal check-in. The tough psychologist had held back tears until now. They had decided that she would not go in to see him off, it would be too painful. Besides, it was impossible to find a parking space; all the hourly parking spaces were already filled. RJ lifted her chin, kissed her glistening eyes, and then her lips. He opened the door. She pushed the knob and popped open the trunk. In the rearview mirror, she watched him take out the suitcase, his laptop bag, slam the trunk shut and then he blew her another kiss. She smiled, it was painful. He waved as she slowly pulled away.

RJ rolled his suitcase through the sliding door, then to the check-in counter. He made his way through security and into the waiting area, then went and sat in the bar waiting for the flight to be called, thinking very heavy thoughts. He took out the ticket from his jacket pocket and put it back again. From the overhead speakers, music was playing Keiko Matsui's *Forever, Forever*, he liked that. Tears came to his eyes. He took a bar napkin and dried his eyes. He'd made the right decision, he thought. There were big troubles at home and it would not be fair to Gia to take her along without first knowing what exactly was happening. He needed her and she had begged to come along. Hearing her voice might calm him, he thought. RJ pulled out his cell phone and speed-dialed Gia's number.

"Honey," she answered.

"I miss you already," he sighed.

"I miss you, too. It wouldn't be long, sweetie. As soon as you evaluate things, I'm coming. You promised."

"Yes," he said, "I promised."

"I love you," her voice quivered.

"I love you more," he said, and then the PA interrupted, announcing the final boarding call. "Flight time," he informed her. "I'll call you as soon as I get there."

RJ kissed the phone and slipped it back into his shirt pocket.

Chapter Eight

I𝐅 RJ didn't know for sure that he could never be happy without Gia, the flight to Liberia removed all doubt. For much of it he sat there, thinking about her. She was good at making things all right. He heard her voice giving him the courage to do what he felt was right. He should have insisted they get married, not knowing what Liberia had in store for him, their future. He was perspiring badly in the cramped and claustrophobic middle aisle airplane seat of Delta 747, so obviously pathetic the pleasant and accommodating flight attendant stopped and asked if he was feeling all right. He told her that he was.

Moments later when she walked by, RJ pretended he was asleep. Sweat continued to trickle down his face and neck; the fear inside him had built way passed the tolerance level. He couldn't get his mind to rest, even for just a few minutes. He had to be on this plane. He had to travel to Liberia. He had to go without Gia. It was all connected to the mess his father was thought to be involved with. And oh yeah, his mother needed him.

Monday morning was finally here and Delta 747 landed on Monrovia soil at Robert's International Airport. RJ marched down the long steps toward ground, walked in line to the terminal, and stepped up to the immigration booth marked VISITORS. He pushed his American passport toward the officer.

"Mr. Douglas," the young immigration agent leafed through the documents. As he went through RJ's passport, he saw the traveler had been to Liberia many times. "Business or pleasure, Mr. Douglas?" the officer asked, in a friendly voice.

"This is home," RJ replied. "Neither, I guess."

"Well, welcome home, Sir," he said, stamping the passport. "Liberia and America are sisters."

He folded the documents together and pushed them back to RJ, making no connection of the identical name the visitor had with the accused senator, whose name had made the headlines daily for the past weeks.

RJ met Katharine and Mellody just as he stepped passed the last traveler standing in line. Then all three of them were hugging and quietly consoling one another as best as they could. Katharine cuddled her children like when they were younger, reminding her of the time she had to leave them with her mother and return to Liberia with the senator. She finally pulled away and headed to the baggage claim counter, where their chauffeur, Mr. Tom, had been waiting.

Mr. Tom greeted RJ with a strong welcoming handshake and a grin, doffing his khaki chauffeur cap he was so proud of. He collected the luggage and laptop, loaded them into the trunk and prepared to leave. At the same time, RJ helped Katharine into the car and later joined Mr. Tom in the front.

It's about a forty-minute drive from RIA to the city, if there were no traffic and if there were no car troubles. Mr. Tom took his time, slowing down around curves, not passing slower cars ahead; deliberately taking more time so he heard all RJ had to say about America. Katharine asked about Gia and RJ bragged about how wonderful things were between them. Then he speed-dialed her personal cell and got her voice mail, a personal outgoing message just for him, ending with a kiss. He smiled and left a message that he had arrived safely. Not satisfied, he dialed her office, but Paola did not pick up and he did not bother leaving a message there.

"Two years is a long time to be engaged, don't you think?" Katharine said to RJ.

RJ turned around and caught Mellody's stare, finding the

expected facial expression like when they were kids. Her eyes were widened, as if to say, 'here we go again'.

"I don't think so, Mom, we're both so busy," RJ said. "We are getting married...Gia just needs to pick a date."

"Well...I think two years is too long," Katharine said, rolling her eyes playfully.

"Mom..." Mellody started.

"I know you, Dr. Douglas," Katharine quickly interrupted, sounding a bit saucy. "You don't want anything to do with marriage."

RJ and Mellody roared with laughter, like when they were kids. Mr. Tom smiled, unable to hide a smirk.

The rest of the way, RJ spoke about how well President Obama was doing regardless of the slow economy, the Cassava Patch new improvements, how proud Osei and Ama were about Michael's studious progress and Gia and her family. Everyone had sent their greetings to the family, especially to Katharine. Katharine exchanged news about everything else. She mentioned nothing about the senator.

Finally, at about 3:30 P. M. they made their way through the front gate of the house. Ma Teete was waiting on the porch, welcoming them warmly with a strong wave and big smile. RJ barely noticed the beautiful new landscaping in the front yard, crushed rocks and lust green lawns skirting clusters of hibiscus that had bloomed in red, pink, yellow and white. Katharine had planned everything with those particular colors in mind. That's the way she was about displaying colors. God had made thousands of colors and she intended using as much as she could find.

While RJ was still hugging Ma Teete, Razaq burst from the garage side door and hurried to the porch, purposely wearing his Atlanta Hawks t-shirt RJ had sent him. He could hardly wait to greet his big brother, his hero.

"You're better at basketball now, I hope," RJ joked, poking at the Hawk's logo on the front.

"Football," Razaq replied, meaning soccer. "I'm the next George Weah...that's what people are calling me."

Everyone laughed about his big dream, and then they ambled to the house.

Ma Teete had prepared a special dinner made of foods RJ especially liked. After a delicious meal of jollof rice, potato salad, pineapple upside-down cake, pawpaw pie, and ginger beer, the family congregated in the living room over bowls of ice cream while Razaq loaded the dishwasher in the kitchen. Ma Teete showed off her matching handbag and shoes Katharine had bought her while on a shopping spree two days before, which were beautiful and expensive. Everybody was pretty much laughing, which was good, it was definitely good to have RJ and Mellody home at the same time.

Soon enough Razaq joined them in the living room to watch TV, claiming the remote to switch between the only three channels that came in on the television. The adults were talking about Mellody's work at JFK hospital and Ma Teete's two daughters who were doing well at the University of Liberia and Cuttington University. Everyone worked hard to avoid the topics of the senator and his arrest. Finally, Mr. Tom drove Ma Teete home and everybody started to wander off to bed, but there were hugs and kisses first.

Katharine followed RJ into his room. She wanted him to know how happy she was that he had come home and how much she needed him there.

"RJ, I don't how it all happened," she whispered. "Your dad tried so hard to help these people, didn't matter who, he helped everybody. This is so awful. They want to take his life, RJ, they want to kill him," she broke down crying.

He pulled her between his shoulders as she cried on his shoulder and he cried on hers.

"I'm here now Mom," RJ whispered. "I'll do everything I can."

Katharine slowly pulled away.

"Get some rest, honey," she said, swiping at her tears. "We'll talk in the morning."

She left his room and went to hers. About 11:30 P.M. RJ finally climbed into bed, hoping for a much, much better tomorrow.

Chapter Nine

It was a rare dry September morning in Monrovia, a little breezy under the tall and stately coconut trees that graced the spacious and orderly backyard of the Douglas's house. Underneath the tree was a picnic bench, chairs and a canvas-topped beach umbrella. Katharine enjoyed her life in her adopted home tremendously. There was always something ripe for picking in Liberia. She had her choice of coconut, guava, mango, tangerine, avocado, depending on what time of year it was. She loved the tropical climate with its little variation in temperature. The wet season was from May to October and the dry season, from November to March. The bite and crispness of the Atlantic sea breeze was a definite plus.

After the war, Senator Douglas had purchased a one-acre lot property with eighty meters of sandy beach frontage for their retirement home. The exterior walls of the house were double wall brick construction with a rock wall facing the street, a two-car garage which had a boys' quarter efficiency with a full bathroom, and paved road in front of the house between two immaculate garden areas. The master bedroom had a private bath, tub and shower. Two other guest bedrooms were fully furnished with queen-sized beds and private baths, setup specifically for RJ and Mellody. There was a large modern kitchen and laundry room. Katharine had no need of servants now that the children were grown. However, Ma

Teete, the family cook-turn-friend, after many years of serving with warm smiles and pleasant words, now prepared dinner occasionally while she continued to draw a bi-monthly paycheck. Most times were spent shopping with Katharine or keeping company. Besides the senator and Katharine, Razaq, the fifteen-year-old boy she had adopted since he was seven, shared the home. Mr. Tom remained hired to drive Katharine around.

RJ awakened to the smell of breakfast wafting into the room. He took a quick shower, tossed on a t-shirt and jeans and went to the kitchen. Katharine was at the table, talking with Ma Teete and Razaq had already left for school.

"Good morning Ma Teete. Good morning, Mom," he greeted. He kissed Katharine on the cheek and took a place at the table.

Ma Teete poured him a cup of coffee before setting a plate of scrambled eggs and a double-sized piece of her famous cornbread in front of him. RJ wished Gia was there to share what he had missed while in America.

"Did you sleep okay?" Katharine asked.

"Yes, Mom, I did… but it's always weird without Gia."

Katharine and Ma Teete glanced at each other and grinned. The fact is he hardly slept during the night, thinking about Gia and the awful nightmare that had brought him home. He'd even tried calling her twice, but got her voice mail.

"Where's Mel?" RJ asked, realizing they were alone after the satisfying meal.

"At the hospital," Katharine said. "She spends more time there than home with me. I created that monster."

"You did, Mom," RJ nodded. "You taught us how important voluntary work is and Mel is giving back where it's needed most. She's doing such a good job here, I'm proud of her. In fact, she loves working at JFK."

"She works harder here than at Roger Williams Medical Center… and she's supposed to be on vacation. When does she rest? She shouldn't be working this hard, but you know your sister, she wouldn't listen to me. She doesn't listen to me on anything."

"Mom, that's what doctors do… work long hours. Mel is used to that, so don't worry."

"Oh, I'm not worried, just concerned."

RJ glanced at Ma Teete as she took away the empty plates. "Thanks, Ma Teete, breakfast was great. I've missed your cornbread."

"Happy to have you home, RJ," Ma Teete said, smiling. "What else did you miss, so you can have it for dinner?"

"I miss everything, actually," he said, and added, "And don't go overboard."

Ma Teete responded with a light laugh and went about her business.

✳✳✳✳

"Mom, I'm proud of how well you're holding up with this nightmare," RJ said, following Katharine into the living room. "I'm so sorry that I couldn't come sooner. I was waiting on a new passport I thought I needed, not realizing I could still use the one I had. Then, I had to get a visa to come to Liberia. Can you believe it? I needed a visa to come home...cost me a hundred and fifty bucks, too."

They both laughed.

"That's how it was when your father and I used to travel. I needed a visa when we were coming home because I am American and he wasn't. He still used his Official Liberian passport, even during the war."

"How is he, Mom?"

"I don't know, RJ...they wouldn't let me see him," Katharine said, with sadness in her voice.

"You haven't seen Dad since he was arrested?"

"No," she said, stifling her fear. "I couldn't go to the American embassy because he is not American...if only he had listened to me when I wanted him to become a citizen."

"How's that lawyer Mel found, is he any good?"

"Well, he comes highly recommended. He went to school in the States, you know?"

"Mel tells me he's very expensive too."

"He is?"

"I'm not worried about that, I just hope he's good. It's better for Daddy to have someone who knows how the system works."

"He seems okay to me, and Mel talked with him…" She trailed off.

"Mel thinks he's the only chance Dad has," RJ finished.

"Yes," Katharine nodded, doubt was written plainly on her face.

RJ looked at his watch. "I'm going to meet with him this morning, Mom. I'd like to know what we have on our hands, and then I'll come up with the game plan."

Katharine smiled, encouraged.

"Mr. Tom can take you," she suggested, "I don't plan on leaving the house today."

"He doesn't need to, Mom. I remember my way around Monrovia. I'll just take the car."

Chapter Ten

LIKE any other modern city scene of joy and stress, lives were expressed daily in new births and growing old. Monrovia was full of people at world speed and hectic days in the ever changing setting of the latest trend and craze. They had partied even during war time and they continued to with more clubs than before. It seemed when people weren't partying, they were already rehearsing for the next party.

Changes were apparent. Politicians, corporations and entrepreneurs were working constructions like magic. Most of the devastation from the war had been torn down and new buildings were going up as fast as everyone could tell. Small businesses were sprucing here and there. There was Sinkor Circle, a restaurant–bar, always packed with well-paid government types having a drink after fleeing the office, a flashy new gym called Beads of Sweat on Newport Street and Frogs & Puppies, a children's clothing store, downtown on Broad Street. A couple of new playgrounds were constructed for the children as well and so was a new Super General Market, covering about four blocks down Waterside. Many three-story buildings built across town had apartments and offices at the top and merchandise stores on the ground level. The government and city planners had many good ideas.

Few things can keep a one-man firm from the joys of sleep.

Diallo Amadou was at his desk most any night until after eleven. He had an impressive resume; age forty-four, married, law school at Duke, undergrad at the University of Liberia. Most people in Africa could not afford him, at hourly rates that seemed obscene, even for the well-to-do, $45 per hour. Most of his clients were desperate politicians and exiled formal leaders. Desperate people would pay anything for their freedom, and for this, he would become rich.

The desk was mahogany, the rug was Persian, the chair was rich crimson leather, and the technology was state-of-the-art. On his desk every morning, in precisely the same spot, were the Liberian Journal Constitution and a cup of fresh brewed coffee, black. Grace Pupoh was responsible for that. She was the heart and soul of the firm that occupied half of the second floor of a new three-story modern building on Broad Street, downtown Monrovia. Two large nicely framed photographs of Franklin Douglas and Martin Luther King Jr. were on the back wall. One wall was covered with new metal file cabinets, the other side, several wooden bookshelves stacked with new and battered law books.

RJ could see inside the office, looking through the French screen/glass door. Behind the front desk, a young attractive woman, with striking resemblance to Queen Latifah, was typing away on a black keyboard before a twenty-two inch flat screen monitor. The computer was underneath the desk, some place.

RJ tapped softly on the door before walking in.

"May I help you?" she said, still typing.

She was Grace Pupoh, according to the nameplate tacked to the side of her desk. RJ soon learns that she is more than a receptionist.

"I'm looking for Diallo Amadou," he said politely and walked forward. "I'm RJ, Senator Douglas's son."

She studied him with a welcoming smile, flashing the small gap between her two front teeth.

"Have a seat," she pointed to the waiting area. "Would you like some coffee?"

"No thanks," he said.

"Well then, follow me," she said and ushered him to the office at the end of the hall.

RJ walked into Diallo's office, fascinated with the place. As far as he could tell, the staff included just Grace Pupoh, his secretary who also worked as his legal assistant.

Diallo Amadou seemed happy to meet the senator's son. He greeted RJ with a strong handshake and a grin. While the men exchanged pleasantries, Grace went back to her desk.

Lunch was always good, especially when the client was picking up the check. Diallo suggested they take an early lunch at Sinkor Circle, however, RJ politely declined; telling him that he'd had a big breakfast. He took a seat, instead, across from Diallo before it was offered.

"How is he?" RJ asked. "My mother tells me the family has not been allowed to see him. I know you have."

"He's holding up," Diallo replied. "He's eager to come home and who could blame him."

"Well… could I see him?"

"I'll make a few calls and see what happens," he promised. "I'll get back to you on that…ASAP."

Then, as concisely as he could, Diallo took RJ through the case so far. A practiced listener, RJ punctuated what was said by uttering 'interesting' several times and seemed open to other points of views the lawyer offered. For the moment he was hopeful, yet eager for new information.

After Diallo went over the pretrial documents and defense plan, they sat mostly in silence for a minute or two. Diallo was sure of himself. He had the solution already, nice and neat.

"All of it looks bad… and for motive, ritualistic murder, juju, greed, you name it," Diallo continued. "But as far as the senator is concerned, all evidence against him is circumstantial."

"Like elsewhere, I believe this system of justice is designed carefully… to prevent people from being unfairly convicted by guaranteeing legal rights to anyone charged with a crime," RJ argued.

Diallo sat patiently.

"For example," RJ continued, "you have the right to have a lawyer present during police questioning. You have the right to remain silent to avoid incriminating yourself, which means that you do not have to answer any questions asked by the police, and do not have to give evidence at trial."

"Mr. Douglas," Diallo said, leaning forward, "I, too, went to law school in the States. Let's not forget… this is not the States. This is Liberia… Africa."

RJ furrowed his brow; it was a bit difficult to handle. *And, my father's life is in their hands,* he thought. After considering the lawyer's points, he thought an apology was in order.

"Sorry. I wasn't…."

"I understand," Diallo cut him off. "Your sister hired me because she knows I can win this case. Please, let me do my job… okay? Ms. Macavoi doesn't have a chance against me. All the evidence they have against the senator is 'hearsay' and I have evidence, in fact, proof, the confession was coerced."

RJ carefully examined the facts and concluded Diallo had home court advantage compared to him. Besides, he understood their legal system.

"That will work," RJ said, trying to pacify.

"I know better than to tell you that this will be a walk in the park," Diallo said. "We have a tough battle ahead of us. I am prepared to fight."

RJ had heard enough, for the time being. He glanced at his watch, Diallo glanced at his. They swapped cell phone numbers and promised to keep in touch. He took a peep at Grace Pupoh on his way out. She looked up and smiled.

✦✦✦✦

As RJ stepped out to the sidewalk in front of the office, a woman suddenly appeared out of nowhere.

"My name is Famatta Kpan," the woman greeted.

She looked thirty-something, spectacularly poised and cool. Then he noticed the Toyota 4-runner, parked close behind his Land Cruiser at the curb, with LJC printed on the door in large letters.

"You must be the senator's son from the States… I see the resemblance. I've made your father an even more famous man than he is already. You are RJ, aren't you?"

The words came out her mouth like running water and RJ heard every word. The Liberian Journal Constitution reporter couldn't hold back a slight smile, the smallest possible parting of her thick, cruel lips. She called him RJ as if they were longtime friends.

Damn you shameless, disrespectful writers, he thought. Did she actually expect to get an interview or was she digging for more lies? He studied Famatta Kpan for a brief moment, a full minute. Ms. Kpan, he was to find out soon, was the owner of the LJC, a soldier of fortune herself.

Under closer scrutiny, she was noticeably tall and fashionably trimmed. She had on DKNY black framed eyeglasses that made her look more sharp-witted than she probably was and the navy blue pant suit was meant to keep RJ off his guard, he was sure.

"Okay, Ms. Kpan, I am RJ," he admitted. "My father is hardly famous and this sort of clever, tabloid journalism doesn't cut it with me. I have no time right now for much of anything…much more an interview. Go back and write more of your nonsense you people call news."

He'd not planned on it, but he had drawn first blood.

"Oh, but he is famous, RJ," she responded with an ingénue toothy grin. "He is so well-known, in fact, that people will not buy a paper these days without him on the cover. These days, people appreciate the truth."

RJ laughed. A cruel little laugh he knew she deserved.

"Appreciate the truth!" he rasped.

Famatta Kpan laughed, too.

"That's what we're printing… would you be helping with his defense? That's what the people want to know."

RJ gave her a long cold stare and walked by.

"Get a close-up… hurry!" she instructed her cameraman as RJ hurried into his car and sped away.

Chapter Eleven

As RJ drifted through the city, he couldn't recall the last time he'd driven the streets of Monrovia when it looked this regulated, working traffic lights, garbage cans on every street corner, vendor stations within precise orderly distances and no squatters anywhere. The heavy luxury SUV moved with the traffic and no particular place to go.

If there was anyone that could calm his fears, it was Gia. He took out his phone and glanced at her face, his screensaver, smiling up at him. He could have sworn he saw her hazel-green eyes twinkle at him and his eyes began to sting with tears.

"Baby, I wish you were here," he whispered. "I miss you."

He was putting the phone on the passenger front seat when it rang.

"Hello," he answered.

"RJ," Mel's voice was clearly audible, but competing with the overhead PA system at the hospital.

"Hi, Mel...I can't believe you're still at the hospital."

"About to leave," she said. "Wanted to know how things went with Diallo... what do you think?"

"Well, he's got the paperwork in order...I'll have to wait and see. I asked if it was possible to see Dad and he'll get back to me on that."

"I see," Mel said.

It was obvious there was a little disappointment in her voice.

"Mel, we'll have to wait and see, okay?"

"I know," she said. "But I wouldn't be satisfied until one of us sees Daddy."

"I agree too, sweetie."

"Have you heard from Gia?" Mel changed topic. "I talked to Mom earlier and she told me that Gia had called the house."

RJ read the time on the car stereo; 4:15 P.M.

"It's a little passed nine there… she should be home by now. I'll call her as soon as I hang up."

"Go ahead and call her now, I'll see you at home," Mel said and the phone went dead.

He turned the phone off and back on before pressing the number one button, set for speed-dialing Gia's number.

"Hello," the sleepy voice answered on the fifth ring.

No doubt her day had been far more productive than his, she sounded exhausted.

"Honey, sorry to wake you."

Gia's voice suddenly came alive, "Honey."

"Yes, baby, it's me…did you get my message?"

"Yes and I tried calling back but couldn't get through."

"Sometimes that's how it is with overseas calls," he said. "I miss you so much. How have you been?"

"Lonely without you," she said. "And, worried too. Did you see the lawyer yet?"

"Yes, I just left him… I'm on my way home."

RJ brought her up to speed on what Diallo had told him, but without too much detail, just his basic defense plan.

"Did you tell your parents?" he asked, concerned about how much they knew.

"Yes," Gia admitted, "but with very little details though. I told them we'll let them know as things progress. Mom thought I should be there with you and you know Dad…he feels anywhere outside the United States is not safe, except Italy, of course."

RJ laughed.

"And baby, Dad wants to help…in any way. You know he means it."

"I know," he said. "But let's not jump the gun yet."

"Of course," Gia agreed. "I want to get there as soon as possible, okay?"

"Okay," he said calmly. "I want you to go back to sleep, I'll call you tomorrow. I love you."

"I love you too."

There was silence, almost a full minute.

"Hello," RJ said, thinking Gia had hung up.

"I'm here," she answered.

They both laughed.

"I love you," she said and hung up.

✶✶✶✶

Rain began to fall, as he pulled into the driveway. RJ walked from the car, into the rain, not really too concerned about getting wet, and disappeared into the house through the front door. Katharine had dinner set in the formal dining room and was waiting in the living room with Razaq, who was sitting next to Mellody on the couch going over his homework. Mellody had showered, changed and looked ready for bed.

"You look tired," Katharine said to RJ after her regular hug and kiss greeting.

"I'm fine, Mom," he said.

Katharine tried to look strong, but he could tell she was dying inside. He told her about his phone call with Gia, and for her benefit, downplayed the meeting with the lawyer. She brought it up anyway.

"Were you able to see Robert?"

"No, Mom, but the lawyer is working on it."

"How are we supposed to know he's okay?" she asked, horrified.

"He told me Dad is holding up just fine," RJ said, and then added, "he's a fighter, Mom…he will be okay."

"I'll just keep praying," Katharine whispered and left to get the food and to wipe her eyes.

Between the small talks over dinner, RJ thought about the senator, wondering what was he eating. He'd pushed himself to set goals, work hard, strived to be a Big Man, with everything aimed at making lots of money and living the American dream in Liberia. He had paid for anything the family needed or wanted. He also wondered why his old man scared him at times. Politics belonged to those willing to play hardball. The senator seemed to know much about life in power circles, but not with the same social conscience, in RJ's opinion. When RJ told him he was going into public interest law, the senator wanted to know 'what the hell is that?', and asked if RJ was Democrat or Republican.

The rest of the evening, they worked hard to avoid the topics of the senator, local politics and the paper headlines, especially the LJC reports. They talked about old friends, old neighbors and got caught up on family gossips, none of which interested RJ in the least. Afterwards, he labored through a ten-minute workout of loading the dishwasher while Razaq and Mellody put the leftovers away.

"The case is worst than I thought," RJ whispered to Mellody as she put the last bowl into the fridge.

She said nothing, only gave him a withering look.

Chapter Twelve

BEFORE the civil war, churches went by names like Providence Baptist Church, Monrovia Seventh Day Adventist, Lutheran Church, United Methodist, The Episcopal Church, and, of course, a few Holy Temples with faith healers. By the time the war was over, people's lives were centered mostly on new churches with prophetic names, like the Fellowship Hall Christian Church, Words of Christ Church, Church of Atonement; all independent of past denominations.

Julius Peabody, a Baptist Seminary student before the war, had helped so many people during the war, who was to say he hadn't been sent by God? Most of his sermons were about the wrath of God coming down on the unrighteous, mainly fornicators and homosexuals. He'd preach, "God is merciful to sinners, but the sinner must be worthy as well."

The dedicated minister slaved over Words of Christ Church, working diligently and watching it grow, prospering slowly over time. He would have made an exceptional politician too, most members thought. Julius Peabody could kiss the ugliest baby known to mankind and still come up with something nice to say.

Over the years, Pastor Peabody perfected his fire-and-brimstone act with weekly sermons on the evils of immorality, and this led to his church's huge conservative congregation build-up. The very thought of fornication or homosexuality gave some of his members shudders, Lynnette Vinton for one, his number one supporter. During most sermons, Mrs. Vinton shouted 'Amen', alone for a while, until the rest of the congregation joined in. It was obvious that was what she wanted, 'on behalf of Pastor'. "Stand up for Jesus" she'd shout, and members would stand up.

Lynnette Vinton had been widowed long before the war, and had remained as such. There were many people who thought she was keeping her houseboy around in a romantic sort of way. Gossip is one thing, hurtful gossip is completely another, especially in the church. Pastor Peabody couldn't have stopped the gossip any more than he could stop the rain from falling.

And not that she was unattractive, but she carried herself plain. Lynnette never wore makeup; that was too worldly. She didn't care much about outward appearance though, not as much as she valued inner beauty. If her looks had not kept the men away, the Bible sure did. Lynnette Vinton carried her Bible wherever she went and threw in words like 'faith' and 'joy' and even 'salvation', in ordinary conversations.

She devoted her life to God and the community, always in charge of one thing or another; vacation Bible school, the women's ministry, Wednesday prayer meeting, new building fundraising, bake sales, thanksgiving dinner and toys collection drive for orphans during Thanksgiving and Christmas. With Lynnette, everything was 'if it was the Lord's will'. She always mentioned the Lord's will whenever you talked to her, no matter what the subject was. Words of Christ Church liked her a lot, though behind her back many teased, calling her the Salvation Lady.

Katharine Douglas was her 'American friend', as Lynnette put it. She always thought RJ would make a good minister, rather than a lawyer. "He's so good with people," Lynnette would say. Katharine thought the concept was absolutely ridiculous and kept it to herself. She'd come back with something like, "RJ's doing exactly what he wants to do, Lynnette," in a matter-of-factly manner.

It was different when it came to Doctor Douglas. The only thing Lynnette had for Mellody was, suspicions. She could no more imagine it the Lord's will to have homosexuals in heaven than two moons in the sky. The only time Lynnette Vinton had for Mellody was when asking for favors, "Mel, could you see this person at the hospital tomorrow? Mel, could you get that poor old lady some high blood pressure medicine? Mel, could you do this for that church member?" As far as Lynnette Vinton was concerned, the Lord willed that Mellody help people, in spite of her lifestyle.

✦✦✦✦

Dr. Douglas thought otherwise. Thirty-year-old Dr. Douglas loved being single, as she always put it. Mellody had worked very, very hard to accomplish a medical profession and did not mind the long hours spent to prepare her for the rigors of becoming a physician. She loved practicing her doctor skills and interacting with patients. Her desire to become a doctor was not for the money. At the tender age of five, Mellody had already tossed aside her toy stethoscope for a real one, playing doctor with her parents and RJ, fascinated over the sounds of their heartbeats.

The thrifty Dr. Douglas was meticulous about her patients and her clothes. Her Internal Medicine salary of $127,000 a year could get her anything and everything she wanted, but she was indeed a cautious spender. Vacations were spent in Liberia, working as a volunteer doctor and most of her elegant Italian business suits, admired by colleagues, were actually tailored while in Liberia. Her suits looked professional, classy, elegant and screamed power without looking too masculine. What people didn't know was, Mellody took with her to Liberia pictures of Italian designers like Versace, Cavalli, Prada, and of course, Armani; which her tailors copied to near perfection.

Two hours earlier, she had been dreaming happily of either sitting under the coconut trees in the backyard or on the front porch—without any interruptions—when the harsh ring of her cell phone burst the scene into quickly forgotten fragments. It was a call from the ER; they needed her for an emergency Cesarean Section. After a blizzard of activity, the emergency was over, and a picture-perfect little boy had been born.

Still soaked with the glow of the miracle of birth, Mellody

glanced at her watch. The emergency had come at that awkward time when she would normally be home showering. Instead, she splashed her face with cold water in the on-call room, no time for a shower. She rushed through the cafeteria line, and grabbed a bottle of coke, which was breakfast, while walking back to her office. Mellody arrived wearing part of her breakfast. It was a very minor inconvenience, but the feeling of wearing a stained shirt or having rumpled hair embarrasses her. She was not looking forward to the rest of the morning.

The waiting area was jammed as usual. The first few patients she saw were mostly children, some she'd seen before, and who had come in with minor complaints. She sped through the morning, pausing to smile at each patient, but hurrying to get back on schedule.

The next chart in her hand had a familiar name on the cover. Mellody stepped into the exam room and recognized the nine-year-old boy; large clefts marred the middle of his face. Although a scar suggested that his cleft lip had been repaired, he was still left without a nose or eyes. She was happy to see him wearing the glass eyes Roger Williams Medical Center had donated on her behalf, an attempt to make his face more presentable.

"Hi, Tapee," Mellody smiled, reaching forward, taking his hand, shaking it warmly. The hand at the end of his shortened arm was missing three fingers.

Tapee's condition is known as Amniotic Bands Sequence, which affects only about one in 25,000 otherwise normal children. When Tapee was still waiting to be born, his forming face fused to the membrane lining of the amniotic sac. Normal development was arrested, resulting in the large clefts in his mid-face. Part of the amniotic membrane ruptured, and the sac that was supposed to protect him, instead entangled his developing limbs in shriveled, fibrous, amniotic strands. Decreased circulation to the limbs caused multiple deformities and amputations. Incredibly, normal intellect and normal emotions were framed in a twisted, blind body.

'I'm glad this sweet little boy will never see his own face,' Mellody thought.

Thumbing through his chart, she looked up to ask a question, and saw tears making their way down the crevices of his face. Surprise that his tear ducts functioned gave way to genuine concern over what had made him cry. Mellody placed her hand gently on his shoulder and asked what had provoked his tears.

"I'm happy, Dr. Douglas...you smiled at me," little Tapee said.

'I cannot believe this little boy, with no eyes, had felt my smile,' she thought, 'The same way as he had felt the averted gaze of many onlookers.' And, her smile had touched him deeply.

This was part of what took Mellody into medicine. How striking, a gift as simple as a smile could be so powerful. When we see someone afflicted, whether emotionally or physically, it is easy to turn away, she thought. What an important act of humanity, to look in the eyes, even if there are none, and see a person, not just a problem.

To Mellody, it was not just the disabled or sick that needed reassurance. In both societies, Monrovia and Providence, the anchors both to place and to people had been loosened. People were drifting in a rolling sea of human community and by looking with fresh warmth and compassion at the people who surround us each day, we create new connections. By seeing beyond surface appearances, to the unique miracle of each individual, we are all kept afloat. As she stood in the exam room with Tapee, the two beaming at each other, both felt beautiful, regardless of how life was on that day.

The rest of the day, Mellody dealt with one patient after another: diabetes, poorly controlled hypertension, obesity, vaccinations (tetanus and pneumonia), lower back pain in an elderly man, bronchitis, unexplained weight loss, ringworm, schistosomiasis, African trypanosomiasis (sleeping sickness), toenail fungal infection, lipoma (a benign fatty growth), malaria, and asthma.

Chapter Thirteen

On Wednesday Katharine Douglas had prepared lavishly for the church monthly women's group meeting at her home, but no one showed up, except for Lynnette Vinton and three others. This meeting had one time attracted more than fifty. No phone calls, no home visits, no excuses; nothing. It was as if the meeting had never been planned although it was announced last Sunday at church.

But the following Sunday morning Katharine felt recharged, sitting in church with her three children. Mellody had taken Sunday off and Razaq and RJ were happy to please their dear mother. Katharine kept her faith in all her troubles and, like it or not, was pursuing the unknown end. Her children turned down family counseling offered by Pastor Peabody, but today's message would do. She was persistent about them accompanying her to church, mainly because Pastor had informed her beforehand of the title of his sermon: MIGHTIER THAN ALL. She had been trying her best to influence her children when it came to her faith, only God knew.

"The roar of a waterfall is truly majestic," Pastor Peabody started his sermon, "but it is a different matter to be in the water hurtling toward the falls. That may be the situation you are in today. Be it physical, financial, emotional or some other troubles looming ever bigger… and you feel like you are about to go over the falls. In any of those situations, you have someone to turn to. He is the Lord!

He is able to do exceedingly, abundantly, about all that we ask or think. He is greater than all of our troubles! You must never measure God's unlimited power by your limited expectations!"

Pastor Peabody's soul-preaching was giving voice to hurt as well as to joy. Throughout the sermon, Katharine responded with an "Amen" and "Yes, Lord". Mellody smirked at some of the stares Katharine got from some members. RJ kept his attention on Pastor Peabody, but his mind was on Gia the entire sermon.

After an hour of soul preaching, Pastor Peabody ended his sermon with, "If you are helpless in life's battle, God's mighty power will be your stay… your failing strength He will renew, He is a God who cares for you!"

Sunday service closed with the hymn, GOD BE WITH YOU TILL WE MEET AGAIN. Pastor Peabody and the officiating deacons marched out first, and then the congregation followed. Katharine had already decided not to stay for potluck, because of Wednesday's no-show. She thanked Pastor Peabody for a heart-touching sermon, shook hands with the deacons and bid farewell to a few members that simply could not avoid her stare. RJ drove the family home.

✦✦✦✦

Around 10:30 A.M. Monday morning, Mellody was wearing hospital scrubs and a lab coat with her ID badge still pinned to the lapel. She had come straight from work after a long terrible shift for her, going straight to the hospital after church. She couldn't wait to get home, take a nice shower and hit her bed. She wanted to escape into blessed sleep. Then the front door buzzer went off repeatedly, three, four times, and then the knock on the door.

"I'll get it!" Katharine called and hurried to the front door. Still wearing a white robe with a pink shower cap, presumably from the shower, she opened the door and stared at Lynnette, surprised.

"Good morning, Lynnette, come on in." It was Katharine's natural instinct to be nice, to be polite and courteous. "Please, wait in the living room while I put on some clothes."

Sitting in the living room, Lynnette turned the question over in her mind for what seemed to be the hundredth time. She pulled herself up from the spot on the couch and walked over to the home office setup in the corner of the room. Lynnette stared at the Douglas's achievements hanging on the wall, credentials and awards, theirs and the children's. Katharine came out from the kitchen to the living room with a tray, as Lynnette was now staring at the family pictures on the desk, one with the senator and Katharine sitting and cuddling on the beach, another with RJ and Gia, Razaq in his soccer uniform, and Mellody in a hospital scrub, all grinning. Lynnette had missed Katharine when she went into the kitchen.

"The whole church's been in a tizzy since they found out about the senator," Lynnette said, realizing Katharine's presence. "And you know, you can't hush everybody… I am sorry for what you're going through."

"Thanks, Lynnette," Katharine said, and then suggested, "Why don't we go and sit on the porch."

The women ambled to the antiquity 5-piece, elegantly tailored, furniture on the far corner of the porch, opposite the hammock. The outdoor cushions, with contrast cording, looked equally great as if in a garden. Lynnette took her cup of tea and plate with slices of sweet cornbread Katharine had prepared for brunch, and the two sat down.

"Katharine, you know what I'm saying is what everyone else in the church has been thinking in the past few weeks," Lynnette started. "The point is… you know people will talk."

Katharine nodded, not knowing exactly what Lynnette was talking about.

Lynnette pursed her lips, wondering whether she should let Katharine know what was being said behind her back. Knowing it was a hot-button issue with some women, especially when it came to their children.

"When did she stop being attracted to men?" Lynnette asked, anyway. She had a faraway look in her eyes, and it was a moment before she went on. "Poor Katharine, it must be hard for you."

"Who?" Katharine asked, somehow, pretending.

"Mel," she said, and took a sip of tea.

Katharine's gaze faltered. "Mel?" she said, furrowing her brow.

"A church member saw her kissing some Chinese doctor the other day," Lynnette whispered, matter-of-frankly. "Now...a fine looking girl like Mel should be married. People wouldn't think otherwise, don't you think?"

Katharine sighed.

"Only God knows, Lynnette," she said. What she really wanted to say was, 'Is it any of your business?'

Just then, Mellody poked her head out the front door.

"Hello, Mrs. Vinton," she greeted. "Mom, sorry for interrupting, but I turned the living room phone ringer low because I don't want to be disturbed. Don't' forget to turn it back up if I do."

"Sure, honey," Katharine said, smiling.

Lynnette leaned toward Katharine as soon as Mellody left. "It's not your fault," she said, as if being supportive. "If truth be told, it's the white people that our children have learned that nasty thing from."

Lynnette was openly a racist, and was proud of it. She was too self-righteous to be socially or politically correct. She didn't so much dislike white people, especially those that came into her country, as she distrusted them.

"Is that why the women didn't come to last week's meeting?" Katharine asked.

"Partly so," Lynnette pursed her lips again, thinking to herself, Mellody's lifestyle seemed to coincide with the senator's involvement of the ritualistic murder.

Not surprised, Katharine stared at Lynnette with her eyebrows raised. "Is it because of Mel or Robert?" she asked.

Lynnette cleared her throat. "Actually, both...Pastor Peabody doesn't want anything to do with gossip, so as your friend, I'm telling you."

"Well... thanks," Katharine muttered.

"You're a good Christian woman, Katharine. I see how you've taken to that country boy as if he's your son. I know it's not the Lord's will that you suffer because of your daughter or your husband."

Katharine chuckled, disgustingly. It was not the first time that Lynnette had referred to Razaq as 'that country boy'. And Katharine had reminded her, always, that Razaq was just as much her son as RJ was. She did not feel any different about him being adopted and did not understand why black people in Liberia felt there was a need for separation of class or tribe.

"You remind me of Job, in the Bible," Lynnette said. "Remember Job?"

"Oh, yes I do," Katharine mumbled.

"Now Katharine," Lynnette continued, reaching for her friend's hand. "God is always available to hear the prayer of His children. You are His child, the senator is His child, and Mel is His child."

Katharine forced a smile.

"We both see things through our faith, right?"

Katharine nodded, 'yes'.

"God's hand is in everything," Lynnette continued. "You must leave everything in His hands now."

"I have, Lynnette… I have," Katharine said. "I know what my husband did for these people in this country. Robert is one of the kindest human beings I know. He's always extended his hands to the needy. Now, they are trying to sentence me to a life without him. As for Mel, she works hard… so hard that I'm worried about her health, not getting much rest. I know what difference she makes in this community. And for that, I will not stick to the bitter. Lynnette, I will stick to the sweet and leave all of it in God's hands."

There's always a price for becoming involved in the struggles of others, Lynnette thought. She regretted being the bearer of bad news.

"No need to worry about me, Katharine," Lynnette said. "I'll always be your friend."

Katharine didn't know what to say. She needed her friend even while her children were home, and especially after they return to the States.

"Keep being my friend, Lynnette," she said, pleased.

Chapter Fourteen

AFTER Lynnette left, Katharine felt herself puff up just a bit at the realization. Her husband was in jail and she'd suspected her daughter of being a lesbian since she could remember. Technically, Mellody wasn't a lesbian because she'd not come out to her, yet.

It was getting close to six o'clock; Razaq was setting the table while Katharine got dinner ready. She heard the SUV drive in the yard and went to the window. She pulled the curtain to one side to make sure it was RJ. Beyond the window, she watched him get out of the car and walk toward the front door.

RJ was adapting to his life in Monrovia, over the last few weeks, waiting for documents that should be available but not getting them until after a few days, waiting on folks at the office who were at work, but had their secretary tell him otherwise and office workers openly asking for bribes.

"Hello! I'm home," RJ called as he came through the front door.

"I'm in the kitchen," Katharine answered.

"How was your day, Mom," he said, walking in the kitchen, studying her face.

"Okay, I guess. Didn't do much… just Lynnette came by this morning."

"That's nice," RJ said, absentmindedly. "I've noticed she's the only one that comes around. Not even Dad's family. Are they already ashamed of us?"

"Oh no," Katharine said, seriously. "Everybody's working and they are too busy with their lives to be bothered."

"I see… where's Mel?"

"She should be up by now," Katharine guessed. "She came in late this morning and went to bed around ten-thirty."

They were soon feasting on baked chicken and scallop potatoes when Mellody walked into the kitchen. From the corner of her eyes, she caught sight of Katharine looking at her.

"So, what did the Salvation Lady want?" Mellody said to Katharine and sat down.

After giving it some thinking, Katharine answered, "You."

"Lucky me," Mellody muttered. "Seriously, Mom, why does she give me those crazy stares?"

Katharine had a need always to tell her children the truth and her commitment to truth-telling between them every once in a while got so hard to do; especially now, with something that would hurt her daughter.

"I'll be the first to admit that it doesn't make much sense, and if I had my way, I'd have told Lynnette it was nobody's business," Katharine said.

"Yeah?"

"Sweetie, the crazy thing is folks here don't mind their own business. They'll talk behind your back, they'll gossip, and it'll take them a long time to forget that we all live in sin," she shook her head. "I know it's a lot to ask, honey," Katharine said and reached for Mellody's hand. "But would you do this for me?"

"Do what, Mom? What are you talking about?"

Katharine swallowed and whispered, "You and Doctor Cho."

Mellody pulled her hand away.

"Since when did you start discussing me with your friends?"

"Be discreet, Mel. It's all that I'm asking," Katharine said, touching her chest for emphasis, trying her best to appear earnest.

"Why does it suddenly feel like I'm sixteen years old and sneaking behind my parents' back?"

"These people are not as understanding as parents, Mel, they're much worst," Katharine stressed.

"Then why do you care what they think?"

Katharine broke down crying.

"Because I love you," she sobbed.

RJ withdrew his chair from the table.

"These people are nuts!" he snarled. "Mom, listen to me. Mel is a brilliant doctor who can be living a life that most people only dream of. Look what she's doing? She spends her vacation time working for free... taking care of sick people who can never earn enough money, in their lifetime, to pay her."

As Katharine listened, she swiped at her eyes and forced a smile. She understood why RJ was trying to make his sister feel better.

"I love my sister just the way she is," he said and kissed Mellody on her forehead. Then, he gave Katharine a stare, rolled his eyes and walked out.

Mellody's phone buzzed.

"Hello," she answered, and then hesitated to continue. "Hold on, baby."

Katharine looked up, wanting to know who had called.

"Shakari," Mellody volunteered the information, as if suddenly accepting the weight of her sin.

Katharine pulled away from the table, left the kitchen and joined RJ in the living room.

Mellody had prolonged her usual two months of service to indefinite after the senator's arrest. Shakari could understand a few more weeks, but not indefinitely . She didn't feel she could make it with Mellody gone longer than usual. Mellody's traveling had become a source of tension, and Shakari had nagged long enough to come along. She'd never taken Shakari's suggestion seriously, but reflecting on her life now, Mellody wondered whether she should. The constant pressure to live together, she realized, had manifested itself in other areas of her life as well. Mellody loved her space, as she put it. It was easy for her to do something, anything, every waking moment without someone else's approval. For the first time in what seemed like forever, spending time with someone other than Shakari, Dr. Cho for instance, was beginning to feel like guilty pleasure. The sneaking around was no longer exciting.

"I'll figure something out," she promised Shakari when she

resumed their phone conversation.

Shakari seemed happy enough with the progress of a new promise to even consider a solution. Needless to say, Mellody sounded
like she meant it. She ended their conversation with how much she
missed her, how she couldn't wait for them to be together again,
and there was no one else she'd rather be with, other than Shakari.
Mellody even kissed the phone before hanging up.

Lost in thought, it took Katharine a second to realize Mellody
was making her way back to the living room.

"Is Shakari okay?" RJ asked.

"She's fine," Mellody said, moving toward Katharine. Then she
sat beside her and slipped her arms around her shoulders. "Mom,
can I tell you what Mahatma Gandhi says about your people."

Katharine raised her brows. "What people?" she mumbled.

"Christians… Words of Christ Church people… the Salvation
Lady… every one of them."

"What did he say?"

"Gandhi said, 'I like your Christ; I do not like your Christians.
They are so unlike Christ,'" Mellody said, staring at Katharine.

Katharine sighed.

"I agree with him, Mom," she added.

Katharine said nothing. Her fragile body trembling, she
wrapped her arms around her daughter, knowing how she loved
her children so much and was very afraid for them.

Chapter Fifteen

At first, there was a steady stream of well-wishers and gossip-ers lingering in and out of the Douglas's home, deeply concerned about Katharine, but also desperate for details. But as time went by, because of the fact that the senator had steadfastly insisted on his innocence, the unfolding of the murder case had forced family, friends, and church members alike, to confront the enduring nega-tive reports on the senator and his wife, devout Christians, pillars of the community.

"*The revelations of his involvement are eloquent examples of the senator's double life, his wicked ways,*" said an editorial in The Liberian Journal Constitution. "*Ritualistic killing is the reason that he hangs his head in shame.*"

But while Senator Douglas was the latest and not the most prominent, dozens of business leaders, politicians, even clergymen had been charged; some convicted and hung of similar charges, long before the civil war.

Even though he didn't know quite what to expect, it certainly wasn't easy. RJ and Diallo had law degrees, both had passed the bar exam, both were fluent in the tongue of legalese, twin warriors to some degree. But they had both been working hard for the past weeks and RJ was amazed how very little progress had been made. He'd come to believe the only thing too many workers did was to procrastinate, expect bribes, what they called cold water, and scam people out of small change. Even when they came by certain Government offices, no one ever actually seemed to be working. Needless to say, he always felt a tinge of chance in his father's freedom whenever he headed to one of those offices.

RJ was suddenly in a hurry to get to Diallo's office. This was Diallo's last attempt requesting a meeting for the senator and his son. They had been given the run-around every which way he took. He showered and changed into jeans, a white shirt and tie, a navy blazer and Air Jordan tennis shoes. He was ready to go without breakfast as food was losing its importance. Then, the phone startled him.

"Hi baby, how are you holding up?"

It was Gia and she was going right to the point, as she always does. He always thought she would have made an outstanding detective with her psychology background.

"Hi honey," he said, and waited with a long pause.

"I asked how you're doing."

"I'm okay," RJ said, "How a' bout you?"

"You don't sound okay to me," Gia said. "I'm sure you're not sleeping, and what about progress of the case? How's that going?"

"Not as well as I would have hoped," he admitted. "I'm praying that something good happens today. Dad's lawyer and I are going to see the judge. Say a prayer, because he's an asshole of a man."

"Oh baby, I sure wish I was there. It wouldn't be long now. I'm doing interviews with a few more doctors so I can leave someone at the office while I'm in Liberia."

He could not believe she was thinking about leaving someone in her practice. That seemed too much to ask, but he wasn't surprised at her thoughtfulness. It's just that they both couldn't abandon their jobs the same time.

"Honey, I don't want you to…."

"Baby, I've already decided it," she cut him off. "I'm coming there to be with you and don't try to talk me out of it. I love you."

"I love you more," he said. He'd always said 'more'.

"Good luck with the asshole judge," she chuckled.

"Yeah," he replied. "I'll call you later, okay? I really miss you."

"I miss you too, baby. Good-bye."

"Good-bye," RJ said and hung up.

✶✶✶✶

RJ arrived at the office a few minutes before nine. Grace was sitting in front of the computer, her fingers poised on the keyboard. She saw him, took a deep breath and lost the frown. He seemed to have read her expression.

"Grace? Are you okay?"

"Yeah," she said, "Just a lot on my mind."

"There's a lot of stress these days," he said. "Thanks for helping Diallo with the case, by the way."

"No need to thank me, RJ... it's my job, really."

He remained standing in front of her desk, a bit hesitant. Perhaps his timing might not be perfect, but he thought about it before asking.

"Do you know anything about Judge Tweh?"

Grace looked up from the keyboard.

"He's tough," she said, stressing 'tough', "And, he's obsessive about a clean docket. I know he is from the Firestone area. Want to hear something funny? He divorced his wife once, and remarried her after a year," she chuckled.

RJ uttered a light laugh.

"All of his children are well educated," Grace continued. "One daughter is a doctor at Firestone Hospital, a son teaches at Cuttington University, two of his children work for the UN and another teaches engineering in America."

"Wow," RJ said, amazed.

"He is going to be tough," Grace promised.

"Is he fair?" RJ asked. His tone was challenging.

"Most people think he is," she said. "He's not like some of the old judges that used to accept bribes, calling them gifts. He moves his cases fast, wants quick trials and makes decisions on the spot. He's especially hard on big shots and those in high government positions."

"So, he hates rich people?"

"No. He feels strongly that the rich man's life is worth just as much as a poor man's. Because of him, many poor people have seen their freedom."

"I see," RJ said. "You must be a fan."

"Well," Grace said, selecting the right words to respond. "I know what it's like to be among the poorest in Liberia. In our justice system, the poor are often unjustly exposed to prolong pre-trial detention. Poor people that are charged with minor crimes are jailed with little hope that they will ever have access to a legal process and with no knowledge of their constitutional rights. What are their chances, if they have no choice except the public defenders? God forbid if all you can afford is a public defender. Some remain detained for months, at times, over a year, awaiting trial, especially in a magistrate court. Judge Tweh was one of those who saw that our justice system had an urgent need of support and reform."

"Of course," RJ said, after evaluating her response. "I applaud justice for the poor. I hope his justice is for all."

"That's what's written on the front wall of The Temple of Justice building," she said, and then quoted, "'Let justice be done for all men'. You are a lawyer, so let's not forget, justice is blind."

"Justice is blind," RJ repeated. "And I can't wait to meet this, Judge Tweh."

"I believe he is a fair man," Grace said, trying to assure him.

RJ nodded.

"RJ," she whispered, "Diallo is a very good lawyer…the senator has the best."

"I know," RJ said. Then, crossing his fingers on both hands, added, "A little luck wouldn't hurt either."

"A little luck wouldn't hurt," Grace said and smiled.

At that moment, Diallo stepped out of his office, dangling his keys. From the look of it, he was handling the driving. He gave Grace some instructions on his other cases; assured her he could be reached for any reason, and then said to RJ, "I'm ready."

RJ squeezed into the front seat of the Miata holding his cell phone, a little nervous. He'd always been uncomfortable with someone else's driving, especially in a tiny car like the MX-5. Of course, Diallo drove badly too, cutting before taxis, overtaking slower cars. He'd even squealed to a stop at a red light, his car partially blocking the intersection. RJ slid lower in the seat, closed his eyes, in his mind, and offered a short but sincere prayer that they reach without a collision.

"Can you believe this?" Diallo snarled, looking at the brake lights on the cars before them.

He had not the slightest clue that they were impeding bumper to bumper traffic three blocks ahead. Horns erupted all around. RJ caught sight of Diallo from the corner of his eye. He was staring anxiously ahead. It was obvious he had his heart and soul on his plan. Traffic stalled for a while, and then about half an hour later they were moving again, somewhat faster.

"Well… thank God," Diallo said, sounding relieved. There was a pause, then he said, a matter-of-factly, "I don't care whose button I push today."

RJ did not say anything, knowing this was a minefield where Diallo was forced to tread. His role was almost limited to checking on the progress of the case in this legal arena. Who could blame him for being antsy?

Chapter Sixteen

THE Justice Ministry's second floor was crawling with busy people. RJ and Diallo spotted Judge Tweh, walked casually by the receptionist, and followed closely behind. He was in a hurry, carrying a stack of files in one hand and his briefcase in the other. He immediately felt their presence.

"Who the hell are you?" Judge Tweh demanded, walking away and talking. "What do you two want?"

"Sir," Diallo said, walking side by side, signaling RJ to tag along. "I'm Diallo Amadou, Senator Douglas's lawyer. This is RJ, his son."

"He got himself a celebrity lawyer, uh?" Judge Tweh murmured, still walking, but with slower steps.

He led the men to his office, slammed the pile of files on his desk, most of which were falling, placed his briefcase on the floor, and sat down behind his desk.

RJ had heard enough about Judge Tweh, now he was face to face with him; a powerful-looking man, not much younger than the senator, sixtyish, potbellied, clean shaved and a receding hairline at the sides of his forehead. Only the sides and back of his head had hair, leaving a horseshoe shape.

While they waited for Judge Tweh to settle down, his desk phone buzzed. He picked up, listened for a second or so.

"Yes, Ms. Barr, I will be there shortly," he said into the receiver and hung up. "I'm already late for this meeting," he said to Diallo. "Speak hurriedly…what do you want?"

"Sir, RJ has been trying for three weeks to see his father, and we've been denied. I'm pleading his cause, Sir…."

Judge Tweh got up before Diallo finished.

"I cannot help you with that," he stressed. "We have a system in place; that is the decision of the people at MCP to make, not me. If you two will excuse me, I am already late for my meeting."

The men had sat briefly when Judge Tweh got up and walked toward the office door. Diallo was up in a hurry and then RJ. The Judge, showing less patience now, for the first time looked RJ in the eyes as the men walked by him.

"Sorry, son, but follow the protocol. I'm sure Chief Dolo is only doing his job. Try him again," Judge Tweh said and took off walking. "Follow the protocol," he said loudly, waving his hand.

It didn't make sense to RJ. Nothing did so far. But especially the back and forth whose-in-charge game being played in their system of *change*. Had a war been started against his father? If it had, who was the enemy? What was to happen next? He thought of taking ownership of his father's trial, but Diallo was doing his job, really.

"Let's go!" Diallo said, after a long pause, pondering the matter.

✦✦✦✦

They were back in traffic heading to Monrovia Central Prison in a hurry, hoping to catch up with Chief Dolo before lunch. It seemed like a long shot, but they had no choice. For a moment, RJ tuned out the highlife music blasting through the car speakers and started thinking about his father, trying to figure what could possibly have tied him to this mess, this disaster, this murder. There was no evidence tying him to the crime, no confession, only circumstantial evidence. So far he didn't know anything about the other four men and one woman also charged. One thing was obvious, and probably useful to the case—the forced coercive confession of an intimidated suspect turned state witness.

"We should be in visual contact with the senator as soon as we clear these mountains we're against," Diallo said. "We're going directly to Aaron Dolo… sneak up on him. Fuck protocol."

Either Diallo had run out of patience with the bureaucrats and government workers or he was having a ball on this gravy train he was riding.

"Just try to get me to my father," RJ said to him. "Don't draw blood, we don't need more enemies," he added.

"Understood," Diallo said.

A few minutes later they were in front of the MCP main office building, out of the car and standing before the receptionist. Chief Dolo had come out of his office, on his cell phone, heading toward the main entrance. On his way, he had gotten a last minute call from his boss, who had gotten a call from Judge Tweh.

"Let the man see his son," his boss had said, "he's going to die anyway. And oh… you don't have to play easy."

"Sir…" Diallo called to get the chief's attention as soon as he folded his phone.

"See my receptionist at the desk," Chief Dolo pointed at a female officer. "Have her schedule an appointment, I'm out for lunch," he said looking at his timepiece, pretending he was unaware of the men's visit.

Diallo followed him outside instead.

"Sir, it's about the senator. His son lives out of the country and since he's been home, he hasn't seen him. We've been trying for weeks. Please, Sir… one phone call from you and they will let us see him. Five minutes is all I'm asking… *only* five minutes."

Chief Dolo glanced at RJ, giving it some thought.

"I'm a reasonable man," he said, loud that others in the parking lot heard him. Then he unfolded his phone and pushed a few numbers.

They did not know exactly who he was contacting.

"Give Senator Douglas five minutes with his lawyer. His son is with him," Chief Dolo said to the person at the other end and folded his phone. Then he got in his dark blue Ford Explorer and drove off.

As Diallo drove to the prison compound, he was thinking that his oddly brilliant plan had worked well. There had certainly been a backup plan just in case something didn't work right.

Chapter Seventeen

RJ was bristling with nervous energy when they got to the main prison. Everything seemed to be falling into place, according to Chief Dolo's orders. The level of security was extremely high. He and Diallo were subjected to a metal detector, then they had to present photo IDs. The officer furrowed his brow looking at RJ's Georgia driver's license and they had to explain that RJ was from America. They entered maximum security, signed the registry and were directed straight to the waiting room, a ten foot by ten foot section with two sets of tables with four chairs.

Twenty-five minutes ticked away, there was no show of the senator or a guard. Then another forty-five minutes went by. The level of frustration RJ was feeling was increasing by the minutes. He had never seen so much chaos, so open, in his entire professional life. This must be a sick joke, he thought.

Another one hour and ten minutes later the door opened, Senator Douglas was escorted by a heavily armed solider; ankle chained and hands cuffed. Inmates couldn't move outside their cells without handcuffs, leg irons and security guards. The senator was wearing a prisoner's uniform, a faded navy blue jumpsuit with the white letters MCP on the front and back. He looked frail, almost anorexic, and much older than sixty-five. His black hair that was peppered with gray was completely white. Senator Douglas had changed so much that he resembled his father more than himself, looking like an old demoralized slave. RJ sucked in his breath, but tried not to show it.

"Papay, don't do anything stupid," the solider taunted the senator. Then he said to Diallo and RJ, "You got thirty minutes and thirty minutes is all you get."

RJ hugged his father and patted his back as Senator Douglas kept repeating, "How is your mother?" and "So good to see you." When they finally pulled apart, the senator's eyes were red and his cheeks wet. RJ remained dry-eyed, strong, for his dad. He had never, ever seen his father cry.

"Diallo is working hard for you, Dad," he said, turning to the lawyer. "He's the best in Liberia."

"That's what I need," Senator Douglas said, forcing a smile.

RJ noticed the space from his missing tooth.

"What happened to your tooth?"

"Happened the night of the arrest," Senator Douglas said. "They tried to beat a confession out of me, but I would not admit to something I did not do. Son, this is so crazy," he sighed. "This is a nightmare, one that I wouldn't wish on my enemy."

"That's why I'm here, Senator Douglas," Diallo said. "I'm doing my best to stop this awful craziness."

Senator Douglas nodded at Diallo, and then turned to RJ. There was a long pause.

"Son, I had nothing to do with that young man's murder," he said. "I swear...I simply let a friend borrow my car. I've always let people borrow my car. It's obvious, someone has framed me. It doesn't make sense to me. I don't have an enemy in this world. At least, I didn't think I did."

"Dad, your only mistake, a big and painful one, is trusting people. You've never done that before...allowing somebody else to use your property without asking questions.

"Tamba has used my car before, in fact, many times before."

"Without you asking any questions?"

"Yes," Senator Douglas nodded.

"I'm sure the man has his own car," RJ said, clearly out of frustration. "Was his car in the garage, or something?"

Senator Douglas started to respond and hesitated.

"Dad, your life is on the line here. This man is saying that you helped plan that murder."

"I didn't, damn it! I didn't," he shouted at RJ, his eyes pleading for understanding.

"Senator Douglas," Diallo interrupted, "did you tell the police that you gave Tamba Nah Wumah permission to use your car?"

"Wumah always used my car when he took his girlfriends out," Senator Douglas murmured, slightly embarrassed. "He didn't want his wife finding out about his affairs. He always borrowed my car. That was not the first time."

"So you knowingly let him use your car to cheat?" RJ snarled.

"Please, RJ," Diallo pleaded, showing respect for the senator. To Diallo's understanding and even experience, it was common for men in Liberia to be of help to each other in that situation.

"For some reason, my sense of balance was off," Senator Douglas whispered. "I took for granted what people are capable of."

"This is a tough one, Dad," RJ said. "So typical of the black man, just like crabs; your so-called friend is going down and he's pulling you with him."

Suddenly the officer came bursting through the door. It scared the three men.

"Time's up!" he shouted and moved to claim his prisoner.

"I will do everything to get you out. You can count on that, Sir," Diallo stressed.

RJ tried to hug the senator, but he backed away; only giving his son a small, sad wave. Then the officer took the senator away. RJ knew, then and there, his father had lost hope of living, in or out of prison.

✦✦✦✦

"I have to pick up a file from the police station," Diallo said, on their way back to his office. He had an appointment with Officer Lonos, Chief Dolo's special assistant, to get some documents on the case.

Officer Lonos was fiftyish with a well-toned, stocky five-feet-eight body. He met them waiting in his office. He was neatly dressed in camouflage with spit-shined army boots. As hard as Diallo tried to be cordial, Officer Lonos was stone-face. He asked them, more or less, ordered them, to wait in this office. Moments later, he came back with a case file.

"Why are you having a hard time putting together a case, a murder as obviously ritualistic motivated as this?" Officer Lonos remarked, rather sarcastically.

"What are you saying?" Diallo said to him.

Officer Lonos leafed through the file until he came to an official document marked *City of Monrovia Coroner's Report*. "Read it and weep," he snarled, handing Diallo the file. "You still want to check out the pictures too?" he asked, seemingly enjoying the moment.

"Sure, yeah," Diallo said with a shrug. "What about the confessions?"

"Right," Officer Lonos nodded. "I almost forgot that."

He went back in the chief's office and came with another case file.

"If you are looking for a connection, it's all there," Officer Lonos said, handing Diallo the file. "I'm sure you know how unusual it is for a killer, who has been caught, to lie."

"Thanks," Diallo snapped back.

Diallo quickly did a mental check, making sure all the files he had asked for were there. Then he and RJ headed back to the office.

✦✦✦✦

They arrived a few minutes before seven and Grace was still behind her desk, but packed and ready to head home.

"You're still here," RJ said to her, surprised.

"Yeah," she said, handing Diallo a stack of pink memo slips. "I wanted to make sure he looks at these before going home tonight."

"If you don't mind waiting, I'll give you a ride home," RJ offered, knowing it was about to rain.

"Thanks," she said and sat down.

RJ followed Diallo into his office.

Diallo took out the file that had forty-seven photos of the crime scene, and arranged them in no particular order, on the table. One particular one caught RJ's eyes, a close-up of the victim's face. His breath emptied out of his lungs. What type of monster would do this to another human being? He thought.

"Nobody deserves this," RJ whispered, staring at the photo. "Anyone guilty of this should be punished. I'm damn sure my father is not capable of doing such."

"Your father had nothing to do with that," Diallo pointed at the photo. "To be honest, he is guilty of one thing."

RJ looked up, as if to ask what.

"For being a Congo man…."

RJ chuckled at the concept. "Why would they think a Congo man would do this?" he said, studying the photo.

"Money… power… that's where the juju comes in," Diallo said, nodding his head.

"Juju," RJ repeated; his voice skeptical.

"My defense is not to prove whether ritual killing is done for juju in this case," Diallo explained. "I've read the confessions, over and again, your father did not participate in any part of their planning or killing. The car used in the night of question, belongs to the senator. He allowed his friend to use it, he cannot be responsible for what reason it was used. He had no idea they were going to use his car for such a purpose. He is not responsible for Johnny Bono's murder. Because he is a successful Congo man, they want to make their lineup a diverse one."

Diallo's theory suddenly made sense to RJ, but then again, it did not.

"Somebody hates Congo people and my father's life is to be used simply for diversity?" he said to Diallo. "Is that your defense?"

"That is my defense," Diallo said. "The senator had no connection, zero connection, to the crime."

RJ furrowed his brow.

"RJ, you've had a long day," Diallo said, "Go home to the family and get some rest. I'll be on this, among other things, for a little while before I go home. Tomorrow is a new day…I'll do this all over again."

RJ looked at his watch. He had kept Grace waiting long enough.

"Okay, tomorrow then," he said to Diallo and walked out.

Light rain was falling as he and Grace ran to the SUV. They sat in silence, RJ behind the wheel, driving off slowly and waiting for Grace to say something.

"I live in Paynesville," she said, slightly embarrassed that it was probably out of his way.

"Just give me directions," he said, politely.

She was glad to hear willingness in his voice.

On the way, Grace shared more stories of poor people's struggles in Liberia. The enormous strains on their paychecks, to clothe, feed and house a family on income as low as $45 per month. And at times, things went from bad to worse when they could not find work. Desperate to survive, people are forced into deceits and shameless crimes. Her struggle was no different, until Cecelia Amadou believed in her dream and begged her husband to hire her. Not only did she want a much better life for herself, she wanted better things for Liberia as well.

The ride lasted about thirty minutes and RJ was amazed at her ambitions. He made the final turn into the yard and stopped. Grace thanked him and got out.

Chapter Eighteen

RJ shared details of his meeting with the senator over dinner. He left out details of the senator's appearance, only stressing that he'd asked about Katharine and was very much concerned about her. It hardly made a difference in Katharine's mood, she was happy a family member had seen him, at least, but it was not good enough. He was still incarcerated. She went to bed right after dinner. RJ and Razaq decided to have their heart-to-heart boy-talk sitting on the porch.

The first rumblings of thunder could be heard as far as anyone could hear. The moon was now hidden by clouds, darkening the sky. Lightning flashed on the horizon and a moment later a soft rain began to fall again, pattering against the roof. In the backyard, the leaves on the coconut trees rustled in the breeze as thunder echoed. They watched the rain intensified into a steady downpour, falling diagonally from the sky. Thunder exploded overhead, and the rain began coming down in sheets.

"You want to go in?" RJ asked, sensing Razaq was a little scared.

Razaq shook his head, 'No', but with obvious hesitation.

The storm seemed to be reaching its climax as another sheet of rain broke from the clouds. Water poured off all sides of the house like waterfalls. Lightning flashed again, closer this time, and thunder crashed like a giant gun. Razaq scooted closer to the door and looked at RJ. Lightning flashed again, and both boys booted into the house, laughing scared.

They settled around the kitchen table, each with a tall glass of lemonade. Though the wind had picked up, the rain finally began to slow.

"Is Daddy going to be okay?" Razaq asked, concerned. "Why hasn't he come home since the police took him?"

RJ hesitated, trying to think of what to say.

"Razaq, you're old enough to know what's going on," RJ said. "I'm going to be honest with you, okay? And, I don't want you to worry."

Razaq nodded.

"Dad is in trouble, big trouble."

Razaq's face clouded. "What kind of trouble, RJ?"

"Nothing for you to worry about," he said, and pointed calmly, "That's why your big brother is here to take care of it."

Razaq smiled, but there was something sad in it.

"Listen buddy, I'll do all I can to get Dad home…even if I have to beat the crap out of those police," he said, furrowing his brow and flexing his biceps.

"I will help you," Razaq laughed, but it was a sad little laugh.

The rain had finally stopped, and in its place, the sounds of light thunder echoed.

"You better get to bed…. tomorrow's school."

He patted Razaq's back, to reassure him that they were in this thing together, whatever it was the family was facing. Razaq walked to his room and RJ went to his.

✦✦✦✦

It was late, but RJ decided to call Osei anyway, before turning in for the night. He dialed the number to the Cassava Patch first. It was around nine-thirty in Liberia; two-thirty on the East coast in the States. On many nights, Osei is at the restaurant way past three in the morning, he thought.

"Thank you for calling the Cassava Patch," Osei answered, being professional even after regular business hours. "How can I help you?"

"I want to report a missing person," RJ joked.

Osei recognized the voice instantly.

"RJ," he screamed, "You are the missing person!"

RJ could feel the love over the phone. His best friend, his brother, was so happy to hear his voice.

"How are things? Man, you wouldn't get off so easy, you don't call, not even a crummy e-mail for almost a month!"

RJ apologized, and then told Osei what had happened so far. He had seen the old man, met with the lawyer, and they were working their asses off to get the senator home.

"I haven't seen Gia since you left," Osei said, almost complaining. "She knows that I'm here for her. I've called her cell, the office; no return calls. Is she here, or did she go to her parents?"

"She's there, possibly buried in work. You know Gia," RJ made the excuse.

"RJ, I've been worried about you. How is Mom holding up? And how's Mel? Is she back?"

"Mom is holding up fine, she's happy that I'm here. Mel is fine… busy as ever. She's expanded her time at JFK to indefinite."

"Is she giving up practice here?"

"No, just until this whole mess is over."

"Good… good," Osei said. "What can I do to help? I hate being here while you're there."

"I know, Osei, I miss having you here. Just keep the family in your prayers. How's Michael, by the way?"

"He's fine…he missed having you at his games."

RJ laughed, happy to hear that.

"Tell my favorite wide receiver that I miss him. How many touchdowns has he made?"

"Only you would ask such a question," Osei laughed and then answered, "Four."

"Tell him Uncle RJ will make it up to him when he gets back. And give your beautiful wife a hug for me."

"I always do," Osei said. "RJ, please, don't let it be so long. And, return my calls!"

"Will do," RJ promised and hung up.

Chapter Nineteen

AFTER his follow-up call to the office, RJ laced up his sneakers and headed outside for a run. His plan was not to sit in the house thinking about his father on death row this morning. So far, Diallo had managed to convince him he was working hard, beyond expectations. The neighborhood had many homes that had been built after the war and many new town houses were going up, which look very American, with sidewalks and many driveways with garages or carports. An LJC article the other day proclaimed that Monrovia was beginning to look no different from the city of Atlanta. Some houses even sported hexagonal red IWSC security signs, courtesy of the Intelligent Watch Security Corporation, the leading security company in Liberia. The IWSC system provided video surveillance for residential and commercial customers. RJ thought about their commercial on TV:

We will protect your family and business
from theft and Burglary; all UNWANTED *invaders.*

"What happened to ya'll the night Dad got arrested?" he said to himself.

Two hours later when he got home from his run, Mr. Tom had made it in and was getting the car ready for Katharine's daily errands.

"Morning, RJ," Mr. Tom greeted. "You're not a footballer, so why do you exercise so much?"

RJ chuckled at the concept. "I need to stay in shape," he answered.

Mr. Tom laughed and shook his head. "You are running for nothing," he said. "The only reason I would run is, if someone was chasing me."

RJ laughed. The typical Liberian's sense of humor was extraordinary, far beyond ordinary and average, RJ thought. Someone ought to write a book, they'll laugh all the way to the bank.

After his shave and shower, RJ went looking for Katharine to check on her. He did not find her in the living room or the kitchen. She wasn't on the porch nor sitting under the coconut trees in the backyard, her favorite spot during most mornings. The next reasonable place to check was the bedroom. He edged open her bedroom door and saw her lying in bed.

"Come on in, RJ, I'm not sleeping," she said, almost in a whisper.

He quietly walked into the room.

"Are you okay, Mom?"

"I'm just lying in bed because I don't have much to do today. Ma Teete is not coming in today, so I've decided to be lazy."

"How about breakfast in bed… I'll make it, not Mel," he joked.

"No thanks," Katharine chuckled. "I think I'll just lie here a little longer."

"Will you be going anywhere at all today?" he asked.

"No, hadn't planned to. Why?"

"I was just thinking. Maybe I'll pick up Razaq today after school."

"I'm sure he'll be happy," Katharine said. "He wouldn't have to take the bus home."

"Well, that's what I'll do," RJ said, and kissed her forehead. "I'll see you later Mom… and please, call me if you need to go anywhere."

Katharine nodded and smiled. She had brilliantly hidden one of her many crying moments.

Yes, he will pick up Razaq and they would head to Sinkor Circle, he thought as he perched himself behind the steering wheel. A little change of pace might do some good. More than that, Razaq would be surprised at his thoughtfulness. RJ drove Mr. Tom home, which Mr. Tom didn't mind the time off, and headed back to town.

Razaq was surprised and thrilled with RJ's showing. He showed off his brother to a few schoolmates before jumping in the front seat.

"Where are we going?" Razaq asked.

"Nowhere, really," RJ said. "I was just driving around to clear my mind. But of course, we can go to Sinkor Circle if you like."

"Yes! Sinkor Circle," Razaq repeated, pleasantly surprised.

RJ fire up the engine and followed the path through town, cruising slowly. Dimly aware of the traffic, the sense of familiarity came back in waves. He passed old landmarks of his youth when he'd visited Monrovia a few times during summer, where memories flashed with pleasant hints. RJ found himself pushing the accelerator slower, trying to bring to memory specific events, specific times of the good old days. He drove through the entire city, on every street, sharing stories with Razaq.

The sun was beginning its slow descent with the sky, showing a swirl of fruity colors that contrasted dramatically with the evening skies. Finally while on Tubman Boulevard, RJ slowed the car and turned into a small parking lot boarding Sinkor Circle. A few dozen cars were parked in front, as they always were.

Razaq wore a juvenile expression as he stepped inside. There was a bar off on one side, large windows facing Tubman Boulevard, and, in the main seating area, table settings for parties of two, four and six or more. A couple of waitresses were moving among the tables, carrying platters of food and drinks. The air held the greasy smell of fried food and cigarette smoke, but somehow it seemed all right. Most of the tables were filled. Most of the customers looked as if they made a decent living.

With his hands on Razaq's shoulders, they wove their way among the tables until they reached a table for two. RJ and Razaq sat across from each other.

"You come here often?" RJ said, mainly joking.

Razaq furrowed his brow and rolled his eyes. He chuckled. "No," he said, "But Daddy used to come here."

RJ started to ask how he knew this, but changed his mind.

Instead, he reached for the laminated menu sandwiched between a napkin holder and the salt and pepper shakers.

"Gee… what would you like?" RJ asked, after going over the menu briefly. "They have Liberian dishes, burgers, fries and chicken."

"Burger and fries," Razaq said, happily. Knowing this was something Katharine and Mellody frowned on.

A few minutes later, the waitress showed up. RJ ordered a cheeseburger, French fries, fried chicken wings and two cokes. Then they settled into easy conversation after the waitress left. Razaq talked about school and their soccer team, how much he liked the new house, especially having his own living quarters. It was as if he lived in his own apartment. RJ chuckled over the concept. He wanted to be a famous soccer star, like George Weah; everybody thought he played like him. RJ wondered why he'd not mentioned Dante. Then again, George Weah had home-court advantage in Liberia. He listened closely, asking questions now and then. Finally, he asked Razaq whether he would like to come live with him in America.

"Who will be with Mom?" Razaq said, concerned.

RJ smiled to the boy's wit and obvious concern for Katharine.

The waitress arrived with the platter of food and drinks and set it on the table with the efficiency of someone who'd been doing it for less than a day. She turned on her heels without asking whether they needed anything else.

RJ paid the tab after their meal and gave the waitress a five-dollar bill as tip, the only time she smiled.

On the way out, as they were weaving between the tables, he heard a familiar giggle. They rounded the corner and he came to an abrupt halt. Grace was there. What stopped him from moving forward was the fact that she wasn't alone. She was sitting beside a guy, almost nestled against him. From the back, it was difficult to make out anything more than that. Until, that is, they shifted, and he realized they were holding hands.

There was no reason that what he saw should bother him, but strangely, he felt a stab of envy. He reminded himself that he'd known her for just three months and they were barely colleague and even chided himself for being a little jealous. He should not do that, he thought, even if he did not have a reason to be.

Chapter Twenty

As November rolled in with the dry season, RJ found himself dwelling on the case side by side with Diallo. Grace was quickly becoming a third partner and the case was a wonderful excuse to keep in touch. He could almost count on her for just about any and everything. Actually he'd searched for anything different about their working relationship, whether he'd kept thinking about her long after business hours or calling back to verify something, but he sensed nothing wrong and decided to invite her over for Thanksgiving dinner.

"Would you mind coming over to our house for Thanksgiving dinner?" he said to Grace. "That is, if you don't already have plans."

She had a faint outline of a smile as soon as he'd said it.

"Sure," she said and took a deep breath. "I would like that very much."

"I'll come to get you. Is five o'clock okay?"

"I'd appreciate that," she said. "What should I bring," she offered, being polite.

"You don't need to bring anything," he said. "I'll pick you up at four forty-five."

"That's good. I'll be ready."

"Thank you for such a good job on my father's case," RJ said, walking out.

He was feeling her eyes on him.

✳✳✳✳

Grace was pleased to see him right on schedule, as RJ had promised.

"You look as if you're going to church," Uncle Moses commented, surprised at Grace looking her Sunday's best and even more surprised to see RJ, not knowing who he was. He'd never seen him before.

Moses Zarway was a huge dark-skinned man, at least five eleven with a wide frame that carried a lot of weight. He was in his late fifties, with a graybeard and low afro. He stared at RJ, thinking whether Alex Massaquoi had approved.

"Grace, where you going?" Uncle Moses asked; not that it was any of his business.

"Uncle Moses, this is…."

Grace didn't know how to make the introduction. She hadn't told them about the senator's son from America.

"I'm, RJ," RJ held his hand out and introduced himself.

"Are you a Peacekeeper?" Uncle Moses asked, detecting the accent.

"Just RJ," he said and shook his hand.

He had no intentions of helping the LJC write more lies in the papers.

"We'd better get going," RJ said to Grace, without catching Uncle Moses name.

RJ complimented her dress and opened the door for her to get in.

Katharine was a little surprised when RJ had asked if it would be all right if Grace came for Thanksgiving dinner. It wouldn't have been a big deal if things were normal. Besides, Ma Teete hadn't planned on anything special for Thanksgiving, considering the situation. Except for RJ, Mellody and her doctor friend, it was always the usual group for holiday dinners: Katharine, Razaq, Ma Teete and her two daughters from college and the senator. But Ma Teete always made enough food for a small army anyway.

Grace felt awed when she walked in the house, although it wasn't as large as most of the houses in the neighborhood. The garage and separate living quarters, where Razaq had to himself, still afforded the Douglass bragging rights. Everyone was dressed nicely, as was RJ. Katharine and Mellody shook Grace's hand with big smiles when they said hello. RJ was formal with his guest, referring to her as Ms. Pupoh. She was a major player in the case and it was important that they make her feel at home.

Dinner was nice and fairly formal, with baked turkey, jollof rice, potato salad, green beans, and sweet potato pie. Katharine and Mellody carried on the most considerate conversation with Grace, limiting it to mostly the changes women were making for themselves in Liberia. RJ injected his two cents worth whenever given the chance. Razaq couldn't wait to get out of his dress clothes and into something more comfortable.

A pleasant surprise was waiting in a woman who had a way of making everyone she spent time with feel as if they were the center of the world. When dinner was over, Katharine and Mellody were hooked. They too found Grace charming.

RJ was ready to take Grace home after dessert was done. As she got her purse, Ma Teete invited her into the kitchen and offered her some food to take home. She had made three packages, two for the girls to take back to campus and one for Grace. She understood what life was for young ladies like Grace. And as far as she could tell, Grace was different. She seemed focused.

"Your family is good people," Grace said as they drove away. "They treat everybody like real family. I like your Ma and your aunty. Your sister, Dr. Douglas, is so funny. I like her too."

"They are nice in their own way," RJ said, "My mother especially; she is the sweetest person I know. She's just like Nana."

He did not bother explaining his relation with Ma Teete.

"Who's Nana?"

"My grandmother in America," he said. "She's ninety years old and still does things for herself."

"Wow! Ninety years old," Grace said, "God bless her."

RJ wondered whether he should mention he'd seen her at Sinkor Circle. He supposed he could come up with some sort of plausible excuse and asked who the guy was, but what would that mean? Suddenly it seemed as if he had two views of her, one in which they made dynamite team players and he respected her for such ambitions; the other, he scolded himself for allowing his imagination to run in an awkward direction. And, oh God, what about Gia? Because you love Gia, an inner voice answered.

"I'm sorry the senator wasn't with his family tonight," Grace broke the silence.

"Yeah," RJ said. "I thought about him the whole time we were eating. Wondering what he had for dinner."

"I was just thinking about… well, what I might be able to do about that."

"What do you mean?"

"I'll see if arrangements can be made, where your mother can have food delivered to MCP for him regularly… like… every day."

"Can you do that?" RJ asked, surprised.

"I'll try," she promised. "I can't guarantee it though."

"Trying is good… sounds good, Grace," he said. "I'd appreciate that. My mother would love that."

"Don't tell anyone until I've tried, okay?" she said. "I don't want to raise any false hope."

"Sure," he promised. "Can I ask you something?"

"Sure."

RJ hesitated, and then he asked, "Do you think my father is part of all this?"

Grace looked at him. He deliberately did not meet her eyes as she thought about her answer.

"Do you?" RJ asked again, still not looking at her.

Grace considered her thoughts some more.

"To tell the truth," she said, finally, her voice softer, "I don't think that he did."

"What took you so long to say that?" RJ asked.

Grace turned from him.

"Everybody who knows Tamba Nah Wumah should also know that he has been accused of this thing before… he has a history about this heart man business," she said, her tone softened. "Why would the senator trust him?"

"I don't know," RJ said. "All I know is that I'm convinced there is no connection between him and the senator." He paused and added, "And I think my father is being framed."

Grace didn't elaborate any further, her point was clear. Deep down RJ knew she was right, she thought like a lawyer. He wondered if she had asked Diallo the same question.

Chapter Twenty-one

WITH Diallo out of the office on other business, RJ used his desk going over forms and other papers. The entire day was nonstop calls and research. Through sheer willpower, he spent several grueling hours looking through more records of Charles Sarpo's confession. He wanted to know when or if Sarpo and the senator had ever met. He kept leafing through the records, but found not any connections. He went through every page a second time. There was nothing in any of the records to indicate they'd even spoken or had been seen together. Not a goddamn word.

RJ sat back and stared at the wall, letting his eyes glaze over the file, contemplating matters. The Court records seemed doctored. But why and by whom, he thought. It was also frightening. Checking his watch, he saw it was almost five and walked out of Diallo's office.

Glancing toward the front door, he noticed Grace's chair was empty. Thinking that she had left for the day, he started to head back into the office when Diallo walked through the front door.

"Some good news," Diallo said, smiling. "They will allow the senator's family to bring him food."

Diallo was arrogant enough to think RJ believed it was his idea in the first place. Grace had suggested it and Rue had made it happen.

"My mother is going to like it," RJ said, forcing a smile.

"She can start tomorrow," Diallo said, almost bragging.

RJ got the confession files off Diallo's desk and decided to use Grace's desk instead. He studied the record for much of the next hour. The entries, one after the next, seemed to blend together. He continued reading, searching for patterns, trying to spot anything unusual. He read through the record, entry by entry, half a dozen times. He began to feel something gnaw at him, as if he was missing something, and he read through the record again, this time starting from the end. Then he read through it again.

"Find anything else?" Diallo yelled from his office.

"Nope," RJ answered, reassembling the files. He rose from the table.

RJ was wondering if his frustration even mirrored Diallo's own when he heard the front door open. Grace came through with a stack of files. That explained her disappearance.

"More files," she said and then asked, "Did Diallo tell you?"

"Yes, he did," RJ said, smiling. "Starting tomorrow we can take Dad's food to the prison."

"Good," she said, "I know that will make your mother happy."

"Yes. And, thanks," he said. "If you're about to leave, I can give you a ride home."

"Thanks," Grace said, seemingly happy for the offer. "Let me give Diallo these files… I'll take those too," she pointed at the files in RJ's hand, "If you're finished with them."

"I'm finished. Thank you," he said, and placed the file on top of the ones she was holding.

Grace balanced the pile and walked to the office.

"He looks exhausted," she said to Diallo as she placed the files on the table.

"Why don't you take him to Sugar Shack," Diallo suggested, tossing a conspiratorial smile.

✳✳✳✳

For RJ, the day had been long, hard, and depressing. More than anything, he needed a break from the nightmare. A laid-back atmosphere at any place would be a relief. He wasn't exactly sure when, where, or how it came up, but sometime during the walk from the office to the car, Grace had mentioned Sugar Shack. From its name, he concluded it was a dive bar, but considered the invite anyway. She had engineered the outing to help him clear his mind, but with an understanding of her own inner motive. Coincidently, her landlord she calls Uncle Moses, but with no genetic link, and Yassah, her best friend, were also at Sugar Shack. Within ten minutes of introduction and re-introduction, the four had settled down comfortably around a square table in the back.

Sugar Shack might have seemed a hole-in-the-wall saloon, but it offered an upscale ambience with a laid-back vibe, a good middle-tier nightlife option. The trendy concrete shack was a favorite of Monrovia's young and hip crowd, who shook their stuff to the latest grooves until the wee hours. The expansive dance floor, bordered by hip-hop hand-painted murals and hypnotic disco lights, got packed every night, thanks to the state-of-the-art sound system. The kitchen served up tasty bar food too.

This little castle of merriment was also the meetinghouse where older men met much, much younger women. Innocent dreamers, with dreams that had no chance without the shadow love affairs with older married men they called Godpa. Shame had no chance either, players got played. In other words, those were forgettable relationships. The men used women and allowed themselves to be used; feelings were kept to oneself.

"Uncle Moses thinks the rich will always rule over the poor," Grace said, looking at Yassah.

"It is because the borrower is always servant to the lender," Uncle Moses added. "Do you not believe it, Mr. Douglas?"

"Call me, RJ," RJ corrected, and added, "I don't know, but that sounds realistic."

Grace broke into a toothpaste smile. Uncle Moses laughed, than he began to even howl. Uncle Moses laughed like hell, the idea the American had agreed with him. As his laughter died down, he nodded to a waitress.

"Bring me one cold, Club Beer... and anything that my friend here, RJ, wants. Also, some soft drinks for the ladies."

"Do you have bottled water?" RJ asked the waitress.

The waitress nodded, 'yes'.

"That's what I'll have."

"No… no," Uncle Moses interrupted. "He will have a large Club Beer also."

"Water," RJ insisted and winked at the waitress.

Suddenly, RJ's cell phone buzzed with the ring tune of 'Mission Impossible' as the waitress took the women's order. Gia's picture appeared on the screen.

"Excuse me," he said getting up, and then hurried toward the exit.

"Hello… honey… hello," he repeated, than the phone went dead. He powered off the phone and turned it back on immediately. Then he dialed Gia back. The phone rang five times and her voice mail started. He closed the phone before it ended, not bothering to leave a message.

Uncle Moses indulged himself in his beer, and then ordered a few more. He was already sipping his third when RJ got back. A handful of people crowded around the dance floor, watching a young man break dance. Sugar Shack gradually became crowded.

"A man's eye never stops searching for beautiful women," Uncle Moses said. "Just look at them," he pointed at a group of women, four, between eighteen and twenty-one. "Eh-yah Liberian girls… even in the dark club, they are something to see, to watch, and occasionally take home," he said, singing, to be exact.

Grace and Yassah roared with laughter, which caught RJ by surprise. As far as he was concerned, Uncle Moses was belittling the women. What he did not know was that Grace and Yassah were actually laughing about the last time Uncle Moses got caught cheating. Irene Zarway beat the woman to the ground and fed her dirt mixed with dog shit. And then, she hit Uncle Moses so hard on his head he nearly died. RJ sipped his third bottled water and watched the women at play.

From the moment the women had entered the club, they were being watched by two men sitting at the next table. The men checked each passing woman, as if eyeing something for their collection. They studied the women, licking their lips in anticipation, but making sure no guy, maybe a boyfriend, had come with them. Both Casanovas were much older men, fiftyish, even late sixties. From their outfit, they looked like profiled men with respectable jobs, wives, and even children. But then and there, none of those things mattered.

One of the women, a tall, slender, exquisite one, leaned against the bar counter as if she was about to order something. Her skirt was short, to the point where everyone could see as far as her butt cheek line.

"You see that?" Uncle Moses said excitedly. "I know they are here looking for Godpa."

One Casanova got up, walked to the bar, and then to the women. He whispered something to them and the four women followed him to his table.

"I told you," Uncle Moses said, almost bragging as if it was a bet he had won. "Every man is a hunter by nature. The so-called husbands are careful and secretive. You see those old men? They pretend to be above a fight, so they are cute with their affection. I bet those two are married and they might be older than me," he chuckled. "But they are men, hunters, constantly watching, selecting, obsessed with hunting young girls."

Was it a biological need? RJ thought, 'no'. But Uncle Moses was certain of that. The women that RJ was used to were not demanding that men hunt them down to belittle them. These men were predators and their hunts were relentless. He didn't know anything about Yassah, but Grace was different. He admired her devilish, heartbreaking smile, the 'you can never have me' smile. Not that she was too good for them, she was just different.

The young women were laughing and chatting up a storm, totally aware of the Casanovas' intentions. Within the hour, the waitress had put a spread of bar-food on their table. They were now eating fried chicken wings and drinking beer, imported beers; laughing it up with their picker-uppers.

RJ nursed his bottled water as time went by, looking around, watching people come and go. By two o'clock the club was crowded, loud and smoky. The DJ's music alternated between soukous, reggae and hip hop. It actually reminded him of the Cassava Patch and he told them.

"My man, you will only drink water?" Uncle Moses asked. He was now sipping his eighth. "Drink some Club Beer."

RJ shook his head, 'no'. "I'm fine," he said. "I could use another bottle of water, though."

Uncle Moses got the waitress's attention and put in their order, "One Club Beer, two orange Fantas and one cold bottled water… ice-cold," he stressed to the waitress.

Grace did not want anything to eat; just the Fanta and Yassah simply went along. The waitress nodded, 'yes' with a smile, flashing her beautiful white teeth. By now RJ realized that every request was affirmative, but the customers got what was available.

The waitress returned with the order and the tab. The Club Beer was icy, and the rest of the drinks were room temperature. She handed Uncle Moses the check, but he pointed at RJ. Not realizing what it was, RJ took the check and glanced at the total; $110. I've been taken, he thought and pulled out his wallet. He handed the waitress two fifty dollar bills, and a twenty.

"Keep the change," he said to the waitress. As she was leaving, he stopped her. "Next time I'm here, do not give me a bill unless it is prearranged with me. I will not pay it next time."

She walked away as soon as he was finished.

"He na stupid," Yassah said to Grace, underneath her breath, speaking Liberian slang.

Grace's face seemed laced with embarrassment. She knew RJ clearly understood what Yassah had said. Yassah did not know that he spoke with an American accent, but he was Liberian and he understood everyday Liberian slang perfectly well.

"RJ, I'm sorry," Grace apologized.

"It's not you," he said, looking at Uncle Moses, who was sipping on his beer without a care in the world.

Quickly picking up on the conversation at the next table, RJ could not help overhearing the two men.

"I cannot believe how good Dante is," one man was saying. "I keep telling you, Ricciola is better than Weah."

He turned his attention at the men, one a police officer.

"Sorry, I couldn't help overhearing," RJ said. "Did you just watch a soccer game?"

"Oh… yeah… the game was hot," the police officer said.

"I didn't think you could catch the games here," RJ said.

"Look at this man," the officer said to his friend, "You think Liberia is a small place?" (Meaning, behind the times).

His friend laughed and RJ broke into a slow smile.

"We just watched the game at the old man place," the officer said.

"Whose?" RJ asked.

"Chief Dolo," he answered, "Who else? Aaron Dolo has the dish at his house. He never misses a game when Ricciola's team is playing. He calls him his son." Then he turned to his friend and asked, "Do you remember when Ricciola scored the winning goal? The old man was so happy, he nearly cried."

"I thought that he likes Weah?" RJ was feeding for more info. "In Liberia, Weah is everybody's man."

"Weah time finished. Yeah, we like Weah," the officer said, laughing.

Both men laughed at their inside joke.

"Okay," RJ said and turned back to his table.

"Look, Uncle Moses," Yassah pointed at the Casanovas. "They are leaving with the men."

A smile broke across Uncle Moses' face.

"I told you they were looking for Godpa," he said and busted out laughing.

The alarm went off on RJ's phone at three-thirty, just when he had set it for.

Chapter Twenty-two

RJ debated whether to call Gia, and then decided not to until he got back to the house. He'd set his alarm at three-thirty in the morning so he could talk with Gia before she left for work. He thought it would be better if he would drop everybody off and then call.

Yassah and Uncle Moses sat in the back. Grace sat in front, when RJ had opened her door before he sitting in the driver seat. Since Thanksgiving, she'd enjoyed his well-mannered treatment toward her. She reminded herself, he's only in Liberia until his father's case is over, so don't make this into something it isn't. Maybe it was just a silly crush on him since that Thanksgiving dinner.

Uncle Moses sat back staring ahead, actually snoring, and didn't know when RJ had dropped Yassah home.

"He's not a bad person, you know," Grace said, as if defending Uncle Moses.

"Why? Is it because he's your uncle?"

"No, and he's not my uncle."

"So why do you call him, Uncle Moses?"

"He took me off the streets when I came back from Ghana," she said, slowly.

"Ghana? My best friend is from Ghana, his name is, Osei Agyeman."

Ghana was a bad experience and she did not want to elaborate any further. Grace looked at him, he sensed her stare.

"You didn't like Ghana?" RJ asked.

"I was a refugee there," she replied. The way she said it, it was heartbreaking.

"I'm sorry Grace," RJ said, "I was not thinking."

They drove the rest of the way in silence, which wasn't long. By four o'clock they were in front of the house. RJ opened Grace's door and then he went to the back. He helped Uncle Moses out of the car and then into the house. The house was quiet and dim. Everyone was in bed, lights out. Uncle Moses straggled to his bedroom and shut the door.

RJ and Grace were standing in front of her bedroom door, which was the first room to the right as you entered the house. She wasn't exactly sure of what to do.

"We can sit in the living room, if you like…." Grace suggested and motioned to the chairs.

One second RJ was thinking about getting home and in the next second he wasn't. Grace took a step closer to him instead of walking toward the chairs. It was crazy. He found himself reaching for her hand and something stopped him. He didn't exactly step back, but his eyes widened just a little, and for a tiny moment he thought he'd done the wrong thing by coming in the house. He debated going any further.

Grace took RJ's hand and raised her eyes at him. He smiled slowly at the wide craze in her eyes. Then, she sort of tiptoed, closed her eyes and moved toward him. She leaned further and kissed him. It wasn't a long kiss, but it felt wonderful.

"I'm… sorry," she whispered, and remained.

"Don't be," RJ murmured. "Don't be sorry," he said and planted his wet lips against hers.

Their lips touched again. Then she took his hand and slowly drew him into the bedroom and shut the door.

Grace slowly pulled RJ's shirt out of his pants, then unbuckled his belt. He found himself scooping her in a fireman's carry and walked toward the bed. She loosened his pants and he helped her out of her dress. Somewhere along the way, RJ kicked off his shoes and Grace did the same with her sandals.

Lost in the moment, he undid her bra and it slipped to the floor. Then he slid off her panties. She pulled down his boxers. Within the next moment, Grace leisurely lied on the bed, bare. She pulled RJ to join her—all happening within seconds.

His touch was gentle, so were her eyes. He kissed her and she feverishly kissed him back. And at that moment, RJ ran his finger between her legs, feeling her moist and ready. Then, he spread her legs and penetrated. A spasm of pleasure went up Grace's spine and she voiced a soft moan, pulling him toward her with a quick, slight jerk. RJ inhaled deeply and sucked in his breath.

"Are you all right?" he whispered, sensing that she was a bit nervous or maybe, inexperience.

"Yes," she said, panting. "It's all right."

RJ throbbed harder.

It felt good that someone, pleasant and so kind had come on to her. This tall, handsome Liberian, even with an American accent, had thought highly of her. This was more of an opportunity than a chance. She would play her cards right, and when he saw her for what she truly was, she would have him for herself. He had mentioned Gia, but never called her a wife, she thought. In fact, his ring finger was bare and had no marking of a missing wedding band. That's how she saw through the false promises of men who wanted to use her. They removed the wedding band, but could do nothing about the imprint.

Grace murmured in a strange tongue as RJ throbbed harder, but with gentleness. He found it sexier although he had no understanding of anything she was saying. The truth is, it hurt like hell, with eight inches of him inside her, but the only thing that mattered now was that RJ was fucking her like she was a delicate flower. He was handling her petal like an exceptional florist.

Time disappeared from his mind. RJ had worked her for little over an hour and the two were too empty, too spent to keep at it. He felt Grace come, and then he came finally; rolled onto his back, breathing hard, his body slate with sweat.

For a while, RJ stared at the dark ceiling thinking to himself, he'd not used a condom. In the past three years, he had not made love to anyone other than Gia. It was too late to think about that either.

"Grace, sorry that I cannot stay the entire night," he whispered, after lying for about ten minutes.

"Sure," she said, a touch of disappointment in her voice, as if she'd expected it. She handed him a clean towel.

"I just can't have my mother worry about me," he made the most logical excuse. "She's going through so much right now."

"Of course," Grace said and added, "I understand."

RJ got up, wiped himself and got dress, slowly, but he was dressed in no time.

"I'll see you out," Grace said and turned on the bedside lamp.

Grace got up, slipped on a pair of daisy dukes and a tank top. Then, she walked toward the door and RJ followed. They walked in silence to the SUV; RJ got in and slammed the door shut.

"I'll see you on Monday," he said, and smiled.

He waited until Grace walked through the front door, shut it, and then he drove off.

RJ arrived home around six-thirty, took a long hot shower and climbed into bed. He sighed, realizing the futility and stupidity of chasing the desire his body had been craving for these past months. It was a vain pursuit and had not brought him what he wanted. The satisfaction he wanted only came from the woman he truly loved and until now, was committed to for the past three years. He wanted Gia, and on that thought finally fell asleep.

He woke up around noon and was still ruminating about the night with Grace, worried thoughts, nothing but guilt. There was a soft knock on the bedroom door. Katharine quietly opened the door halfway and poked her head in.

"RJ, are you okay?"

"C'mon in Mom," he said, half asleep.

Katharine opened the door completely.

"I was up until way past four, and you'd not come home. I was a bit worried," she said with a deep concern. "Not that I'm check-ing on you. It's not like Mel... at least I know she's at the hospital."

RJ remained silent and only stared at the door.

"Gia called last night, you know," Katharine went on. "Said she'd called your phone several times... you didn't answer."

He thought about his reply, waiting for her to add something else, but she didn't. He continued to stare.

"You heard me?"

"Yes, Mom," RJ said, trying his best to sound more tired than he really was.

Katharine could tell he didn't want to be disturbed. Maybe the case was catching up with him. "I didn't mean to wake you RJ, I was just concerned," she said, and slowly closed the door.

Chapter Twenty-three

RJ forced himself out of bed at two o'clock in the afternoon and headed out for a walk around the neighborhood. A man was working on his car, before his house, and they greeted each other with the usual "Hello, how are you?" Then, in a concerned tone, the man shouted, "I don't care what anybody say, the senator is a good man!"

RJ nodded his appreciation for the support and continued walking. One supporter for the senator, he counted and liked that very much. The neighbor seemed sure of himself; the senator is a good man. How well he knows the senator when I, his son, don't really know him, RJ thought. Not even Katharine, his wife, knew the senator. Only one person knew him well enough, Mr. Tom, his right hand man, his shadow. The senator had spent more time with his driver than his own children, even more than his wife. RJ figured Mr. Tom had not said anything about the case and it was because he had not been asked. He took out his phone and dialed Mr. Tom's number.

"Hello," Mr. Tom answered hesitantly, after about six rings.

"Mind if I come over to your house?" RJ said. "I know that it's your day off. I just wanted to go someplace and clear my mind. I need a change of scenery."

"Sure," Mr. Tom said. "I am at home and you know where I live, right?"

"Yes, I know where you live," RJ chuckled. "I'll be there in an hour."

****

Mr. Tom's wife was warm and friendly. She offered RJ only a bottle of water because of her husband's suggestion. He took the water and followed Mr. Tom out to his backyard. The men sat and exchanged pleasantries for about half an hour, and then RJ took control of the chitchat.

"May I ask you something, Mr. Tom?" he said. "You've known the senator for how long now?"

"For a long time," Mr. Tom said proudly. "More than forty-five years."

"That is a longtime."

"Yes," Mr. Tom said, and then added, "I've known you all your life," stressing the 'you'.

"Yes," RJ agreed, "I've known you all my life. When we came home for the summer, you were there for me more than the senator was. We played games together; you told me stories…you even hugged me. The senator provided well for me and for the family, but sometimes all a kid needs is a hug, a simple hug."

Mr. Tom caught RJ's eyes and frowned.

"African men don't hug their sons," he snarled. "You want your son to grow up to be a man. We show love by providing means for their needs. We pay for food, school, clothes…that's how a man shows his love for his family."

RJ should have known better. Mr. Tom's hug was part of the job; sucking up, letting the senator know that he gave a damn about the children. Still, he was a good man, kind, caring, even fatherly. Mr. Tom used to carry young RJ on his shoulders, so he could see faraway in the distance.

"I'm worried about my father," RJ said, admittedly.

His voice had a pleading note, betraying his fear. Mr. Tom took out his pack of Marlboros, tapped out a cigarette from the pack and lit up.

"The senator is not a killer," Mr. Tom said, after taking a drag.

"No, he's not. But perhaps life is paying back for other things in this way."

"What do you mean?" RJ said, furrowing his brow.

"What's going on with him…that's called life," Mr. Tom said. "And life has a way of throwing stones when you least expect them. I don't know how things are in America, but in Liberia, things are the way they are."

"What do you mean by it?" he asked.

"The way the big shots treat our daughters," Mr. Tom snarled. "Do they think they can get away with it? It is life who teaches them. Just when you think you've gotten away with something, life hits you with a stone."

Mr. Tom took a drag on his cigarette, staring away. In the silence that followed, RJ took in the anger and sorrow that flowed with Mr. Tom's words.

"RJ, I have something to tell you," Mr. Tom said, with a little hesitation.

RJ's heart skipped a beat at Mr. Tom's words. He waited. Mr. Tom exhaled sharply and RJ felt himself stiffen. Mr. Tom sat straighter and RJ leaned forward. Then Mr. Tom took what seemed to be the last drag of his cigarette.

"A man was born to hunt women, but this is not the way," Mr. Tom said, exhaling the smoke outward and upward.

He flicked the cigarette bud onto the ground and smudged it out. Then he went into the story as best as he could.

Once he had driven the senator to Bong Mines on a business trip and on their way back, the senator had asked him to stop at the mission school in Kakata, where he knew the principal well. After their initial pleasantries, the principal made a call and moments later, a female student, about fourteen or fifteen, came to the office. She greeted the senator and they were off. Mr. Tom was not surprised by this, as many of these occasions had taken place. He knew the routine after they got in the car. He would take them on a thirty minute drive along deserted roads.

During this drive, the senator undressed the girl and fondled her breasts while she did nothing to stop him. It was mostly because of obligations rather than fear. Then he laid her on the backseat and arranged her legs, one leg against the rear windshield and the other, against the front passenger seat headrest. When he made his way between her legs, the sudden thrust made her gasp. She started to cry.

"That's pretty young," RJ said, "Fifteen is too young." And then he asked, "Did the Senator stop?"

"No..." Mr. Tom shrugged. "He begged her to stop crying."

"He was raping her and he asked her to stop," RJ scowled. "She was a child, for Christ's sake!"

"This is common here," Mr. Tom said, also carrying a concerned look on his face, somewhat bothered by it. "Like I said, they treat our daughters like whores... only because they are paying their school fees. It is normal here."

"That is not normal," RJ said, trying to keep his voice steady in an attempt to stifle his growing sense of anger. "So, they support these poor girls with a few dollars so they can rape them?"

"They all do it," Mr. Tom said. "Some of them keep mats in the office. You do not know if it's for praying or adultery."

A long icy shiver ran through RJ's body and he took a deep breath.

"Make me understand this," he said. "Why do men claim to love their mothers, but treat women so badly? Whatever happened to dignity?"

"Dignity," Mr. Tom chuckled. "These girls cannot get jobs to keep a place of their own; their parents are poor and they have no means of paying their school fees. Perhaps dignity and having a real job cannot exist as an income. Did you know...?" Mr. Tom said and stopped.

"Did I know what?"

"That boy at the house is the senator's own son?"

RJ's face registered his surprise. He wasn't sure where Mr. Tom was going but knew enough to stay silent until he had finished.

"That's what I thought," Mr. Tom said, staring at RJ.

Silence settled between them.

"Does my mother know that Razaq is Dad's biological son?" RJ finally asked.

"No," Mr. Tom said, shaking his head. "But, I know his mother and her people. Her name is Foyah and she lives at Bob Gray Estates. Her grandfather is my brother."

RJ knew his father was a smart businessman who could charm the pants off anyone, but never dreamt of the secret life he had away from his wife. He felt as if someone had hammered a cold chisel right into the center of his chest.

Then Mr. Tom started at the beginning, finally telling him about the thirteen-year old girl the senator had devirginated. He'd taken Senator Douglas to his home in Bong County to buy land to start a rubber farm, when he saw Foyah and got her pregnant. The problem was Foyah's dowry had already been paid. But the senator was more than happy to pay the bride price to the man and things were quietly settled. Later, it was known that Foyah got pregnant. Because the child would have never been accepted, Mr. Tom took him to the orphanage in Monrovia. It was there that Katharine met Razaq, during one of her social voluntary works, and fell in love with the seven-year-old. With a little persuasion from Mr. Tom, she adopted him. The senator never asked about Foyah and Mr. Tom never told him about the boy. Mr. Tom spoke in a voice that omitted blame, as if talking to himself as much as to RJ.

When he finished, RJ felt as if he could not breathe. He glanced at his watch and realized that he'd taken too much of Mr. Tom's time on his day off. As he jingled his keys, in preparation to leave, he suddenly felt an undeniable urge to meet Foyah, one so powerful that he felt little choice in the matter. He thanked Mr. Tom and said good-bye.

✶✶✶✶

RJ drove slowly, but as he drew nearer to the area, a curious sense of anticipation made him press down more firmly on the accelerator. He turned onto the road that fronted the subdivision and read the billboard announcing the property in large block lettering, WELCOME TO BOB GRAY ESTATES.

Just about everyone at Bob Gray Estates lived in what is known as Affordable Public Housing. The APH is based on family income and size. Most of the small ranch houses were homes run by single mothers, mainly schoolteachers and police officers. Several of them had manicured flower gardens, but many looked like they needed serious maintenance work. Over sixty percent of the occupants were returnees from refugee camps. The woman RJ was going to see did not own a phone; otherwise he would have called. Mr. Tom had simply given him a name and house number with directions.

Fighting the urge to jump from the SUV, RJ stepped out slowly and began to walk up to concrete house number ninety-eight. He reached the door but frowned on the idea of knocking. RJ turned around and retraced his path back to the car, opened the door and sat.

A few minutes later the front door opened. A woman wearing a faded batik lappa and a pale yellow blouse appeared. She looked twentyish, lean, and attractive. Behind her were three small children, they looked two, four and six, trying to run out the door. RJ got out of the SUV and hurried to meet her.

"Excuse me," he said, trying to stop her from reentering the house.

She stopped and turned.

"Yes?" she asked.

"I was looking for Yassah Johnston's house," he lied.

She didn't respond; didn't even blink.

"Do you know where I can find her?"

She studied RJ for a minute or so and shooed the children away, back into the house.

"I don't know anyone by that name," she said, folding her arms across her body.

"I'm not with the government," he assured her. "I met her at Sugar Shack and…."

"Who are you?" She cut him off, prying further.

Just then, two of the children came running through the door— the six-year-old was chasing the four-year-old for an old broken toy. The little boy stomped his foot and fell hard, where RJ was standing, and he started to cry. RJ squatted close to him, and as soon as he pulled him to stand, he stopped crying.

"What's your name?" he whispered to the little boy.

The little boy offered only a faint smile and swiped at his tears.

RJ put his hand in his pocket, pulled out a ten dollar bill and held it out. The little boy's eyes glowed and he grabbed it.

"Papee," he said, slowly and plainly.

It took a few second to sink in. RJ wasn't sure what he'd do or ask next.

"It's okay," he said, getting up. "I'll just keep looking until I find her."

Foyah looked at him and smiled, her lips slightly opened. With a complete lack of thought, he turned around and walked to the SUV. She remained standing in front of the house, watching as RJ drove away.

Chapter Twenty-four

EARLY Monday morning, just past seven, RJ was heading to the shower when his phone started to ring. It has to be Gia, he thought.

"Hi honey," he answered, without looking at the screen. Then he heard a man's voice, familiar, with a heavy German accent.

"RJ, this is Dr. Klause, Lennard Klause."

"Yes, Dr. Klause," he greeted, "How are you?"

"Good," Dr. Klause said. "I have the report you'd asked me to look up."

RJ closed his bedroom door and sat on the bed.

"I'm ready," he sighed.

"It's a hard one to swallow," Dr. Klause warned. "When I'm done, you will see why."

"I'm ready," RJ said.

"Even as we speak, officials in Gurgaon, India are trying to round up members of a criminal gang accused of stealing poor people's kidneys and transplanting them into bodies of wealthy customers," Dr. Klause reported. He spoke slowly, as if making sure every word was heard.

"Can someone actually steal a kidney?" RJ asked, astonished.

"Well, yes and no," Dr. Klause said. "It seems like the making of a fairy tale, but in India, it is no tale."

"How so?"

"It's not like people are lured into a building and then robbed of their kidneys. The actual victims, according to police, are poverty-stricken locals. They're enticed with promises of employment where they are forced to donate their organs."

"So, what are you saying, Dr. Klause, is kidney theft a myth, or not?"

"I suppose that depends on how the tale is told. And, so-called foreign tourists are involved too."

Dr. Klause's comment seemed to stop RJ's train of thought. In the silence that followed, he waited for him to continued, trying to assess whether he knew if anything like this was also happening in Africa.

"How do you feel about the heart man's tale… do you think it is real?" RJ finally asked.

"Could very well be," Dr. Klause said. "I've heard that before, many years ago."

"What do you mean?"

"As far as the scenario of the heart man's tale," Dr. Klause continued, "unless there's a makeshift operating room somewhere, where people's kidneys and hearts are stolen for sale on the black market, I really can't say."

RJ felt his stomach sink when he thought about Duo Boley, the male nurse, one of the defendants in the Johnny Bono's case. Besides, he thought, it's all but impossible for such activities to take place outside properly equipped medical facilities. The removal, transport, and transplantation of human organs involves procedures so complex and delicate, requiring a sterile setting, minute timing, and the support of so many highly trained personnel, that they simply could not be accomplished on the street, as it were with Johnny Bono. He wondered if he should share details of the autopsy report with Dr. Klause, but decided not to, not yet.

"Too many things happened in Africa that is unexplainable," Dr. Klause continued. "I'm sorry, RJ, the heart man's theory is just too complex. However, I cannot say that selling human organs in Liberia is not possible."

"I was afraid of that," RJ said.

"In fact, the World Medical Association and the World Health

Organization regard the sale of human organs as inhumane and unethical. But in recent years the rise in demand for organ donation has dramatically increased because of advanced medical technology. The supply of human organs cannot meet demands, and as a result, there has been an incredible rise of illegal human organ sales."

"Sounds like we're talking about human beings like a commodity here," RJ said.

"We are," Dr. Klause said. "The lack of regulation, in conjuncture with increased demand and of course, an inadequate scale of supply, makes human organs a rare commodity. Unfortunately my friend, modernization and advancement have facilitated and produced a double-edged phenomenon."

"The illicit trade of human organs," RJ added.

"That's it," Dr. Klause said. "By the way, how is Mel? Has she heard anything?"

"Not that I know of," RJ said. "She's busy taking care of sick people. I guess, too busy to notice anything."

"Ask her anyhow," Dr. Klause suggested. "Maybe she'd be able to find something out. I am snooping around while I travel throughout West Africa. I'll let you know what I find next."

"Please do," RJ said. "Thank you, Dr. Klause. I will let you know what I get from Mel."

"Before I hang up, any news about the case? How is Robert holding up?"

"It's tough," RJ admitted. "This is a mountain… and I don't know how we're going to climb it."

"But have you seen him?"

"Yes… he looks terrible."

"I can't imagine. I don't see how they could implicate him with such nonsense. Robert never had any dealings with such matters. I know him well."

So far, RJ concluded that as a senator in Liberia, his father flirted around the edges of laws and ethics, but there was nothing illegal or unethical on their books, until now.

"It's more of being a scapegoat, rather than guilt," he explained. "We're up against people who want to use him as an example for the so-called change in Liberia. I guess because he's Congor."

"That's too bad, RJ. Can't anyone at the UN do anything?"

"I don't know."

"Well… I'll see what I can do," Dr. Klause said. "I'll give you a call next week."

"Thanks, Doc," RJ said, and then added, "You take care."

✦✦✦✦

It was a little before eight-thirty when RJ came out of the shower. Nothing like a little pressure, he thought. He hurriedly got dressed and was running to get a cup of coffee when the house phone rang. It was Mellody checking in on Katharine.

"Just the person I want to talk to," RJ said. "When can I see you today?"

Mellody's answer came slowly, "Maybe after four. We have a full house here."

"Can't we meet earlier?"

"RJ, I have a full schedule today. Can't it wait, what is so important? Right now I have ten other patients that I haven't seen yet."

He struggled to remain perfectly calm. It made no sense alarming her. Stealing human parts was a serious matter, but he wasn't even sure that's what it was.

"Okay, four o'clock," he said and handed the phone to Katharine.

At four-thirty, RJ trudged down the corridor toward the Emergency Department. The foot traffic was heavy and a few patients were standing against the wall, waiting; they had a full house, as Mellody had put it. His mind was filled with images of hearts, lungs and questions, many questions, about the possibility of getting human parts without the proper procedure. A nurse rounded the corner of the passageway and nodded her head politely as she approached RJ. Her cheeks were immediately warm. She knew he was Dr. Douglas's brother, she had a crush on him, and she wasn't the only one. He was an eyepopper.

"She's waiting for you in her office," the nurse said, showing a lot of very white teeth.

"Thank you," RJ said, with genuine warmth.

He reached the office and knocked, and since the door was partly open, he pushed it open while still tapping it.

"Hello, Dr. Douglas," he said, entering.

"Hey," Mellody said, looking up from the chart she was reading. The creases in her forehead, the tiredness in her eyes, and the tone of her voice left little doubt that she was beyond exhaustion. She got up, quietly closed the office door, tapped RJ on his shoulder and sat down. "What's going on?"

RJ thought for a second, then said, "Got a call from Dr. Klause this morning."

"Dr. Klause?" Mellody said, seemingly surprised.

RJ nodded, 'yes'.

"By any chance this place could be bugged?" he asked, his eyes shooting in all directions.

Mellody rolled her eyes, a favorite communication that meant something seemed particularly crazy to her.

"Please, RJ, tell me you're joking."

"Are you sure?" he said, seriously.

"Not here," Mellody stressed. "What's going on?"

"After going over the autopsy report, I asked Dr. Klause to find out the possibility of organ transplant in Africa."

"Why? I thought this was a case of their so-called African voodoo?"

"The way some of the victim's organs were removed…I know it sounds crazy. Mel, is it possible for the kidney or lung to be taken out of the body outside an OR? According to one of the defendants, specific instructions were given to the nurse, who removed the lungs, kidneys and heart."

"In the real world, RJ, if an organ has been removed to be implanted for several hours, it is desirable the organ be cooled and kept at 32° F, the transition temperature of ice to water. How many people here in Liberia have ice water?"

RJ shrugged his shoulder. He was listening, with nothing to say.

"The organ has to be kept sterile in a consistent normal saline solution which could vary if ice were used in the same container with the organ," Mellody continued. "It is important that an organ, being removed from the donor, be placed in a sterile container, which in turn is placed in another sterile compartment; so when the organ container is removed from the compartment at the facility for implantation, the container is sterile and can be handled in the operating room without fear of contamination to the room and its contents. Do you understand?"

"What about all this happening on the black market?"

"Come to think of it, I don't know if there's an independent organization that regulates international human organ donation. Maybe it is possible for black market trade. It sounds so far fetch though… human organ and illegal activities."

They stared at each other for a few seconds.

"Think for a second," RJ said. "If a wealthy man needs a kidney, don't you think he will get it by any means possible?"

"A rich man can go to any country where there are poor people and buy a donated organ," Mellody said. "Poor people sell their kidneys everyday… all over the world. It is not illegal and everything is done in a hospital setting."

"That's how you see it?"

"RJ, listen… I'm all in for organ donation and saving lives, but it is an artificially-created need invented to dangle before the eyes of the sick and dying. Medical advancement is feeding into the typically human denial and refusal of death. People never want to die. Personally, the best possible solution for organ transplantation and donation might be for humans to deal with the fact that we are all mortal."

After thirty minutes, RJ was done; all possible questions served up and answered. Mellody's arguments were well reasoned, but he was not totally convinced.

"Well, Dr. Klause wants you to keep your ears and eyes open," RJ said. "Can you do that?"

"Sure. I'll give him a call as soon as I get the chance. They are crazy if they think Daddy would be involved in something like that."

"That's why I want to make sure Diallo covers everything," RJ said and got up to leave.

RJ and Mellody walked out of the office and then down the hall. She saw RJ out and then rushed back to the ER to care for the next patient in wait.

Chapter Twenty-five

THE weeks that followed passed in a dreamlike state. It was time. RJ and Mr. Tom were an hour early to meet the flight coming into RIA from the United States. The airport was crowded. People were waiting on another flight from Europe. Mr. Tom waited at the airport terminal curb and RJ went in to meet her. He found an empty chair near the large window where he could see where the jets come in. He sat down, and then popped up again. RJ was nervous; it was a good nervous, with anticipation. Gia was coming to Liberia.

Finally, the big American jet slowly taxied to the gate. Gia was in the first wave of passengers getting off the plane. She had on jeans, a cream-colored cotton blouse and her laptop case striped across her shoulders. She looked great. RJ followed her with his eyes as she came through custom. When the immigration officer returned her documents, he was right there to meet her.

"Oh, baby," he took the laptop case off Gia's shoulder, grabbed her in both arms and gave her a kiss. "I'm so happy to see you. Was your flight okay?"

"Yes," she said, smiling. "You're almost as nervous as I am."

"Not nervous, excited," he said and kissed her again.

Gia held his face, and kissed his lips lightly. "That's much better," she said, and smacked her lips. "You taste good."

"You must like peppermint."

"No, I like you," she winked.

RJ introduced Gia to Mr. Tom and they were soon on their way to Monrovia. This was Gia's first trip to Liberia. They talked about everything that had been happening since the civil war ended. At first, it was the destruction, and then they got into the so-called changes and help from different western governments that was making it possible. They talked about her parents, Dante, Mrs. Douglas, Mellody and finally the senator and the case. It was only when they pulled up to the house when things became a little tense.

"You ready for this?" RJ asked as he got out of the car.

"Bring it on," Gia said, looking relaxed.

He grabbed hold of her hand and they headed toward the house. RJ was glad to have his Gia home with him, finally.

✦✦✦✦

Katharine and Ma Teete had obviously been thinking about the proper welcoming dinner for Gia. Katharine wanted to keep it as close to American as possible. Ma Teete suggested if RJ liked her Liberian dishes, so would Gia. Besides, it would allow her to show off her work. Standing with her favorite apron on, white and spotless, Ma Teete took enormous pride in her work. Gia overheard them debating over the choice of entrée.

"How about some steaks, sweet potato casserole, fried chicken, green beans and your special cornbread," Katharine suggested. "Oh yeah, and some salads, potato and Caesars salad would be good."

"Maybe add jollof rice, pineapple upside-down cake and cassava bread," Ma Teete added. "I want to make some goat soup too."

As they were discussing, Gia poked her head in the kitchen. "Did I hear someone mention yucca?"

"Yucca?" Ma Teete repeated, "I didn't hear nobody say 'yucca'… what's that?"

"Cassava," Gia told her. "My mother is Mexican and I eat all of those things that you mentioned." She stepped between the women. "Mom," she kissed Katharine's cheek, "Don't trouble yourself about what I would like, I'd like everything." Then Gia planted another kiss, this time, on Ma Teete's cheek. "And you, Mama Teete, I heard about your cornbread, I definitely would like to try it tonight."

"You smell like America," Ma Teete said, smiling.

"What does America smell like?" Gia asked.

The three women giggled like schoolgirls.

Dinner was served in the formal dining room at six. It was odd to have fun without the senator. Razaq sat looking at Gia and grinning the whole time.

"You're looking at my girl like you've never seen her before," RJ said, with an arched eyebrow, pointing an accusatory finger at Razaq. "You need to get your own girl."

"Razaq, don't pay him no mind," Gia said and winked.

After ten minutes of cautions flirting, Razaq's attention went back to his dinner. Dr. Cho, a regular guest at the house, especially on special occasions, stared at Mellody most of the time. Mellody stared back, as if they were in a staring contest with each other. Dinner and small talk was a success, the laughter was constant, and mostly relaxed.

Gia put down her knife and fork and pushed the plate away. After dessert, she rose from the table. "I absolutely forbid Mom or Mama Teete to do the dishes," she said. "I'll do them and RJ will pitch in. That's our job."

"Oh, no, you won't," Ma Teete commanded. "You and RJ will not lift a finger in this house, not while I'm here."

"Baby, she's serious," RJ confirmed. "She won't let us."

"Well all right then, all right," Gia chuckled. "I'll let it slide this one time."

Razaq followed Ma Teete out to the kitchen with about half of the dirty dinnerware stacked in his hands and arms. He set the dirty dishes in the sink and turned on the hot water. Ma Teete went back to clear the rest of the dishes.

"Welcome to Liberia, Gia," Ma Teete said smiling. "Thank God, RJ has picked the right woman; I don't even care if she's white."

"Well, thanks," Gia said and chucked at the thought of being called white to her face, so innocently.

Ma Teete went back to the kitchen.

✦✦✦✦

Moments later Katharine came in through the kitchen door while Razaq and Ma Teete were finishing the dishes. She couldn't resist taking a peek out the window at RJ and Gia as they, seemingly, were going for a stroll. They were moving at a slow pace, looking sleek, even beautiful, in the dusk light of day, and holding hands. Their legs moved in synch like lazy, but efficient, pistons.

"I've missed you," he said, giving Gia's hand a slight squeeze.

"A lot?" she asked, squeezing back. "You had better miss me a lot. I came all the way across the Atlantic. Oh baby, I missed you too," she said, with seriousness.

RJ stopped, grabbed her in his arms and kissed her, pressing into her, and then he slid his tongue into her mouth. She liked that a lot and was starting to respond, which probably wasn't a fantastic idea in the streets.

"Get a room," they heard a voice behind them.

Mellody was walking her guest, Dr. Cho, to her car, cracking up at their expense.

"Dr. Douglas," Gia whispered at RJ, shaking her head. "Why doesn't she bring Shakari sometimes?"

"Who knows," RJ sighed. "That's Mel, for you."

They watched Mellody kiss Dr. Cho on the lips, and then waved as the car sped away.

The evening felt a whole lot better with Gia in Liberia. RJ and Gia continued their walk, silently taking everything in. Then they stopped to kiss and discovered how much they'd missed each other. They would take two steps and kiss some more.

"I have a much better idea," he said to Gia, "A better way to burn these calories."

"You do," Gia said and stopped, reading between the lines.

They both turned to go back, and this time, hurried their steps to the house.

The bed was the visual focus of the room, but it would look even better a little messed-up. RJ tossed the three throw pillows onto the floor and before they knew it, the two were at the center of the queen-size bed.

"It's been too long," Gia whispered against his cheek.

RJ kissed her mouth. Her soft lips continued to press against his and he felt himself melting. Soon they were holding each other, folded in real close. RJ was strong, but knew how to be tender. It felt good. They remained cuddled together for a little while, and then he moved his head. His lips brushed the hollow in her throat, and just lingered, then slowly, gently, he moved toward her breasts and nipples. They looked at each other, appraising, admiring, and building up eagerness and passion. He wanted Gia badly and Gia couldn't wait. She rolled on top of him.

RJ raised his head to her breasts and she lowered herself to him. He kissed one, then the other, playing no favorites. Gia was smiling in a way even he'd never seen before. He ran his strong hands up and down her back and over her buttocks. Then, he eased himself into her. She leaned over and kissed RJ a long, lingering kiss as he moved inside her.

They moved together, real slowly at first, then faster, and faster still. Gia rose and fell hard on him and they made love with an intensity that surprised them both. It was as if, in their lovemaking, RJ was trying to erase all of his betrayals. When they finally collapsed with the pleasure of it all, Gia looked into his eyes.

"Phwe," she sighed, "I think we both needed that."

Chapter Twenty-six

Pastor Peabody's office door was partially open. He was sitting behind his desk, glasses propped on his nose, looking over some papers, when Lynnette Vinton walked by. She knocked at the door, and he looked up with interest, as if he was not expecting anyone.

"Hello, Pastor," she said politely. "Do you have a moment?"

"Hello, Sister Vinton," he said, barely excited.

"May I come in?"

Pastor Peabody nodded slightly, and she entered the office. He motioned for her to sit in the chair across from his desk.

"What can I do for you?" he asked.

Lynnette adjusted herself in the chair. "Well, I wanted to ask a favor."

He stared at her, studied her face, before finally asking, "Does it have to do with the senator?"

"No," Lynnette answered and sighed. "I wanted you to please ask members to volunteer this month. DOC adopted the MaryMartha Orphanage this Christmas."

Lynnette Vinton was leader of the Daughters of Christ women's ministry and couldn't have been prouder. She had met with Mrs. Ricks, the director of the orphanage, to let her know the DOC was taking care of Christmas for the children this year. She had also recruited Katharine Douglas and they'd gone to every office building and store in Monrovia, soliciting support by placing penny jars marked *DOC Ministries—MaryMartha Orphanage Christmas Fund* on counters and desks.

He sighed. "Is that all?" he said.

"Well, yes," Lynnette said. "It is very important, Pastor, that we make a good impression on those children. They can have some good food, a tree, and a few gifts, something for all of them. I want them to have the best Christmas, ever, if it's the Lord's will."

"That shouldn't be hard, Sister Vinton," Pastor Peabody said.

He took off his glasses and wiped them with his handkerchief before putting them back on. He was taking a moment to think about how much it would cost the church.

"It won't cost the church a dime," Lynnette said. She seemed to have looked right through him. She stood from her chair and pulled out one of DOC penny jars. "I've put one of these on every office desk in Monrovia," she said proudly. "One on every store counters too. Here is yours," she put the jar on the desk.

Pastor Peabody looked surprised.

"I need folks to decorate, cook, clean, wrap presents and serve," she said, walking out.

✶✶✶✶

Christmas was a few days away. RJ could feel little butterflies starting to form in his stomach, thinking how they would spend it with the senator still sitting on death row. There weren't too many sad moments when Lynnette Vinton was around, always cheerful and happy. She suggested RJ would make a wonderful Santa, if he could get a costume in time for Christmas. Mellody got one of her tailors to manage that task, a Santa suit for RJ and even an elf suit for Razaq, Santa's helper.

Mr. Tom drove Katharine and Lynnette around town to pick up all the DOC jars from stores and businesses. By the end of two days collection, all they'd taken in was $105.83, mostly pennies. Lynnette felt awful, especially considering the jars had been out for almost five months. She added the $50.00 Pastor Peabody had handed her, supposing from his jar. All they had was $155.83 and

Christmas was just four days away.

"Here," RJ handed Mrs. Vinton some cash, "this is from Santa."

Lynnette counted $545, money he had managed to collect between him, Mellody and Gia.

"Thank you, RJ," Lynnette said smiling. There was more emotion in her voice. "Thank you so very much."

The women insisted RJ went shopping with them to pick up toys. From the list Mrs. Ricks had given her, they picked out two toys for each child, sixty in all. Gia and RJ bought thirty outfits, shoes and socks, charging their personal credit cards. The rest of the evening was spent wrapping presents and drinking eggnog, lemonade and ice teas.

The morning before Christmas, RJ drove Katharine and Gia to the MaryMartha Orphanage to help with the set up. Lynnette was there, waiting in the office with a few DOC members. Mrs. Ricks walked the group down the corridors to the end of the hall, where two doors opened into a good-size room.

"We'll have the Christmas dinner in here," she said.

Gia glanced around the place. Balanced in the far corner were about fifty metal folding chairs stocked against the wall. In the opposite side were four long tables, most of the surface cracked and worn out. Along the wall on one side were set of shelves, with few toys here and there, blocks, puzzles, headless dolls, cars with no wheels. There weren't too many toys, and the few that were there looked as if they had been in this room for a longtime.

"These are all the toys they have?" Gia asked.

"Yes," Mrs. Ricks nodded, "except some of the children take toys to their rooms and they not suppose to."

Mrs. Ricks seemed used to it. To Gia, the bareness of the room made the whole place depressing. She couldn't imagine growing up in a place like this.

By six o'clock, the formation of the room had changed. In the center of the room was the artificial Christmas tree Lynnette Vinton had ordered from the States, as if it was the Lord's will the orphans have a real Christmas this year. She and her committee had decorated it with shiny flecks, colored lights, and dozens of different handmade ornaments donated by the Sunday school class.

Beneath the tree, spread in all directions, were wrapped gifts of toys in every size and shape. The Children were on the floor, sitting close together in a large semicircle, dressed in their best clothes. They all looked as if they had cleaned up before the big event, the boys had new haircuts and the girls had colorful barrettes and ribbons attached to their braids. On each of the four tables set for dinner, were a bowl of punch and two platters of cookies, compliments of Ma Teete and Gia.

Katharine, Ma Teete, Gia, Mellody, Dr. Cho, and a few other DOC members, were sitting with smaller children on their laps; their faces rapt with attention as they listened to "The birth of Christ", told by Lynnette Vinton, sitting on the floor in front of the tree. The little girl Gia was holding kept twirling with Gia's hair, as if Gia was her baby doll. Lynnette paused to look up when she noticed RJ, dressed in his Santa suite, standing in the doorway, smiling. 'He'd make a good minister,' she thought, 'and I don't care what anybody thinks.' Then she went back to telling the story.

After Lynnette's story, the children walked to their tables. Pastor Peabody said the grace, thanking the Lord, Lynnette and the DOC members. Then he prayed that the Lord will remember the Douglas family this particular Christmas. The children wished they had dinner like this every night, with presents, punch and cookies. Christmas dinner and the small talk were a success; at least it went according to the Lord's will, and Lynnette Vinton thought so.

Following dinner, Mrs. Ricks rose from the table and proclaimed, "Time for presents!"

The children cheered.

"Help me hand out the gifts," RJ said to Razaq.

Razaq looked down at his elf's costume, pouting. RJ had practically forced it on him; since he had vouched he'd rather be dead than seen in it.

"That's why I got you the costume," RJ chuckled. "Come on, do it for the children."

Razaq didn't think it was funny, but after a little while it was even far better than he'd imagined, handing out gifts.

Afterwards, RJ stood next to Gia and they watched the children open their gifts one by one. She was happy to have helped Lynnette and Katharine shop all over town, picking up a few things for each child, individual gifts that they had never received before. There were squeals of delight everywhere as wrapping papers were tossed around in enthused frenzy. Seemingly, the children had received far more than they had expected, many were hugging their new toys and clothes instead of playing with them.

✶✶✶✶

By ten all the children had opened their gifts and the atmosphere began to calm down. RJ, Pastor Peabody, Razaq and about three deacons from Words of Christ Church tidied up the room while the women cleaned up the kitchen. Soon all the children were gone back to their rooms with their gifts. Everybody else had slipped away except for RJ and Gia. Mrs. Ricks dimmed the overhead lights on the way out.

Gia was away from her family on Christmas Eve and RJ hadn't had a chance to talk to her all evening. Because of the preparations, not that she had mind. As they prepared to leave, they noticed the lights on the tree had cast a delicate glow in the room. They both gazed up at the lights on the tree, wondering what the other was thinking. Then RJ glanced at Gia. She had a tender look about her, she seemed pleased. He was thrilled with how the evening had gone, even with the senator sitting on death row.

Gia turned from the tree to face him, smiling softly.

"This is by far the best Christmas Eve I've had… Flaky," she whispered, as tears filled her eyes.

"Flaky," he repeated, sounding almost musical.

All he could wonder was how blessed he'd been to have a girl like Gia.

Chapter Twenty-seven

CHRIST'S day was a time of joy and peace around the world. On Christmas morning, the sun rose over a calm Atlantic Ocean, casting prisms of light across the water. A light mist lingered in the quiet neighborhood, making it even more special.

"Merry Christmas, Mom," RJ said, staggering into the kitchen. He squinted in the bright kitchen light and saw Katharine sitting at the kitchen table alone, staring at the gifts on the table. It looked as though she'd been crying.

Katharine had put everybody's presents on the table, Ma Teete's and her daughters', Razaq's, Mr. Tom's, his wife's and their two grandchildren. RJ had insisted that she didn't get him and Gia anything, so did Mellody. He poured himself a tall glass of orange juice, wandered to the table and joined her.

"Where is Gia?" Katharine said.

"I left her sleeping."

"I hate it that she has to be here during this time," Katharine said, concerned. "I wish things were different."

"She wouldn't have it any other way, Mom, she's family."

Katharine pointed at her wedding band, indicating RJ's finger was bare.

"Don't worry about that, Mom," he chuckled. "That will be taken care of soon enough."

"There you are, honey," Gia said, entering the kitchen, barely two minutes behind RJ. She was holding two gifts; one for Ma Teete and the other was Razaq's. "Interesting tree," she joked and placed the presents on the table with the others.

"I thought you were sleeping?" RJ asked.

"You know I can't stand being in bed without you," she said and poured herself a cup of steaming hot coffee. "Where's Mel?" she asked and plopped herself on the chair next to RJ.

"She was called in after we got back from the orphanage," Katharine said. "She should be home around noon."

Mr. Tom dropped by to wish them a merry Christmas and picked up his gifts and Ma Teete's as well. After Mr. Tom left, Katharine, Gia and RJ kept company and sipped coffee and OJ until half of the day was spent. After showers were taken and clothes changed, everybody, for no particular reason, assembled back around the kitchen table. Mellody joined them around one.

Katharine, Mellody, Gia and RJ made phone calls and sent e-mails, making sure friends and family everywhere had gotten their Christmas greetings. With no special dinner planned, it was almost like skipping Christmas and Gia would not have that. With everybody sitting around the kitchen table, she rummaged around in the cabinets and refrigerator for food she could prepare quickly.

Two hours later, Gia had prepared a simple, but tasty meal of green beans, mash potato, chicken sandwiches, and an eight-pound baked red snapper. The food had been arranged and rearranged until it looked festive. Razaq heard the news about dinner and abandoned his iPod Gia had given him for Christmas. Katharine graced the food and they ate and toasted to better days ahead.

Thankfully, the end was in sight. Around five-thirty, everyone had gathered in the living room. For the first time she could remember, all three of her children were home at the same time, but her husband was sitting in jail, Katharine thought. It was the sad truth. Her eyes were moist. Then, soon the tears were halfway down her cheeks. "I wonder what he is doing right now?" she whispered, referring to Robert.

"Probably thinking about us," Mellody said.

They hugged and cried together.

"Sometimes I do feel like Job," Katharine whispered.

"And it's okay, Mom," Mellody patted her arm. "We both can't pretend that nothing is wrong. It's okay to feel the way you do."

Razaq was staring at them while lying on the couch, with extreme sadness on his face. He did not understand what everyone else seemed to, perhaps something that no child should be burdened with. But the senator was in jail and, his mother, Katharine, whom he had clinched to since seven, looked sad. She had not conceived him, nor had she bore him; she had raised him and it pulled at his heartstrings that she looked depressed , not horribly depressed, but depressed, scared and miserable. Gia took one look at him and her heart lurched.

"Razaq, let's watch a movie," Gia suggested, "Pick a real funny one."

Not that it would do any good. Nonetheless, it would be easy to forget the trouble for the time being. Razaq got up, off the couch and rushed to the library of DVDs. He looked for one Katharine loved, one that he'd seen her watch and laugh so hard, she cried.

"How about Coming to America?" he said in a whispery voice, holding up the DVD, looking at Katharine for approval. She smiled a reassuring smile and Razaq hurriedly loaded the disc.

In time, with little interest in the movie, RJ drifted away from everybody else and went on the porch to the hammock. It was one of those perfect evenings with just enough breeze to keep from being either hot or cold. There was a moon and some clouds. He was alone on the porch for a while, rocking gently in the hammock, lost in a dream world, listening to the crickets. The front door closed, the screen slammed behind it, and Gia walked to the hammock. She lifted his arm and tucked herself next to him. She was easy to hold, he held her firmly.

"Mom and Mel gone to bed?" he asked.

"They're still watching the movie."

He squeezed her tighter, wondering how everything in his life seemed perfect, yet knowing at the same time that it wasn't.

"What are you thinking?" she asked softly.

His eyes turned to the beautiful face of the woman he loves, brought the back of her hand up to his lips and kissed it.

Gia smiled.

Chapter Twenty-eight

WATCH MEETING NIGHT

IN Liberia, New Year's Eve is observed in watch meeting services with the greatest respect for its purity and with no thought of blasphemousness. Even before the time for this service to commence, sometimes two to three days ahead, the more devout begin to make themselves ready by fasting, thus getting themselves in a spiritual frame of mind for the blessings toward which they look. Lynnette Vinton, Katharine Douglas and many other members of Daughters of Christ had habitually fasted for three days.

In the meantime, Mellody had slid into the silliness of extreme workaholism and had no plans of joining the family for watch meeting. Katharine did not like it one bit. How was her church members to understand when the least the Douglas family was expected to do was attend every spiritual assembly, and didn't. Gia convinced Katharine that what Mellody was doing equaled to what Jesus did when he healed on the Sabbath day and Katharine wondered if Lynnette would agree that Mellody was doing the Lord's will.

They arrived early, around ten, and sat on the third pew, center aisle, next to Lynnette Vinton. The sanctuary looked beautiful. The old oak brown linoleum floor was restored to a high gloss finished, the dark wood pews had been polished to a shine, and the stained windows were sparkling clean. Earlier, members of Daughters of Christ had arranged bouquets of flowers around, making the church more handsome.

Gia had never been to a watch meeting before and had no idea what to expect. There was no haste by the audience to begin the service, which increased in number by eleven-thirty. At eleven thirty-five, the choir took its place behind the pulpit and remained standing, right before Pastor Peabody assumed the pulpit and directed the assembly to stand. The choir started to hum and sway and then he served up a lengthy prayer. The Lord was appealed to in intense strains, to come down and be present in their midst. Afterwards, he directed the assembly to sit.

A woman choir member did a solo, and then there were moments of silence. Pastor Peabody read several Scriptures, and preached for a bit. He was followed by a deacon who delivered his own testimony and asked volunteers in the assembly to offer theirs. As they did, an audible murmuring and groaning could be heard, and then a noticeable swaying to and fro of the bodies of the more emotional ones and, now and then, an exclamation of "Thank you, Lord".

Lynnette Vinton was always ready. While giving her testimony, she shouted about the Lord's will in her life and the countless blessings she'd received throughout the year. But she saved her best testimony last, her harshest criticism, for the gossipers, those who didn't care who their lies hurt. She was articulate and angry. They clapped for her, nonetheless, when she finished, and some even said, 'Amen'.

Pastor Peabody spent more time preaching, reading more Scriptures, and the assembly sang more songs. There was another solo by the same woman choir member, backed by the choir in a soulful hymn that made Katharine cry. She was stroked and soothed by Gia and RJ. As the choir cranked it up several notches, others began to cry.

The service lasted for an hour and a half. Pastor Peabody prayed again, with organ music in the background, to close the service. When he finished, a long dismissal began as the people paraded to the large conference room where homemade shortbread and coffee was served. Lynnette was proud of the work the DOC had done.

Chapter Twenty-nine

ALL prospective jurors had responded to the summons and reported for jury duty for the final selection. Diallo and Grace had joined them, with Bly Macavoi and her assistants, and they were waiting for the judge. When Judge Tweh stepped into the room, everyone bolted upright in their seats. Some instantly became enthralled by the man most were meeting in person for the first time. He slowly closed the door behind him, took a few steps toward the edge of the table, and stared calmly at everyone sitting around it.

"How many are we selecting?" Judge Tweh asked of Bly Macavoi.

"Ten," she answered quickly, eager to please.

"Mr. Amadou, do you agree to that?" he asked.

"Yes, Sir," Diallo said, looking away.

"Good," Judge Tweh said, shaking his head slowly, allowing the severity of the moment to filter in. His luck had paid off with an appointment to the bench, where the sight of a jury bench, packed with qualified voters would warm his heart. There was change in Liberia before his eyes.

Each of the juror candidly responded to questions by Judge Tweh and the lawyers on both sides. Throughout the process, they struggled to select the final ten and Diallo created a file on every juror. In each file were photographs and personal history information. It was a diverse group they ended up with, but he wondered if they could even be trusted. He hoped they would not be tightfisted with the concept of change, for sure, and to be so unsympathetic. Most of all, for his client's sake, he prayed no one there was an anti-Americo-Liberian zealot, though no one had shown it.

Juror number one was Amara Dorbor, a middle-aged school-teacher, who had escaped the war while living in England on an invitation of a former student. Ruth Somah was juror number two, a market woman, who was supporting a son at the University of Liberia selling fried bony fish. She'd lost three sons in the war when they became Small Boy soldiers for Charles Taylor . Twenty-seven-year-old entrepreneur, Aisha Sio, was juror number three. With training offered by the Mary L Yeke Foundation, she'd opened her beauty supply store and was looking forward to normalcy in the new Liberia. Juror number four was a teller at Bank of Liberia, Philomena Russell. Ms. Russell was a strong supporter of Daughters of Christ, a feminist in every sense of the word. She was among the women that prayed the devil, Taylor, back to hell. Dr. Mahdia Yekerson was juror number five, a dentist, born to Liberian parents and raised in England. She'd moved with her family to Liberia and was set on making a difference, based mainly on the stories she heard about her indigenous, meaning non-Congor, grandparents. Most Indigenous people had succeeded purely on determination, against lack of opportunities that only few were privileged with. Juror number six, Keturah Zaeh, a nurse. Keturah's story was no different, a self-supporter who had managed with very little. Pastor Cyrus Wleh was selected as juror number seven. Not much was known about Pastor Cyrus, other than he had successfully maintain his prophetic church even during the war and had always preached the sinfulness of voodoo. Juror number eight was a plumber, Sidiki Sundaygah, who reluctantly accepted the responsibility because he would make more money fixing toilets and laying pipes, tees and elbows. Professor Joseph Zion, a history professor at the University of Liberia, was juror number nine. He was already considering writing a book on the trial. And, juror number ten, Mambu Kamara, a tailor; unfortunately Diallo thought, he was not one of Dr. Douglas's tailor-impersonators.

After the selection, Judge Tweh stressed to the jurors that they were to be critical, listen carefully, and analyze what they heard. They were to collaborate and stand strong. Once deliberating, they were to listen to the other jurors. Finally, his advice was that they will have to live with their decision, so it better be a good one; it was someone's life they were judging. They were to vote their conscience. All of his instructions were given in English as well as dialects selected by the jurors.

Chapter Thirty

Iт was a lazy, clear January morning the day the trial began. Monrovia was finally on its way towards true justice, after weeks of countless headline obsessed with the brutal murder of Mr. Johnny Bono. The struggle for a fair trial would be painful, and all knew what sacrifices had to be required. Every citizen in Monrovia was affected, either directly or indirectly from the massive human rights abuse. It was not hard to imagine the need each felt to address the crime, to seek justice, truth, and even vengeance to overcome such an atrocity against an innocent man; but, mainly to move forward.

The guards checked the summons of each juror, admitted them one by one through the metal detector, and told the rest of the spectators they would have to wait awhile. Then the doors were opened to the public at eight o'clock sharp. At eight-thirty the courtroom was packed, beyond its capacity of a hundred people, yet quiet. The slow-turning fans on the ceiling were a blunt contrast to the sweltering atmosphere. Nearly everyone was waving a piece of paper before their face for cooling.

The lawyers for both sides filled up the first row of the courtroom. Bly Macavoi, the government's prosecutor, was younger than she looked; maybe thirty-two, tall, self-assured, with long neat braided cornrow extensions, and an agreeable smile. But inside she was a fighter, a real believer in the change. Everyone was talking about her as a future star in the Justice Ministry. She had just returned a little over a year ago from the States with a law degree from Princeton University on a well-publicized government scholarship, graduating at the top ten of the class.

On the other side, Diallo Amadou sat paging through his notes. Grace Pupoh had prepared and made every piece of document he would need ready.

In the front row of the gallery sat the Douglas family, except Razaq, who Katharine had insisted that he continued his usual school attendance. Mrs. Douglas, a pleasant-looking woman in a plain but tasteful suit holding on to her Bible. Dr. Mellody Douglas, out of uniform, but most people knew her from JFK, sat loyally by her mother, wearing a brown copied Prada business suit.

Mellody looked elegant and refined. Her pants had a slimming seam down the front and a straight-leg cut which would work with both heels and flats. The blazer had two-buttons down the front, cut skimming the hips and waist, and pockets on either side. She looked professional and sexy at the same time.

RJ sat on the other side of Katharine and Gia sat next to him. He was dressed in a gray suit, light blue shirt and navy tie. Gia wore a plain black dress, one done by Vera Wang. She looked stunning, obviously getting more stares.

Security at the Temple of Justice was tighter than ever. Chief Dolo was probably responsible for half of the fuss. Every bag was being opened, every juror's pass double-checked, every press credential checked back against a photo ID. Armed police officers and soldiers were manning the barricades in front and on all sides of Temple of Justice. The senator was being transported from the MCP heavily guarded, at an time unknown to everyone other than the chief. This was the biggest crime trial in years, since the end of the civil war, to be exact, and Samukai Tweh wanted to make a name. He had his eye on the presidency next election and had assurances from the lawyers and from the defendants that he wanted the trial conducted speedily and in the open light of day.

The door finally opened near the rear of the crowded room. A buzz of anticipation rippled through the air as two husky-looking police officers led the defendant inside. Senator Douglas's hands were cuffed in front of him. He was dressed in a regular prisoner uniform, a navy blue jumpsuit with white letters MCP on the front and back, his graying hair nicely combed and his face was clean shaven. But, the indictment had aged him badly. Worst, he'd lost his dignity.

"Why is he not wearing a suit and tie?" Gia whispered at RJ.

"Baby, this is not America," he said. "At least, he's clean."

Gia rolled her eyes. "He would certainly look guilty as hell in that jail suit," she sighed. "The jury is predisposed to convict him dressed like that."

"I know, baby," RJ whispered, hoping he'd calmed her, knowing this was a frustrating resistance to reality. One day the explanation would be lengthy and detailed, he wanted to say.

The senator took a quick look around, saw his family and nodded; forcing a smile in a halfhearted effort to be polite. It was the first time he'd seen Katharine since his arrest months ago. The police officers took him to a chair next to Diallo, and there he sat. RJ expected them to free his hands, they did not. Diallo leaned over and whispered something into the senator's ear that made him smile. He turned, caught a glance from his family for a second or so, his eyes lit up, and he smiled again.

The judge's clerk stood and voiced, "All rise."

Judge Samukai Tweh entered the room through the side door, wearing a suit with a red bow tie beneath his judge's cloak. This was the biggest case of his life. He took his seat behind the bench and motioned everyone down.

"Ms. Macavoi, is the government ready?"

"We are…your honor," the prosecutor stood and nodded.

"Mr. Amadou?"

"Yes, your honor. The defendant is ready also, and eager to prove his innocence."

Judge Tweh nodded to the clerk. "You can bring in the jury now," his words cut through the hushed courtroom.

The jury marched in and took their seats.

Bly Macavoi was ready to showboat. Judge Tweh allowed her to rant and rave about the evidence from the local and international experts, the willing confessions from the defendant's four other conspirators, all of them somehow coordinated the crime for selfish gain, and especially the defendant's key role in providing the only means of transportation to make the crime successful.

Greedy big shots and heart men had been despised for a long-time. Now it was time to get rid of them publicly. The Liberian people were hungry for justice; she was telling the truth and demanding the consequences. She was shining a new light for change into the country and had allowed it to hang in the air for the jury benefit.

Macavoi's first witness was Chief Aaron Dolo. They walked through the crime with photographs of Johnny Bono's corpse as a series of photos were handed to the jurors and passed around. Their reactions were amazing; every face was shocked and some winced. A few mouths flew open. Philomena Russell grasped at first sight and turned away. Then she looked at Senator Douglas as if she would shoot him at point-blank range. Mambu Kamara covered his mouth as if he might throw up.

As the gruesome photos were passed around, not a single juror was without an expression. The pictures were inflammatory, highly prejudicial, yet admissible.

Every attempt to suppress the evidence to his liking was having the opposite result. Diallo Amadou was not having a good start to his day. Arguing didn't work. Objecting didn't work. Pleading didn't work. Bly Macavoi had methodically killed all his arguments, one by one, until finally Judge Tweh broke for lunch.

Judge Tweh was a fanatic for punctuality and no one appreciated brevity more than him. Within precisely forty-five minutes, court was back in session. Diallo looked toward the jury bench. It seemed like Bly Macavoi's words had found a way to their brains and was loosening their thoughts. The thought of Macavoi having such sway over the jurors was not comforting. But he was ready for war.

"Ready for round two?" Diallo said to Grace, with an edge.

She nodded, 'yes', knowing he would have to be bold, gusty and downright brilliant to beat Bly Macavoi.

According to Macavoi's arrangement, someone from the victim's family would be the second witness, Oldman Bono, Johnny Bono's old father from Sinta, Bong County. Death became real when the loved ones took the stand and looked at the jurors. Macavoi wanted to remind the jury that Johnny Bono had his old father to care for, with his wife and five children and he had been taken away from them in premeditated murder. Oldman Bono's testimony was brief. Wisely, Diallo had no questions on cross-examination.

Then it was back to the gore. A forensic pathologist from the United States was called to discuss the autopsy. The pathologist described the wounds, giving details of the mutilation of the face, the exposure of the abdomen and the missing major human organs. The main organs were skillfully removed, almost surgical, he'd stressed. The details were unsettling. At some point, every single juror looked at Senator Douglas and silently voted accountable.

Bly Macavoi was thorough.

Diallo began his cross-examination pleasantly enough, careful not to revisit the crime scene. The jury had heard enough of the cuts and gashes; it would be foolish because he had far less to work with. He was brief.

Everybody in the courtroom was exhausted after four hours of graphic testimony. Judge Tweh sent the jury away with strong warnings about avoiding outside contact.

Chapter Thirty-one

At precisely eight-thirty the following morning, the jurors were led in. Bly Macavoi called her last witness, Charles Sarpo, an ex-child soldier, who had admitted to the crime and named his conspirators, including the senator. He identified the cutlass on the exhibit table, one he and another defendant had used. The knife part was twenty inches long, four inches wide; heavy-duty steel. The wooden handle was about five inches, warped, and badly scratched, with big rivets like kitchen carving knife. Sarpo stumbled through his testimony that should have been much easier, but the point was made that everything connected.

He and Duo Boley kidnapped and killed Johnny Bono at the request of Tamba Nah Wumah, on the suggestion of Wonde Gedeh, the medicine woman. Senator Douglas was linked to the crime on account that in exchange for using his car, he would be given the heart and kidneys. No questions were asked as to why.

Sarpo's testimonies gave a full account of what had happened. His boss, Tamba Nah Wumah, solicited his help in finding and executing the subject. He was specific about what he wanted, precise about whom he wanted. He'd guaranteed Sarpo the payment and the payment of Duo Boley, $1,000 each. A matter of fact, Tamba Nah Wumah personally chose Duo Boley and transported the two back to his house after the killing, using Senator Douglas's car. Some of

Johnny Bono's organs were abstracted from his body with specific instructions.

Charles Sarpo confessed that Tamba Nah Wumah took Bono's penis, anus and testicles; Duo Boley took the throat, armpits, a piece of the intestine, and the liver; while the heart and kidneys were put in a special container for the senator. Tamba Nah Wumah took the senator's parts to him, but he, Sarpo, did not know where to. Wonde Gedeh only asked for one eye and some human blood, which they contained in a small bottle.

During the cross-examination, Sarpo was terrified of Diallo Amadou and began stuttering at the first question. Diallo wisely ignored the fact that Bono's blood was found in the senator's car, and chose instead to hammer Sarpo on the fact he had never met the senator and he had no proof the senator had made his car available for the crime.

"You ever met Senator Douglas, Mr. Sarpo?"

"No."

"Had you ever heard his name before the night of the crime?"

"No."

Diallo assumed a position behind the podium and conveyed slowly, clearly, and with precise diction, presenting the written statement of Charles Sarpo's admission of the abuse during his interrogation; how the officers grabbed him and threw him to the ground. They kicked him in the head, the chest, stomach, and the genitals. He cried out in pain, but the beating continued, almost as if they couldn't hear him. That was not a willing confession as the prosecutor wanted them to believe.

Diallo peppered him with more questions, all unanswered by Sarpo because he simply did not know the senator, had never met him, or heard of him. Diallo's tempo was slow, with thoughts given to each word. Even his speech was perfect, every consonant treated equally, every comma and period honored.

More than once Macavoi objected and she and Diallo haggled over it at Judge Tweh's bench.

It seemed Diallo had the Government's main witness tied in knots. The defense then moved to blame Sarpo's testimony on the pressure of the moment.

"Imagine," Diallo asked the jurors, "being beaten and facing either life in jail or, worst, hanging. The stress was so big that he did not mind naming a stranger as a conspirator. He did not know Senator Douglas, so it was easy to go along and named him as a conspirator."

"Damn it!" RJ said through clenched teeth.

Perhaps Diallo's defense was off a bit. Perhaps the reality of tribalism in Liberia was not matched to the trial. Perhaps Diallo, in his quest to win, thought it was a done deal, not having to prove anything other than his client had simply allowed his friend to use his car. Whatever the case, it seemed an uphill climb and he had never lost a case.

Throughout the testimonies, Mellody sat low in her seat, staring ahead, not at anyone or anything in particular. Gia held on to RJ's hand, squeezing lightly, to let him know she felt whatever he was feeling. Katharine was still clutching on to her small New Testament, softly rubbing the wedding band on her finger.

Chapter Thirty-two

JUDGE Tweh explained to the jury that it was now time for the closing arguments, after that, he would read to them his formal instructions, and they would have the case to decide in a few hours or so. They listened carefully.

Bly Macavoi went first. She pushed the old wooden chair away from the prosecution table; it made a harsh scraping eeek noise in the nearly silent courtroom. Then she rose and slowly approached the jury box, where six women and four men waited with anticipation to hear what she had to say. She looked seriously into their faces.

By now they had high regards for Ms. Macavoi and she knew it. She even expected it. She knew that she had already won this dramatic murder case, even without the stirring summation she was about to give. She was going to give a specially prepared closing, as she felt the need to see the senator and his associates held accountable for the crime against Johnny Bono. The senator had committed the most heinous murder and the people of Liberia expected him to be punished, like the rest of them, and she would not disappoint them.

Macavoi crossed her arms and pinched her chin like a thinking professor. "I, Bly Macavoi, represent Mr. Johnny Bono," she said in a pleasantly rich voice. "A father, who was murdered simply because heart men wanted to steal his heart."

She watched the faces of the jurors; she had their attention. There seemed no sympathy for the defendant. Russell, the bank-teller, was actually nodding as she followed Macavoi. Professor Zion had uncrossed his arms and was listening to every word. Sidiki's stare followed her.

"Why?" she continued. "You look at why. And I submit to you that the evidence tells you why. It tells you that they were looking for a human and they were going to kill whoever they found just to steal human organs. They all knew the place where the killing was going to take place. And that's what the evidence tells you. And in looking at this plan, looking at the intent to kill, look at the reason that place was chosen."

Macavoi watched most of the heads shake in agreement.

"Again, consider the evidence. What else does the evidence tell you about intent? About the state of mind of this defendant, when they caught Mr. Johnny Bono and took him to that beach? Perhaps the most graphic, certainly the most graphic, but perhaps the strongest evidence of intent is the pictures from the crime scene. As distasteful, as unpleasant as they are, while you're deliberating look at what they did to this innocent man. Look at the manner of these executions. This was an assassination, a calculated execution."

More nodding came from the jurors. Macavoi studied their faces, especially the blank one belonging to Dr. Yekerson. Her face revealed nothing but engrossed attention.

"What does the killing tell you about the intent?" Macavoi said slowly, her words echoing in the silent courtroom. "The intent to kill… I have presented to you, the intent to kill Mr. Johnny Bono was formed over that period of days, from August 20th through around the 24th or through the point where he was murdered. Before Johnny Bono died, that intent was formed. You have evidence of premeditation and the plan to kill.

"And you heard from Charles Sarpo's girlfriend… that in a dresser in that bedroom is where this knife and the container were kept. And this is the knife… this is the container. Sarpo identified the knife by the sheath with his name on it. That's the knife. He identified the container that Tamba Nah Wumah gave him, that special container belonging to the defendant.

"He was waiting for the car to carry the parts they stole. Do you think he would have taken a taxi? No. The car was part of the plan, to get Charles Sarpo and Duo Boley away from the crime scene…as quickly as possible. There was Johnny Bono's blood in the car, belonging to the defendant. His car, that he provided, carried Johnny Bono's heart, lungs, and other parts to the witch doctor. They could not get rid of traces of blood; they could not get rid of the evidence.

"Whoever sliced Johnny Bono's throat, whose car was used, they're all acting in consent, performing an act together. It is called aiding and abetting. If you help someone or encourage someone in acting, you are just as guilty, so both are equally guilty. This was a cold, calculated, planned execution.

"I haven't talked a whole lot about the statements Charles Sarpo made. As you would know out of common sense, these statements are only valuable because they relate to the evidence. The evidence is the important thing. So when considering those statements, consider whether they are independently confirmed by the evidence. The evidence at the scene supports what he says.

"If you are to believe that this defendant was not there in person, or held Johnny Bono down so his organs could be stolen out of him, remember this… it was his car that picked up Sarpo and Boley from where Johnny Bono's mutilated body was discovered. Talking about the elements of the crime, these are not that complicated. This defendant set out with the others to kill Johnny Bono, and they accomplished that mission. And that's first degree murder, and they're guilty. The defendant is guilty. And I ask you to so find."

Bly Macavoi was thorough as she made her last appeal for a verdict of guilty.

✦✦✦✦

"In this case, I represent Senator Robert Jenkins Douglas II," Diallo Amadou started. "The prosecution never called him Senator Robert Douglas. They called him "defendant". I want to tell you that Senator Robert Douglas II, like all defendants, is presumed to be innocent and he is entitled to the same dignity and respect as all the rest of us."

Diallo thought it wise to interpret the presumption of innocence.

"As he sits there," he continued, "Senator Douglas is covered in a presumption of innocence and you will determine the facts of whether he is set free to walk out those doors or whether he loses his life. The prosecution must prove Senator Douglas guilty beyond reasonable doubt and must do so to an honest pledge."

A couple of jurors nodded in agreement.

"Let me ask each of you something," Diallo said. "Have you ever, in your life, been falsely accused of something?"

He got more nodding heads.

"Have you ever had to sit and wait, all the while knowing you didn't do it? All you could do during the process is to maintain your dignity, knowing that you were innocent."

Just about every head was nodding.

"I am proud to represent Senator Robert Douglas," Diallo continued, "who has upheld his innocence and has conducted himself with dignity throughout these proceedings."

Diallo went from teaching to preaching.

"This is a homicide case, a serious case," he said, as if evangelizing. "It is important for us to understand that and a competent, non-corrupt law enforcement system must carefully investigate homicides. They are to get the killer or killers and try to protect the innocent from suspicion. The victim's family has an absolute right to demand exactly that in this case.

"The only person Senator Douglas knows is, Mayor Tamba Nah Wumah, whom he allowed to borrow his car. He did not question as to why Tamba Nah needed the car, as his friend had used it many times before. The senator, like any friend, allowed his friend to use his car. The senator had never met Sarpo, or Boley, or Madam Wonde Gedeh. He simply allowed his friend to use his car, not knowing anything about their plan.

"Senator Douglas has dedicated his life to serving the people of Liberia, so has his daughter, Dr. Douglas, at JKF hospital. The Douglas family has helped people regardless of social status, unlike many others. Mrs. Douglas, an American, has willingly given her life to service the people of Liberia.

"Please, don't compromise your principles or your consciences in rendering this decision. Don't rush to judgment. Have a judgment that is well thought out, one that you can believe in the morning after this verdict. I want you to place yourself, the day after you've rendered the verdict, when you get up and look in the mirror and say, 'Have I been true to my oath? Did I do the right thing? Did I believe in the truth? Did I believe in justice? Did I do my part with integrity and honesty?'

"That is a job you've been chosen for… you're on this journey toward true justice. You and I are fighting for freedom and for justice for all, not just Senator Douglas, not just Mr. Bono…justice for everyone. We must continue to fight to expose hate, corruption, tribalism and these types of tendencies. We must become the guardians of the new change in Liberia.

"I hope that I have demonstrated to you that this is a case about making an example of nothing, an obsession to win at all costs, a willingness to twist the facts in any fashion to get you to vote guilty. This is about an innocent man who is wrongfully accused. You have the keys to his future. You have the evidence by which you can acquit Senator Douglas. You have not only the open-mindedness, but the integrity to do the right thing. We believe you will do the right thing, and the right thing is to find this man, Senator Robert J. Douglas, not guilty. Thank you, ladies and gentlemen."

Because the Government had the chance for a rebuttal, and the defense did not, Bly Macavoi got the last word. She ignored the evidence and did not mention the defendant, but chose instead to talk about Johnny Bono. His desire to support his old father, his simple life out of Bong County, and the challenge of raising five small children with his wife, a hard-working woman. Macavoi was effective, and the jurors absorbed every word.

"Let's not forget about Johnny Bono," Bly Macavoi stated. "And, let's not forget about those that are to live without him; his old father, old mother, his young wife and their five small children," she said as she looked into the eyes of the jurors. "They have a voice in this courtroom, and their voice belongs to you. You will speak on their behalf."

Judge Tweh waited for Bly Macavoi to take her seat. Then, he read his instructions to the jury and sent them back to begin their deliberations.

Chapter Thirty-three

RJ began to feel a gnawing anxiety at how soon all of this would be ending. Much of the crowds stayed behind in the courtroom, others remained in front of Temple of Justice, smoking, gossiping, and predicting how long a verdict would take. Others crowded the sidewalk, watching the activities of protesters.

After deliberating for less than two and a half hours, the jury was ready.

When the lawyers and spectators were in place, Judge Tweh told the bailiff to bring in the jury. The door opened and Ms. Russell led the jury out. As foreman, she handed a folded sheet of paper to the bailiff, who then gave it to the Judge. Judge Tweh examined it for a longtime, and then leaned down close to his microphone.

"Would the defendant please rise," he ordered.

Senator Douglas, Diallo Amadou and Grace Pupoh stood, slowly and uneasily, as if the firing squad was taking aim.

In a sturdy, emotion-packed voice, Judge Samukai Tweh read his verdict, "Senator Robert Jenkins Douglas, you are found guilty of the murder as presented in evidence before me and this court. You will be taken to the Monrovia Central Prison jail, and there be hung with the other four defendants, no more than one week from today's date. May God have mercy on your soul."

Katharine collapsed, falling in Mellody's arm. She came thru in a short time and screamed out above all the other noise, "Oh Jesus... is this your will, Lord?"

Senator Douglas, looking straightforwardly at Judge Tweh, did not flinch. Diallo placed his arm around his client's shoulder and gave him a light squeeze. Grace slowly lowered her head until her chin was an inch off her chest. They had been beaten, her heart sank, as the client she'd worked so hard and long for, was sentenced to die.

"You may be seated," Judge Tweh said, and then he turned to the jury. "Ladies and gentlemen, thank you for your service."

There seemed, on each juror's face, a certain amount of pride. Most were sitting where they had never dreamed of sitting, shoulder to shoulder with fellow Liberian citizens, judging a senior senator, venturing into untested waters.

It was over so quickly that most of the spectators didn't move for a moment. Two officers grabbed Senator Douglas immediately, in handcuffs; the Douglas family seemed completely baffled. Grace looked toward the family to catch a glimpse of RJ. Tell me this is a nightmare, his eyes said, as she caught his stare. Then he grabbed Katharine's hand and quickly led the family out of the courtroom. Diallo had no time to chat with them.

As they hurried to the SUV, the sidewalk in front of Temple of Justice was barricaded with Police officers standing around. He remembered parking farther down, where the television and newspaper reporters were. Near them, a large crowd was listening to a speaker yell into a microphone. There were a few hastily painted posters held above the activists' heads, mostly for the benefit of the cameras.

As the Douglas family passed, a man shouted, with great excitement, "That heart man there should die like Johnny Bono!"

Mellody turned and looked at him. He had the audacity to keep a stupid grin on his face although she recognized him from the hospital.

Within minutes, the news had spread all over the country;

DEFENDANT: SENATOR ROBERT J. DOUGLAS II
VERDICT: GUILTY
SENTENCE: DEATH BY HANGING

Straight away, many people gathered in front of Temple of Justice, insomuch there was no room to receive them. The market women organization, headed by Johnny Bono's aunt, exploded in jubilations, waving white hankies. Bob Marley and his Wailers were being blasted from loudspeakers on top of an old beat-up Renault bus, singing "Redemption Song. Every radio station, yelling out of oversize transistor radios, Victory for Johnny Bono! Young, innocent-faced schoolchildren waved hand-painted banners—JUSTICE FOR JOHNNY BONO. A shirt-less man with white chalk writing on his chest—CHANGE IS IN LIBERIA—ran up to a TV camera and made a peace sign. "Change is here!" he shouted, and became famous across the country.

At four forty-five, the officers pointed at the main door out of the courtroom and Senator Douglas obediently followed. Then they led him out of the Temple of Justice and drove him back to MCP where the others awaited their punishment.

Chapter Thirty-four

THE Supreme Court of Liberia started its March term with the Bono Murder appeal. After hearing arguments, at the end in a thirty-page judgment, the Court announced its decision: it upheld the conviction by the lower court and hence affirmed the death sentence for the five murderers, four men, and one woman. The fate of the convicted murderers was now in the hands of only one person, the President of the Republic. From the front of the Temple of Justice, the Press Secretary announced the president had indeed signed five warrants, sparing none.

"This president would not be influenced in one way or the other by sentiments," she read from her paper, "but execute the duty of the country in the fear of God, in keeping with the oath of office of the president."

Many people had gathered in front of the Temple of Justice, insomuch there was no room to receive them. Diallo pushed his way through a surging crowd that had built up on the steps. The case was in his rearview mirror now. He felt hallowed out and terribly sad, but knew he couldn't show it there. It was packed with reporters and news crews, shoving their microphones at anyone who came out of the building, down the steps. Diallo knew most of the reporters, but waved them off. Then a set of hands grasped his shoulders, and a familiar voice chimed, "Diallo, want to talk?"

He spun and came face to face with Famatta Kpan.

"I wouldn't bother you now," she said, above the noise, "But how about tomorrow at nine, at your office?"

Diallo managed a smile. It wasn't a yes or no.

✳✳✳✳

While RJ waited at the office, Grace traced a finger along the back of his hand he had resting on her desk, to get his attention. Not surprised, his skin tingled beneath her touch.

"Can I get you something to drink?" she asked, concerned.

Her voice seemed tender, so tempting, that he suppressed the urge to look at her. He swallowed, trying to soothe the sudden dryness in his throat. He shook his head, 'no'.

"Sure you don't want bottled water?"

"I'm fine," he said, smiling. "Thanks."

Then the office phone buzzed and Grace answered.

It was Chief Aaron Dolo from Monrovia Central Prison. Diallo Amadou was being officially informed of his client's execution time, things were proceeding in an orderly fashion; he had been moved with the others to the prison's death watch area.

The erosion of the senator's chance had been slow, but certain. The clock had run out. Grace pursed her lips before breaking the news.

"RJ, I'm so sorry," she said, almost trembling. "I don't have better news for you. They've scheduled the execution for tomorrow," she said, sounding much sadder now, taking his hand.

RJ sighed. He grunted in their defeat, closed his eyes, and slowly shook his head. "I don't believe this," he mumbled.

"I'm sorry, RJ," Grace whispered.

Diallo walked in the quiet office suspecting they'd already heard the bad news, it was evident. He put down his briefcase and stood ramrod straight, obviously distressed.

"I've always seen my father's hanging... such burning desire in Judge Tweh's eyes," RJ said to Diallo, barely relaxing his face, staring. His words were filled with both sadness and frustration. "My father never had a chance in all of their change. No matter how detailed you were about the SCIU illegal and unconstitutional manner in which they obtained their confessions. I expected the Supreme Court to have remanded the case... even because of Justice Tweh's erroneous and illegal rulings. Daddy is innocent."

"I'm sorry, RJ," Diallo said.

"Thanks for all you did," RJ said.

"Tried to do," Diallo corrected. "Tried and failed, that's what I did."

"Not your fault," RJ shook his head. "The deck of cards was too stacked against us. I know you did your best, and I hope you know that too. Like I said, the deck was stacked so goddamn high."

Diallo took in a breath. "RJ, I truly believe the senator is innocent," he said, exhaling. "It is important for me to say it. Tomorrow, this government will be guilty of murder."

RJ went to shake Diallo's hand, Diallo hugged him instead. He thought about his father, how he would feel if it was his father.

"Let me get home and tell my family the bad news...I don't want them hearing it over the radio," RJ said and quietly walked out.

There was a small group of protesters, mostly university students and a few market women, on the sidewalk in front of the building. A young man about twenty-something walked up to RJ; his eyes narrowed and his jaw tensed.

"I don't understand how a man could willfully murder another human being, as your father most definitely did. He stole Johnny's heart, what for?"

RJ stood speechless, his stomach dropped.

The man leaned forward.

"Take this message to your family," he barked. "When the senator is executed tomorrow, I will be there with the family of Johnny Bono. I'm looking forward to his hanging. What your father did to that poor man disgusts me. Now, get the hell out of my face! Get the fuck out of my sight!"

RJ had a flash of anger, but he let it pass. His self-control was amazing. He hurried away. The group cheered.

✦✦✦✦

Traffic was horrendous during rush hour; it took almost forty-five exhaust-fumed minutes to get back to the house. Darkness had fallen when RJ got home. The Douglas' home had the unnatural, claustrophobic look of a wake. In the living room, the senator's three sisters and their husbands, Lynette Vinton, about a dozen church members, some neighbors, and a few other relatives had gathered. The women had been singing and crying; their faces were all puffy and their eyes red, except for Ma Teete who was serving coffee and biscuits, which no one seemed to be eating.

Ma Teete isn't one to get weepy, even with a good reason, though she was a tremendously warm and caring person. She was dry-eyed as she did her serving. She just doesn't cry anymore, not since the civil war. She says she doesn't have that much of life left, and she won't waste it on tears.

"When God leads you to the edge of the cliff, trust Him fully and let go," she had quoted someone. "Only one of two things will happen, either He'll catch you when you fall, or He'll teach you how to fly!"

Chapter Thirty-five

TOMORROW'S DAY

IT was a dark night, with no moon. About the fifth hour, a line of heavily armored military vehicles, their headlights twinkling in the predawn morning, lumbered past the barbed wire and metal gates marking the border of the Monrovia Central Prison compound. Five defendants, guilty as charged and sentenced to die, were escorted six miles to the old military barracks where the gallows were placed for their hanging. A crowd of more than fifteen-hundred spectators had gathered there hours before to witness the execution. The Atlantic sea breeze was blowing well; many were verbalizing the thoughts racing around in their heads. The spirits of these convicted souls had tinted the air to be more chilling than normal.

Executioner Paul Korto, a local prophet's son, trained as a pastor but had not practiced as such, rode the front seat of the van carrying the prisoners. He did not mind the small income derived from executions and in fact accepted his role as a privilege of helping humanity or acting on principle. When the job vacancy became available, only male applications were accepted and the only required skills were dexterity and the ability to tie a knot. Anyone prone to hesitation or mercy need not apply. A hangman should never have second thoughts nor be remorseful about his job.

Legion, as he was known, was a name Korto had taken from a story in the Bible about a man Jesus freed of more than two thousand devils living in him. According to his belief, God had given him the role of executioner for the purpose of releasing the evil spirits that caused people to kill as these condemned had. Only a possessed person did such acts of violence. He learned the job on his own, even mastering the crafts of a perfect noose. Every collar Legion made had his signature of the type and thickness of rope and thirteen coils, to be exact, that he winds, and winds to get just the right hang knot.

The caravan came to halt about one hundred yards from the gallows. First, soldiers poured out of the vehicles, heavily armed with M-16s, they meant business. The soldier men and women were outfitted in battle dress uniform—boots, camouflage shirts and pants. Then, Legion climbed out of the front door and opened the sliding side door to let out his travelers. One behind another, they climbed out of the heavily guarded van dressed in white jumpsuits, shackled by the ankle and hands tied behind their backs. Then, the condemned marched up to the gallows in unhurried steps to the five nooses attached to the horizontal beam. Even those who maintained their innocence to the end retained great composure. Legion waited for each prisoner to stand on his mark.

Experienced to operate a more complex piece of equipment than it looked; the executioner always made it his business to lessen the suffering of the condemned. His job was to have them go through the process quickly so they are pronounced dead on the end of the rope within seconds.

Legion reached the first man, conveying deep kindness and sadness as he stared into the eyes of one imminently doomed soul. He placed the noose around the senator's head, over his salt and pepper facial grown, then his neck, making sure the knot of the rope was placed just behind the left ear. Then he applied the white hood and moved on to the next. He prepared the other three men and reached the condemned woman last.

'This is my sister to whom something dreadful must be done,' he thought.

He was gentler with her, giving her what dignity he could. After all, he was the last to look her in the eyes. Legion prepared her and took his place near the lever.

Close to six, a hush of silence hung in the air, so strange and eerie, as if the whole world had stopped to listen. Then the officer started the countdown, nine, eight, seven, six, five, four, three, two, and one.

Six o'clock sharp, at the sound of the whistle, Legion pulled the lever. The floor under each convicted murder shifted, advancing each body downward. The five dropped in unison to the end of their ropes, their bodies went limp upon strangulation. There was no struggle. Legion had planned the force from the thirteen coils on the noose will break their necks instantly.

"When you kill, the law will kill you," a man said to his friend.

"Yes," his friend agreed, and then asked, "Do you remember, Obi?"

"Yes, the Nigerian man. I remember him. He came to our country to kill, so the law killed him too. That's why I said, 'when you kill, the law will kill you.'"

Both men chuckled.

✶✶✶✶

Meantime at the Douglas' home, at six o'clock, Katharine let out a high pitch scream, "Oh, God… no! How could you let this happen?" Then choking sobs poured from her open mouth. "He's all I had," she continued to weep.

RJ felt his heart sink. He grabbed Gia's hand and squeezed, fighting back his tears.

"Jesus," Gia sighed as her heart sank.

Mellody sobbed into the shoulder of her comforting friend, Dr. Cho.

Pastor Peabody began to cry himself.

Suddenly, Katharine receded from the sofa and dropped to her knees. "Noooooooooo," she screamed.

Razaq and Lynnette Vinton ran from across the living room, got on their knees beside her, and both began rubbing her back. Katharine screamed louder and longer.

"I know," Lynnette whispered in her friend's ear, "I know, my dear friend."

Suddenly, Katharine collapsed sideways to the floor and broke down crying, big heaving cries that left her shoulders shaking.

"You don't knooooow! None of y'all know!" She cried.

There is nothing worst than the sound of a mother crying. RJ found himself wanting to comfort her. He left Gia's side and joined Razaq. Lynnette got up and RJ sat on the floor next to Katharine.

"There… there," RJ murmured. "It'll be okay, Mom."

It took a longtime before Katharine was able to regain some appearance of control. She looked at RJ, her eyes red and puffy.

"No, baby, it won't," she blubbered. "It's never going to be okay."

Chapter Thirty-six

RJ drifted through the city, simply moving with the traffic. There was no particular place to go, until the thought of a decent burial crossed his mind. This late in the day, he did not think Diallo would be at the office still. He decided to try his luck.

To his surprise, Diallo was at his desk, projecting the appearance of a very busy lawyer. He was perturbed by the intrusion, and rightfully so. Proper protocol would have been for RJ to call ahead and let him know he was heading there.

"Where is he now?" RJ asked, referring to his father's body.

"Probably at JKF, in the city morgue," Diallo said numbly.

"What happens if the family wants the body?"

"We have to go back to Chief Dolo," Diallo suggested. "The government buries the unclaimed and prisoners. On the books, it's called a pauper's funeral."

"I know what it's call," RJ snapped.

It was a soft jab, but Diallo was not in the mood to spar.

"There's an area set aside at the cemetery on Center Street where they pack them in," Diallo continued. "You'd be amazed at the number of people who die unclaimed."

"I'm not concerned about homeless people now... I'm talking about my father."

"Sure," Diallo said reluctantly. He picked up his cell and punched in some numbers. "Grace, I know you're off… and I know that you're home, but could you get me Chief Dolo's personal number?" he said and hung up. He removed his glasses, wiped them with a tissue, and then rubbed his eyes. "RJ, you know how hard I've tried."

"Yeah, I guess," RJ sighed. "So, when can I expect a call?" he said, looking at his watch. He had taken up too much time. "Please… call me as soon as you have an idea, ok?" he said and let himself out.

✶✶✶✶

The last person RJ wanted to see was Pastor Peabody, especially after hearing how the members felt about his father's situation. He drove straight to Words of Christ Church, jumped out of the car and ran towards the back. When he entered the church, he slowed to a walk and made his way to the opened office. Pastor Peabody looked up when he heard RJ, and knew why he was there.

"Pastor," RJ said softly and went in without being invited. He marched right up to his desk.

Pastor Peabody's face looked beaten, even troubled; almost as weary as Moses' face looked in the eyes of his father-in-law, as the Israelites described it in the Bible. He had to keep up his spirits around the church members, and the stress of doing so was wearing him down. Lynnette Vinton had broken the news to Katharine, even before Pastor Peabody had the chance, the board had voted not to allow the senator's body in the church, not under those circumstances.

Before Pastor Peabody said a word, RJ croaked, "Since my father was arrested, hell, before the trial and their conviction, no one would even look my mother in the eye. She has worked so hard to help get this church to where it is now."

Pastor Peabody sighed and remained sitting in his chair.

Was it okay to get angry before a pastor? RJ thought. His anger, however made him realize something else, something that made more sense. Julius Peabody was just a man, like him. With his lips pressed together, the whole thing made him want to cry. Instead, he forced a sad smile across his face, and Pastor Peabody knew right then RJ was trying to express his true feelings. His eyes never left the pastor.

"I know the senator wasn't the kind of man you all suppose he should have been, but I think even your God cares about the worst sinner… and Dad wasn't the worst," RJ said in one breath. "I'm not asking that you eulogize him in the church. It would break my poor mother's heart if you don't eulogize him at all."

Pastor Peabody only sighed again.

RJ felt his heart beginning to race with sadness, anger, and fear. He wasn't sure what the pastor was thinking, until he finally spoke.

"You're right," Pastor Peabody said, nodding. "One sinner isn't less important than the other." His tone sounded defeated, as though he had no strength to fight RJ or members of his church. "Of course, I will eulogize your father… not in the church though. I'll think of something."

"How about the funeral home, they have a chapel there; I've already checked," RJ said. "We'd rather have something simple, with only a few friends with the family."

Pastor Peabody smiled, faintly.

"I'm truly sorry about your loss, RJ," he said and got up. "Sometimes we forget… the foolishness of God is wiser than men; and the weakness of God is stronger than men."

RJ considered the remarks, but made no extra effort to understand it.

"Thank you, Pastor Peabody," he said and shook his hand.

Chapter Thirty-seven

DIALLO walked out of the office straight to his small red convertible. He climbed in, leaving the convertible's top up, windows
partially up and the visors down. He put on his dark Ray Ban
sunglasses, fired up the engine and immediately rolled out into
the streets. As the MX-5 Miata turned onto Tubman Boulevard,
his brilliantly clear and definite plan was mapped out. Only Rue,
his number one client, could help him win this one.

CeRue Manor was an eminent businessman, a wheeler and
dealer, known as GQ for his dress style, Rolex watch and BMW
720. With lean brutally chiseled features, a razor clean fade hairdo
and perfect gleaming white teeth, he always looked like a model
in a Vanity Fair ad.

"Thank you, Jesus!" Diallo said when he spotted Rue's BMW
parked in the driveway.

Diallo rehearsed in his mind he would go straight to the point
when his car came to a stop. He hurriedly got out, ran to the door,
and then began buzzing the bell and knocking on the door the same
time. Even luckier for him, Rue, himself, opened the door.

"Diallo!" he greeted. "Hey… sorry about the senator, but are
you okay?"

"Well… yeah."

"Come on in," Rue led his guest into the living room and straight to the bar. He poured Xante liqueur over two glasses of ice cubes, handed Diallo a glass and motioned him to sit. "You don't sound too good, though. What's up?"

"I need your help," Diallo gasped.

The master of masterminds laughed.

"Well, that's why I'm in Liberia. People always need my help," Rue said.

Diallo chuckled.

"This is for me, personally," Diallo said and went directly to the point. "I want you to help me get the senator's body for his family."

"Consider it done," Rue said and took a sip of his drink. "And, I thought you were about to ask me some impossible favor. Is my lawyer slipping or what?" he joked. "This would be easy... Aaron Dolo owes me one."

Just like that, Diallo exhaled, thinking to himself.

"Are you going to call him, yourself?" Diallo asked.

"I'm going call him right now," Rue said and put down his glass. He pulled out his Blackberry Bold 9700 from his shirt pocket. "My little friend here does everything," he boasted. "E-mail, internet, even keeps all of my secrets."

'Just dial the damn number,' Diallo said in his mind.

"Chief!" Rue yelled in the phone, trying to steady it against his chin and ear. "Hope I didn't catch you at a bad time. Do this for me," he demanded. "The family has suffered enough…let them have the senator's body, okay?"

There was a moment of silence, one, two, three minutes perhaps, which seemed a lifetime to Diallo. Then Rue ended his call without saying 'good-bye'.

"Diallo, you can relax. Stop… I can hear your heart beating," he joked, having some fun at his lawyer's expense. Then he broke the news, "Aaron Dolo will release the body to you… tomorrow at four."

Diallo took a sip of his drink for the first time.

They sat and chitchatted for another ten minutes, and then Diallo made up an excuse about having plans with his wife.

"You are the Big Dawg!" Diallo kidded CeRue as he was leaving.

Big Dawg was a pet expression they used for any person having much influence or authority.

✦✦✦✦

The morgue was on the ground floor of JFK hospital, out a back entrance and accessible from an asphalt path that led from the lobby. It took RJ no more than four minutes to rush down two flights of stairs. He met Diallo in the reception area. Diallo's face bore a look of professional concern, but as soon as he saw RJ, he eased into a smile and shook his hand.

"How is the family holding up?" Diallo asked.

"Good, I guess…just swamped with so many things to do in one day and do them as quickly as possible."

The Chief Coroner came out of his office and led them down an antiseptic-linoleum-tiled hallway toward the morgue's operating room, called the Tomb. They burst through a closed compression door into the dry cold air of the Tomb. The icy chill and chemical smell made RJ feel sick to his stomach. A single inhabited gurney was visible from its refrigerated vault. A human-size mound was on it, covered by a white sheet. It filled the entire length of the gurney.

"Are you ready?" the Chief Coroner warned.

RJ nodded.

He pulled down the sheet and Senator Douglas's face shot into view. He seemed so out of place against the cold, clinical surroundings. RJ stared at his father, a part of him wanting to just reach out and lay a hand against his face, wake him up and take him home. Then a fit of nausea gripped at his gut at the sight of a dark print of the hangman's knot on the left side beneath the senator's chin.

RJ held his father's lifeless hand and thought about their last conversation at the prison, the ineffable sadness in his eyes.

"Executions do not solve anything," RJ groaned. "They are only an antiquated relic of a primitive desire for avenge. I love you, Daddy… I hope you died believing that."

Chapter Thirty-eight

ONE week after the hanging, on a sunny and warm Friday morning, a few dozen black-clothed mourners were jammed into Turay's Funeral Home chapel. Senator Douglas was getting a real funeral after all, though it was not one Liberians are used to–– the ritual of the wake, often lasting the entire night; wake and funeral services with open caskets and much wailing; the mile-long funeral processions; and lastly, the final graveside farewells loaded with emotions.

At this funeral, Diallo Amadou was there, with his wife. Mr. Tom and Ma Teete were stationed an arm's length from the family. Several doctors from JFK Hospital, mostly foreign, were there too. Lynnette Vinton took a seat among a delegation from the church. Standing in the rear of the chapel, in a short black dress, RJ spotted Grace. They both nodded as they caught each other's eye.

Soon, the piano rendition of I'LL FLY AWAY was coming through the four giant speakers, one in each corner of the chapel. There is nothing more stirring than uplifting hymns resonating through a filled chapel. There is almost, always, a need to privately ask God for mercy to shine down on your sinful soul.

At the end of the recording, Pastor Peabody stepped up to a microphone. He spoke about the senator as someone he had known for a long time––his work as senator, a servant of the Liberian people; the many businesses he had managed to bring from overseas for the country he loved; how he had helped rebuild the city after the war; how his children, especially his daughter, Dr. Mellody Douglas, had worked as a volunteer physician at JFK; how, now only the angels would get to hear his voice, touch his hands, walk with him.

Pastor Peabody's eulogy was hopeful, emotional and real. He preached about forgiveness and peace. It must not be about politics or even tribalism. It must be about the right to be free from hate. Liberia needed change to mend itself.

People cried and shouted, Amen.

It was over within an hour. Katharine broke down during the singing of GOD BE WITH YOU TILL WE MEET AGAIN. At the front of the funeral home, the sleek black body of the hearse finally slid into view, to transport Senator Douglas. Somehow, Katharine Douglas looked strong as she followed the casket out, her beloved husband being carried to his final rest.

"Father, into your hands I hand over Robert's spirit," she whispered.

One could almost hear the lump forming in RJ's throat. His jaw muscles stood out as he prevented himself from shaking, moving, breaking down completely. He walked out feeling numb and broken, holding Gia's hand.

After the final ritual prayers and singing, Senator Douglas was laid to rest on a hill overlooking an unobstructed field, a newer section in Palm Grove Cemetery were the graves were neater.

RJ gestured toward the sky as he finished his graveside words. "Daddy, do what you did so well in life, watch over us. We will never forget your sacrifice for us. I love you."

After Gia dropped her rose among the many different flowers on the casket's varnished lid, she and RJ embraced. Then he grabbed her hand and they started their walk through the winding shaded lanes of the cemetery toward the car.

"I'm proud of you, baby," she said and squeezed his hand.

"Couldn't have done it without you," he said, and put his hand around her waist.

Gia laid her head against his shoulder as they walked.

"The wrong man died," RJ said, looking straight ahead. "The

trial was ugly before it started, so ugly that Diallo almost couldn't use any other defense."

Gia listened.

"I am a lawyer, and I've represented people charged with all sorts of crimes," RJ continued. "Fortunately, I'd never had a client convicted of capital murder and sentenced to death. I never had to go to death row, never had to look into the eyes of someone who knew the date, hour... even the minute of their death, until now. I practice law because I want to fight for the victim's rights. I've always been a fighter... until now. Seeing my father march bravely toward his doom, I've been reminded that though I'm a fighter, I have a bleeding heart."

Gia lifted her head and kissed his shoulder.

They continued to walk, now with slower steps.

"The senator was a good father to us," RJ said, "And he was a thoughtful, loving husband to Mom. Diallo did not have to say what he told me."

"What did he say?" Gia asked, softly.

"You know, the night before the execution, Diallo was the only one allowed to sit with him. Diallo swears that Daddy looked him in the eyes and said he had nothing to do with Johnny Bono's death. He begged Diallo to make sure he let Mel and I know that. I believe him," RJ said, and looked at Gia.

"I never doubted his innocence," she said.

"So, I am going to take care of my mother the only way Dad could have."

"Yes, baby, maybe she can come live with us for a while... get away from here. It's going to be hard after we leave, you know."

"That's a good idea, baby, but that's not what I was thinking."

"I'm listening," Gia said.

RJ stopped. He took her hands in his and stared into her eyes.

"I'm going to sue the Liberian Government for wrongful death," he said bluntly. "My father was innocent, and I have enough evidence to prove it."

Chapter Thirty-nine

GRACE waited at the Douglas family home, mingling among mourners and weeping relatives. When RJ and Gia made it back home from the gravesite, most of the people were on the porch. Grace watched him help Gia out of the car, and then held her hand as they walked toward the house. He spotted Grace sitting with Yassah, but had not caught her eyes. After a few curious glances drifted in his direction, he decided to make the introduction, as her presence in the same room with Gia was making it impossible to fully relax.

"I'd like you to meet someone," RJ said to Gia and led her to the women.

"This is Ms. Grace Pupoh, Diallo's fine legal assistant," RJ made the introduction. "Grace, this is my fiancé, Dr. Ricciola."

"Call me, Gia," Gia said, smiling, shaking Grace's hand. "Glad to meet you… and thanks for the good work you did. RJ told me how hard you worked."

"I was happy to help," Grace said. "I only wish it had turned out different. I'd like you to meet my sister, Yassah," she introduced her friend.

Gia shook Yassah's hand, then looked at RJ and grinned, "You were right honey… Queen Latifah."

"RJ thinks I look like this actor named, Queen Latifah," Grace said to Yassah.

Yassah stared at Grace for a moment. "Yes," she agreed and laughed. "You look like her, kind of… remember that movie, Set It Off?"

Yassah gave Grace a quick recap of the movie and she agreed for the sake of agreeing.

The house was packed; everyone who planned to come was already there, and it seemed no one was quiet ready to leave. There were hardly strangers, so RJ had to excuse himself to make time for other guests, mostly family he'd not seen in a long time. As he spoke, he scooped Gia's hand and slid his fingers through her fingers.

"So good to meet you both," Gia said and they walked away.

✶✶✶✶

"Move your heart from there," Yassah warned her friend, in plain Liberian slang, meaning forget about RJ.

Grace responded only with a heavy sigh. She'd always had the passion for life, the excitement between the tedious spaces of possibility, and it didn't matter where it was directed. To her, the saddest people were those who didn't care deeply about anything at all. Passion brought satisfaction and without it, happiness would be temporary; especially when happiness is usually infectious.

Grace had a particular effect on every guy she met, her talking, smiling, or turning that earnest gaze on them, but she was a sucker for only guys who respected women. She resented the ones that were living their fantasies in the real world and using women in the process. This all came about after moving in with the Johnstons.

Grace had lived with the Coleman family since she was seven years old. They brought her to live with them after Marie, their five-year-old daughter, met Grace while visiting the family farm. Grace didn't know what she had been called before then, as Mrs. Coleman had given her a new name, a new life. The Colemans continued to care for her until she turned fourteen, when Mr. Coleman was assigned ambassador to England and his mother-in-law, Etta Johnston, reluctantly agreed to take Grace in. She already had another girl living with her, which was the reason her daughter encouraged her to take Grace in rather than send her back to her people.

The girls shared a room and it was Grace's first night that Yassah told her all about Mr. Johnston's secret night visits. He'd molested every girl that came to live with them, got them pregnant, and Mrs. Johnston would put them out. He'd climb in the bed, on top of Yassah, since she was twelve, and fucked her even as she pretended to be sick or sleeping.

Things progressively got worst. Mrs. Johnston sensed that something was changing, but she was at loss about what to do about it until Yassah's rebellion reached a high point. Her chores were never completed, her grades were slipping, more from lack of interest for school than laziness. She didn't give a damn about anything much.

Then, though Yassah was skinny, her skirt nipped at the waist, making her look as if she was pregnant. Everybody knew except for her, she was two months pregnant. Like the other girls before, Mrs. Johnston was embarrassed by the sight of Yassah and put her out.

Grace fought Mr. Johnston off of her the first time he'd tried to fuck her. He tried many times against her warning, until one day she got the courage and told Mrs. Johnston the terrible secret. Mr. Johnston swore before God, holding on to the family Bible, the girl was lying. He concocted the story about Grace's boyfriend he'd caught her sneaking out the back door. Since it was obvious that every girl that came to live with them ended up pregnant, Mrs. Johnston decided to have Grace thrown out of the house, better safe than sorry.

Grace needed a place to live and Yassah was gracious to share the one room she rented at a boarding house. All of life's frustrations came to the surface, while living with Yassah. Yassah lived her life by her own rules and didn't always care what people thought of her. Grace, however, wanted a job, not to buy clothes, shoes, or any of those material things she'd lived fifteen years without. She was most content at school and dreamt that every extra dollar or coin she got would go into saving for college when she graduated from high school.

Little by little, Grace began to notice differences in the way she lived when she compared herself with most of her friends. While they had money to spend to go to the movies, or clubs, or buy a stylish pair of sunglasses, she found herself scrounging for quarters to buy a notebook or pen. They cared more about looks, simply feeding into the ruthless seduction by the men who degraded, debased and depraved women. These men pretty much avoided anything that might require a shred of responsibility, so most unwanted pregnancies were aborted, like Yassah's, who claimed children only disrupt lives; they are so demanding. Her friends were attractive, dressed like models in fashion magazines, but were illiterate and wrote like that of a child's handwriting.

Grace grew sick and tired of lousy job offers in exchange for sexual favors. She wanted no part in becoming one of their sexual merchandise and decided to start her business, selling used clothes. She studied her friends and learned what they liked. Then she hand-picked the best designs, washed and pressed the pieces to almost looking new, and sold them to friends and neighbors. Soon every young woman in need of a formalwear came to buy from Grace. While her business went on, she attended adult school at night, eventually graduating from Tubman High with a diploma and a secretarial certificate.

As with all Liberians, the civil war disrupted many dreams. With a high school diploma, a secretarial certificate and determination to go to college, Grace found herself caught in the middle of a senseless war, a new assault on her dreams. Side by side, she and Yassah fought rape, hunger, and murder in exchange for life in dilapidated refugee camps.

But a little courage is good for the soul and hope can be ignited by just a spark of encouragement. One day as hope slipped away, Grace encountered Leymah Gbowee and her entourage of women, a diverse group of Liberia's daughters, who were demanding peace for Liberia. They joined forces and actually prayed the devil back to hell. The war ended and through their collective efforts, helped elect the first female president in Africa's history, Ellen Johnson-Sirleaf.

Transition from refugee to normalcy had its challenges. Yassah returned to her style of hustle, getting a place at Bob Gray Estates, and Grace picked up from where her dream had been arrested. With different dreams and directions, the girls parted ways but remain family, best friends forever.

Grace resumed her used clothes business, rebuilding clienteles. Good customers are priceless, especially when they inspire you and you end up learning things you didn't know, like your potentials. Cecelia Amadou and Irene Zarway were such customers. When Grace needed a job, Cecelia Amadou arm-twisted her lawyer husband, who was looking for an assistant, to hire Grace and Irene Zarway didn't mind renting a room to someone she'd worked with during the 2005 presidential campaign. Both women believed in Grace's potential, stomping out possible affairs with their husbands. Sometimes chances are given simply for the sake of one's passion for sisterhood.

Moses Zarway quickly became Uncle Moses to Grace, impressed with her desire for a good education in spite of the challenges in her past. Somehow she did not fit into the sickening odd social baits, sometimes called Jarworlee, which most young women used when sexually selling their pride. Education was important to Moses Zarway and he had, sort of, made Grace a personal project, becoming fatherly toward her, giving to her the same advice his father gave him:

'*When you are struggling with something, look at all the people around you and realize that every single person you see is struggling with something, and to them, it is just as hard as what you are going through.*'

"How did you get this name? Grace." Uncle Moses asked one day.

"My mother never told me," Grace chuckled, and then confessed, "Actually, the Congor people that raised me gave me that name. I don't think they know the meaning either."

"Everybody's name has a meaning," he said. "You must find yours."

A few weeks later Grace opened her dictionary and looked up the word, 'grace'. It read *beauty, charm, and attractive quality, thoughtfulness toward others, the unmerited love and favor of God toward mankind.*

Grace shrugged her shoulders and smiled when she finished reading.

Chapter Forty

GIA decided to stretch her legs, desert the noise for a bit, and explore the beach community. She walked about a quarter mile from the backyard, the ocean was right there, less than half a mile away, if that. The day was just about perfect. Low eighties, sunny, cloudless blue sky, the air was unbelievably clear and clean. A light breeze fanned her cheek, and she could hear the ceaseless motion of the waves as they rolled up the shore. She liked the scene stretching out before her, facing the ocean, all rich blues and greens and creamy foam; it made her feel relaxed. Minus the senator's death, the Douglas's new house was paradise.

"I'm looking for the love of my life, have you seen her," the voice came from behind.

Gia turned to find RJ standing about three feet from her, staring at her, smiling.

"Thought I check out the beach," she said, getting up. RJ helped her to stand.

Gia put a hand on his shoulder for balance as she removed one sandal, than another. When she finished, RJ did the same. The warm sand felt good against their bare feet.

"I was thinking," he said as they walked a few steps down the shoreline. "I am totally convinced that Daddy was innocent of that murder, I am sure of it. He told me so, even when he had no hope of being freed. I can't get pass that, baby, I just can't."

Gia sighed. She could see the pain in his face.

"I'm worried about you," she finally admitted.

"No need to."

"Oh, but I am," she said and stopped.

They were standing in front of an expensive beach house that must have had at least five bedrooms. RJ moved close enough to slip his arm around her. She tilted her head against his shoulder as she relaxed into him. Gia couldn't peel her eyes away from the house, two stories high with wraparound decks on the first floor. A large sign posted on the sandbank near the house read: *Property Protected by IWSC Security.*

"It's amazing how fast things are developing here in Liberia," Gia said, staring at the property. "These people are serious about rebuilding their country."

RJ nodded and he was not having her change subjects on him.

"Stop worrying about me, honey," he said, and then kissed her hand. It felt warm and comforting. "I won't break, you know."

"I know," she murmured. "I love being here with you, too."

"I love having you here," he said.

She gave a dreamy smile, studying the property.

"It's so beautiful here. I mean, the ocean, this is wonderful in its own way. It's…peaceful."

RJ wasn't sure what to say. He held her tighter to let her know he was listening.

"I can't believe that I've only been here a little less than three months, it seems like I've known this place much longer," Gia said.

They had gone a good way down the beach and decided to turn around. Strolling back, they moved away from the water's edge, into the softer sand. Gia's feet slipped with every step, and she tightened her grip on RJ's hand.

"Does Mom like it here?" she asked and glanced at him.

"She's always liked it here," RJ said. "I don't know about now."

"We better get back home, I feel a little tired," Gia said and stopped to put her sandals back on.

RJ put his shoes back on, and then they followed the narrow pathway, through the sea grass, and to the house.

✵✵✵✵

"Hey, you're back!" Mellody called out, her voice worrisome.

She was standing in the backyard behind her doctor friend, who was leaning into her chest. When Dr. Cho saw Gia and RJ approach the house, she seemed undecided about whether to pretend to be comfortable, so she walked away from Mellody and Mellody made her way toward them.

"How was your walk?" Mellody asked.

"Great!" Gia and RJ said together.

"Sounds like fun," Mellody commented. "Just about everybody is gone and Mom's in bed. I was just going to walk Dr. Cho to her car, and after that I'll sit out here for a little while."

"Actually, Gia's a bit tired," RJ said. "I was going to see her in, make sure she's comfortable, and then I can join you."

"You both look tired too," Gia said. "Hope you're not going to be up all night."

"We won't, honey," RJ assured her. "I know we have a road trip tomorrow."

Mellody and Dr. Cho went toward the front of the house and RJ followed Gia inside. Moments later, RJ met Mellody on the front porch.

"Dad had a good home-going, considering everything that happened," Mellody said, sounding pleased.

"Some home-going," RJ swallowed. "They killed an innocent man, Mel."

"Yes, RJ, they did. But Daddy…"

"But Daddy what?"

"I was going to say, Daddy had too many odd people for acquaintances."

"He was a senator, Mel and senators have to associate with everybody."

"I suppose," she said, "that depends on who you ask."

A car passed by, blowing its horn.

"I'll probably never get used to these people," RJ said, almost complaining. "What's the purpose of the horn in a residential area, after ten o'clock at night?"

Mellody laughed. "These people?" she said and laughed harder.

RJ couldn't help but laugh also.

"I believe Daddy is innocent too," Mellody said in a voice so soft, RJ barely heard it.

"Yeah?"

"Yes," she said and nodded.

RJ stood up, ambled toward his sister and sat down in the chair next to hers. She knew their conversation was about to turn heart-to-heart, just like when they were kids, welcoming each other's secrets.

"Hmm… tell me what's really bothering you," Mellody said and squeezed his knee. "And, don't tell me it's Daddy," she murmured, "because I think I know what it is."

"Mel…," he said, and then hesitated.

"You and Grace did *bad-thing*, didn't you?" she asked bluntly.

She had suspected since Thanksgiving dinner. Plus, the many phone calls, mostly unnecessary, that followed.

RJ looked around; to make sure they were actually alone. He laughed a nervous laugh. Not loud, but a laugh nonetheless. It was the way Mellody had put it, *bad-thing*, meaning sex, and the way Liberian children says it. It was impossible for him to deny it.

"Yeah," he said, almost whispering. "I made a horrible mistake, Mel. And, if Gia finds out, she'll leave me. I cannot lose her."

"Then, don't."

"What?"

"Don't let her leave you."

"What are you saying, Mel… don't tell her?"

"Were you going to tell her?"

"Yes… no… maybe, but I can't tell her… I can't tell her," he said, shaking his head. "I can't hurt my Gia."

"What she doesn't know won't hurt her then. It's that simple," Mellody said and shrugged her shoulders.

"If it is that easy, why am I panicking?"

"Are you panicking? Good! It's because you were a bonehead to do something that stupid! You're the good kid, RJ… stop copying me."

RJ caught the joke and chuckled.

"How stupid of me," he said. "I want to be the perfect husband."

"Well, good luck on that!"

"I am serious, Mel."

"No, RJ, you cannot be a perfect husband. You want to be a god. There can only be one God. Go and ask Katharine Douglas or Lynnette Vinton, the Salvation Lady," she said and chuckled.

"Would you be serious for once?"

"Okay… okay, but seriously, please tell me you used protection."

RJ retreated and grew quiet.

"Hello," Mellody called. "Did you use a condom?"

"No," he mumbled.

"Damn it, RJ! You're here fighting to save Dad's life and risking yours," she blurted out, sounding upset. "Do you have any idea how many AIDS patients I get to see every day at JFK? What were you thinking?"

"Mel, I wasn't thinking."

"You weren't!" she shouted. "It's so fucking selfish of you, not only to risk your life, but Gia's as well."

RJ voiced all the excuses that came to mind; being stressed out, not thinking straight, stupidity, etc… his comments grew further and further apart. He felt as embarrassed as he obviously was.

Mellody shot him a playful scowl.

"Mean to tell me… you are one, with a mass number of men in Liberia, who have caused women great suffering and extreme humiliation," she said, accusingly.

That hurt.

"You know that I am not that type of man," he said and then heaved a heavy sigh. "I fight for women's rights."

"I know," she said, sounding more sincere. "You made a mistake. But, here is not the place to make those types of mistakes. Most of the women, a lot of the women here, use sex so these men support them. I'm sure they always have unprotected sex because they want to please the men. I know this because of the high number of abortions at the hospital and backdoor clinics. I've helped out a lot of doctors at those clinics, when things go horribly wrong."

"I know, Mel, but it's the men that use these women, not the women's fault. I know that for a fact."

"Like Daddy?"

RJ feigned shock.

"Daddy?" he asked.

"Look, you know what I say to those women? Your body, or love, or whatever they like to call it, is yours to give, without strings or expectations. Last year while I was here, about four different women came for abortions. Guess whose name came up?"

"Daddy's?"

"You bet… but three out of the four weren't even his. I did DNA tests. He paid for all four abortions, thinking they were his. Some of the women even fake having abortions. They offer some employees bribes for bogus documents, like receipts, showing how much the abortions cost. And, those stupid men pay. I pretend as if", she quoted with her fingers, "this American doctor" doesn't understand a bit of Liberian English, and I listen to them going on wheeling and dealing."

RJ didn't doubt it. He saw it unfold at Sugar Shack.

"Grace is not like them," he said. "She's different."

He thought about the way she goes on talking about her classes at Grimes Law School, at the University of Liberia. She had the rare ability to be exactly what people needed when she was with them, yet remain true to herself. She was gifted and sweet, grew up practically on her own, with a desire to help those in need. She had nothing to begin with, but had everything to offer. It is strange how knowledge changes perception. RJ found himself listing Grace's good qualities. She was special, but he must never let that ambush him.

"What are you thinking," Mellody asked.

Her voice pulled him away from his thoughts. He looked at her.

"RJ, don't screw up your life," she warned and patted his knee.

"You want to know what I was thinking?" he asked.

Mellody waited with a mischievous gleam in her eye.

"I was thinking that, whoever Grace ends up with would be a very lucky man. I mean, any man would be lucky to have her."

Mellody smiled. All she could do was to keep staring and he met her gaze without a hint of embarrassment. They sat in peaceful silence for a while. Then a voice in his head reminded him, a wonderful woman crossed the Atlantic Ocean to be with you and you love her very, very much.

Chapter Forty-one

THROUGHOUT the night, RJ found himself tossing and turning in bed, reliving his conversation with Mellody.

"Someone didn't sleep well last night," Gia teased as they got dressed for the trip.

"Who, me?" RJ asked, not looking up, tying the strings on his sneakers.

"I wasn't the one tossing and turning last night," she said, now concerned.

He finished, caught Gia's eyes and forced a smile before leaving her to go and help Mr. Tom in loading up the SUV for the trip. Ma Teete had prepared a picnic lunch for the day, sandwiches, fried chicken, and potato salad, all neatly packed in separate Ziploc containers. They packed a cooler filled with bottles of water and other essentials Katharine had insisted they take, concerned for Gia's comfort.

The two-hour drive would have given him time to think, but when RJ is with Gia, they fall into easy conversation immediately. The trip started quiet, but not for long. Her anticipation grew, she was eager to see what the countryside of Liberia was like, as Mr. Tom had ignited that ticker.

From Monrovia, they traveled a graded asphalt highway that paralleled the low sandy coastline for about ten miles; then turned

northeast to pass through Mount Barclay, then the city of Careys-
burg, and then toward the city of Kakata. They quickly reached
Salala, then Totota, all the while speeding over sturdy bridges and
slowing down before blind curves. As Mr. Tom approached Sanoyea
intersection in Totota, his first thought was to warn his passengers
about the condition of the gravel road.

"The road is bad from here on," he cautioned. "It's a good thing it
is still dry season… we'll have plenty dust, that's all. During the rainy
season, cars get stuck in the mud… only trucks make it through."

"Are you okay with all this?" RJ teased Gia.

"I suppose I have to be," she said.

"Really?" he said, amused.

"Positive… we can't turn back now," she grinned.

He grinned, pulling her closer. "That's why I love you so much."

Not that Gia expected the countryside of Liberia to be like
parts of old Italy or old deep South Alabama for instance or, even
Mexico. Even so, it was the people who lived there that made the
place special. As they edged down the gravel road toward Sinta,
she sat up straighter.

Since they'd left the asphalt road in Totota, the view on either
side of the highway had been one long version of National Geo-
graphic, tiny towns along the way, small groups of travelers ambling
in single lines processions, mostly topless women with bundles or
loads on their heads and young children tied to their backs, stands
of trees…mile after mile. Sure, they'd passed through the occasional
towns, but only, those had been indistinguishable; unless you live
in Liberia and actually know the difference between an African
village and an African small town.

At times gravels flew from cars ahead like hail, and bombarded
the SUV windshield. Every time they approached a car ahead, Mr.
Tom pressed the back of his hand against the windshield to prevent
it from breaking because of the flying gravels.

Gia's eagerness sidetrack the rough ride as they drove through
dried up mud holes, bouncing through it, getting airborne for what
seemed to be ten seconds, then landing hard. Mr. Tom managed
the dusty hill climbs, drove over plank bridges over cross—bridges
built with three or four pieces of planks placed side by side—and

wobbles from washout ditches running diagonally across the way. With RJ beside her, the drive still wasn't half-bad at all. Strangely, a lot more cars were traveling in their direction.

"I thought this was too far from Monrovia, that we wouldn't have this much traffic," RJ said to Mr. Tom.

"It is," Mr. Tom said.

"Don't tell me they're starting to build up Sanoyea to look like Monrovia," RJ said, almost joking.

Mr. Tom laughed. "No, it's the third Saturday of the month."

"And that means?" RJ asked.

"It's the town's Market Day. Once a month, each town has a big Market Day… people come from everywhere," Mr. Tom explained.

"Ah, just like on certain days we have flea markets," RJ explained to Gia.

"Flea market?" Mr. Tom asked, puzzled.

"I'll tell you about that later," RJ promised.

Chapter Forty-two

THE noble beauty of Sinta Village was breathtaking, to say the least. Oldman Bono's compound had about ten mud-built homes topped with thatched roofs. His hut was seated in the front, in a meticulously clean yard nearby a patch of pepper blossom. About twenty yards from the hut was a wall-less shack, obviously the kitchen. A young woman, more likely a teenager, was beating rice in the mortar while another woman, her mother perhaps, was tossing rice grains in a fanner to rid it of chaffs. A few chickens and ducks were busy pecking at the ground here and there. Another woman was braiding a little girl's hair, who clearly she would rather be playing with the rest of the children than sitting there. She was crying, but stopped on hearing the noise of the car. Gia could not get over the fact that there was no fence cutting off one's neighbor. Little did she know that in the village, the entire clan was one family.

Everyone in the kitchen stared at the car when Mr. Tom drove into the yard. They had gotten used to visitors in the past few months. Oldman Bono had not seen so many cars come to his compound until Johnny's death. The group of young children abandoned their game and ran to meet the car.

"Where is the old man?" Kai Flumo, the interpreter Mr. Tom had brought along, asked in Kpelle, Johnny's language.

"Are you going to take the old man to Monrovia again?" a little boy asked in Kpelle.

"No," Kai Flumo said, laughing. "He has a guest and the man wants to talk with him."

As the boy was pointing toward the hut, a woman came out of the kitchen, and then to the car.

"Hello," she said in Kpelle and wanted to know who the guests were, looking directly at Gia.

Kai Flumo explained, in Kpelle, the senator's son had come to see Johnny's father.

She glanced at RJ, then back at Gia. "Who is she?" the woman asked.

"A peacekeeper from America," Kai Flumo lied.

"Maybe I should talk to the old man first," she suggested and walked away.

She went back to the kitchen, said something to the others, and then went around to the back of the hut.

Kai Flumo interpreted their conversation for RJ.

"Am I a problem?" Gia asked, concerned.

"No," Kai Flumo assured her. "She's just being nosey." He started to say, that's how women are, but stopped himself. Gia only detected a note of teasing.

A few minutes later, the woman came to the car and told Kai Flumo the old man would be happy to receive his guests. Then she escorted them toward the back of the hut where Oldman Bono was, lying in his hammock attached between two breadfruits trees. He got up to greet his guests and offered them the four wooden benches that had been placed for their comfort. Kai Flumo told him who each person was and that he was there as interpreter. Oldman Bono shook hands with Kai Flumo, then RJ, Mr. Tom and Gia. His hand was warm and callused. RJ was suddenly aware of how the old man's life had been; nothing but hard work.

"Thank you, Mr. RJ," the old man said out of respect. "You have done a good thing by coming here. Johnny did not come from the ground like a rock. He has roots, we are his roots. Thank you for recognizing that."

As Kai Flumo interpreted, the old man had an open, honest face. RJ nodded.

"Tell me about your son, Johnny," RJ said.

That was what he always said to the victim's families that he represented. Knowing the victim personally made them real.

The old man held RJ's gaze for a moment, evaluated the request, and then turned his attention to the interpreter.

"My son was a quiet man," Oldman Bono said, by way of his interpreter. "He asked few questions and rarely grew angry, he rarely joked, either. Johnny lived for routine; woke up at five o'clock every morning, talked to his wife, then listened as she talked about plans for the day. He renewed his promise of a better life for them, if he ever made it to the city. Then he left his house every morning at exactly six o'clock. With the duties of his day finally completed, my son came to visit with me. I could see in his eyes, he was most content while telling me about his plans, sitting in my presence… right where you all are sitting now."

RJ glanced at Gia, then back at the old man.

"Johnny was socially awkward," Oldman Bono continued. "He spent long hours at home with his wife, rather than with friends. He never complained, even when people disappointed him.

"The idea of his wife starting a market seemed foreign and ridiculous to most people here in our village, but Johnny was not one to be content with just living life and floating along. He had big dreams for his family, education for his children, for instance. He and his wife wanted the same things, and the only way they could get it was if he went to the city and looked for work. There was something exciting about Monrovia, he told me. The first day Johnny arrived there, his friend took him to get his picture taken."

Oldman Bono handed a photograph to RJ, with a painful expression. In it, Johnny's friend had his arm draped over Johnny's shoulder, and they were both beaming. His wife had given it to the old man since Johnny's death; she could not stand looking at it.

"He'd wanted to let his wife know that Monrovia was just the place to be," Oldman Bono continued. "He didn't mind the sacrifice of being away for a while. Johnny worked hard in Monrovia and sent every penny home to his wife. His once a month visit calmed her mind; it also made me happy."

By now, the compound seemed to be coming to life. More

people had materialized, and now and then laughter could be heard. The same woman that met with them at the car came and went a few times, each time she spoke softly and Oldman Bono listened deeply.

"What business did Johnny and his wife want to start?" RJ asked.

"I'll have her tell you," Oldman Bono offered, and then he yelled, "Korlu! Korlu!"

The mediator came into view, she was Johnny's wife.

"Sorry about your husband," was all RJ could say.

She nodded after Kai Flumo interpreted. Then Oldman Bono told her of his calling.

"Johnny and I wanted to sell can goods," Korlu said. "Most people cannot get to Sanoyea so easily, especially when they have to walk. So, we wanted to open a small shop here."

Kai Flumo interpreted, and told them that Sanoyea is twenty miles away, and as they can see, no one owns a car.

RJ expressed his deep sadness over her loss, apologized that bad fate had brought their families together, and if it meant anything to them, his father was not part of Johnny's senseless death. However, he had not come to defend his family's name; he only came to know the man that fate was crudely unkind to.

After Kai Flumo interpreted, Korlu slowly reached for RJ's hand and expressed her sincere gratitude thru the words of their interpreter. She excused herself and went back to her business.

RJ expressed his thanks to the old man, for allowing him into his home, and asked permission—Kai Flumo interpreted permission to mean blessings—so that he could help fulfill Johnny and Korlu's dream, by donating the money to jump start their business.

"Because you have shown respect for my son's life," Oldman Bono said, "I will give you my blessings."

The burden of sorrow was removed, RJ felt lighter than he had in months.

"Thank you, Oldman Bono," RJ said.

He took out the envelope from his jacket pocket and handed it to the old man. Oldman Bono accepted the envelope.

As his guests prepared to leave, Korlu and two youngsters brought three baskets full of plantain, pineapples, cassava, mango, pawpaw and oranges. They placed them before Gia.

"What's that for?" Gia asked.

Kai Flumo interpreted that Korlu had asked the old man what was best to offer the guests and he had suggested the vegetables and fruits, things they will not refuse. Gia heartedly accepted the gifts, smiling and thanking them over and over.

It was past dark when the Land Cruiser SUV turned into the driveway. After a long hot shower, the bed, sleep and Gia met the same time.

Chapter Forty-three

MAY started with three straight days of drenching rain. RJ and Gia had no interest in leaving the house in such weather, though most afternoons they sat on the porch for just a few hours to breathe the fresh sea breeze. Friends, relatives and few church members were still dropping by, some with fruit baskets, others just to say hello.

Diallo called and asked if it was okay to stop by, he was already in the area. Within thirty minutes he wheeled into the space where the SUV was usually parked and prepared to run through the rain. He got out and slammed the door. His third step was into a shallow pothole as water soaked his right ankle and oozed down quickly into his shoe. He froze for a second and caught his breath, then stepped away on his toes, trying desperately to spot other puddles while making his way to the porch.

It took him a couple of minutes to dry himself off and finally get to the point of his visit. He had come to deliver his final bill, and say good-bye, he said, and he could not imagine why all this had happened to such a loving family. He also had something for Katharine, and he handed the envelope to RJ, his hand shaking and his words ringing with the most heartfelt emotions.

"The senator asked me to personally give this to his wife," Diallo said, his voice almost cracking. "I've never been sorrier about anything in my life. Your family deserves better," he paused and swiped at the corner of his eye.

"Thank, you," RJ said, shaking hands and taking the envelope addressed to Katharine Douglas.

RJ offered him a chair, and he sat down. Gia offered him something to drink; he didn't want anything, just wanted to talk and to say good-bye.

Diallo seemed troubled though; the last few months had been the most difficult of his practice. He confessed the money he'd made had given him little comfort and he was finding sleep difficult because of the verdict. He'd also realized how hard Grace Pupoh had worked without him showing the slightest amount of gratitude other than her paycheck. He had even thought about implementing pro bono into his practice; he had not performed free work at any time, he admitted sadly. Rich people did not give a damn about poor people in Liberia, and that was a fact of life.

RJ was too surprised to say much, and mesmerized to hear him say he was tired of chasing money; but his mind was racing.

"You can start with Grace," RJ suggested. "Help her finish law school and the two of you can make a bigger difference."

Diallo pondered it. He smiled. RJ could only wonder if he knew anything about what had happened after his outing at Sugar Shack and suspected he was reading between the lines.

"My family saw how ambitiously she worked, and she's not a paralegal, to say the least," RJ pushed further. He was careful.

"That's an excellent idea," Diallo said, thoroughly enjoying his soul-cleansing, not worrying about the sins of others. "When are you leaving for the States?"

"In a few weeks," RJ said. "Looking forward to getting back on track... can't wait to get back to litigation again, you know, tough trials against tough prosecutors in front of tough juries... fighting for poor people's rights."

Conversation went on, each listened until the other was finished, then the conversation slowly drifted to the other. Diallo had stayed almost two hours, and apologized when he realized he had taken so much of their time. He got up to leave.

"Remember, RJ, you still have friends here," he said, extending his hand. "Don't be a stranger to your own home."

"I won't… and thanks, Diallo," RJ said, shaking his hand.

The rain had stopped.

RJ walked Diallo to his car, and then took the letter to Katharine. Diallo seemed much happier when he left. He was going straight home to his wife and children with a new purpose, a man on a mission.

RJ rejoined Gia soon after.

"Change," RJ sighed loudly, taking his seat. "I almost feel sorry for the politicians and bureaucrats in Liberia, especially at the thought of real change, when more people are suddenly seized with dedication to protect the rights of every Liberian."

"Don't expect an overnight change, honey" Gia warned, and she'd read him correctly. "Folks who make a life out of suppressing others don't come willingly to change, they do more than moaning and groaning.

She caught a glimpse of him staring at her.

"Besides," she continued, "there has to be a change in the mind-set of the masses. Simple minded people are easily misled… everywhere, not just in Liberia."

"You're right, honey," he said. "I've never seen people so glad to see injustice. You'd think change means wanting truth to win; that way hope will last."

"I know," Gia agreed. "But not if people are misled. We have to constantly fight racism at home. In Liberia, it is tribalism…I've noticed. I've been greeted so warmly by everyone I've met; Country or Congor, rich or poor, old or young, man or woman, that I cannot imagine Liberians being cruel to each other."

"Remember what that man said to Mel after the verdict?"

Gia thought for a second. "The man that works at the hospital?" she asked, finally remembering.

"That's the one," RJ said, rolling his eyes. "Besides treating sick people, Mel is always helping somebody out… giving them money for food, to buy medicine… even paid their children's school fees. And, that man in particular, she remembered giving him money to buy medicine for his wife… only a few days ago."

"Baby, they are human," Gia said. "Remember what people

did to Christ. He fed them, clothed them, cured them; even raised their babies from the grave… and what did they do? They chose a murderer over him."

"The thing about Liberia," RJ said, growing resentful again. "Everybody wants something for nothing, looking for a tip, a bonus, bribe, a handout… something, something, and something."

Gia eased out of her chair and walked to him. She took his hand, staring into his eyes, she whispered, "The best thing about it is, most of the young people I've met are promising. They are the ones that will make the change and live it. We can start… and they will finish it."

Chapter Forty-four

MELLODY was already tired and stressed when she walked into the Emergency Department. She looked at her schedule and sighed. For one thing, she was happy she'd been assigned Sydni Thorpe as an intern for the day. Dr. Thorpe was the sharpest knife in the draw and Mellody always found her incredibly useful.

Mellody's first patient was an eight-year-old girl who had fallen and broken her wrist. She gave her some pain control and sent her for x-rays. Later, the x-rays showed a fracture that was not displaced. Mellody had Thorpe put a splint and schedule an appointment.

They were on the roll when suddenly Mellody's cell phone rang. She pulled it off her clipper and looked at the number. It was Gia.

"Hey, Gia," she said, "What's up?"

Gia wanted to know how busy she was and if she could fit her into her schedule; she'd been feeling light-headed lately and it seemed to be happening more frequent.

"I have a couple of patients before lunch…can you get here by one?"

"Sure."

"Okay, see you at one," Mellody said, and closed the phone.

Dr. Thorpe had the next patient laying on the examination table when Mellody came into the room. The twenty-six year old woman, possibly pregnant, was cramping and bleeding. The night before, she was on her way to Sugar Shack to meet some friends when she started cramping. The man in the room with her, who had brought her, stood with his arms across his chest, leaning against the wall, obviously wishing he was somewhere else.

"Is this your husband?" Mellody asked, after noticing the patient's wedding band.

The woman seemed stunned and had a sleepy look of someone awakening from a dream.

"No," she said softly, "But he's my baby Pa."

Mellody turned to look at him; he looked at neither she nor the patient, just there was profound silence in the room. She wrote orders for pregnancy studies and an ultrasound. Dr. Thorpe started IV fluid and afterward set up the patient for a pelvic exam.

While waiting for lab results, Mellody saw other patients, and then she returned to the pregnant woman, finished the exam and sat down. Thorpe handed her the lab results. She read the result in silence, and then looked up at the patient; she looked exhausted. The ultrasound was showing an intrauterine pregnancy with no signs of a heartbeat.

"I am very sorry," Mellody said, furrowing her brow. "You are experiencing a miscarriage."

The patient drew in a long breath and let it out slowly.

"It isn't your fault," Mellody said to her, but looking at the man. And then she looked at the patient. "It doesn't mean you cannot get pregnant again. Miscarriages, this early, usually mean the cells came together wrong. Half of all fertilizations end in miscarriage."

She hoped she'd explained miscarriage simple enough for the patient to understand.

"Do you have any questions?" Mellody asked. "Do you understand?"

"I understand," the patient said. "God killed my baby because I cheated on my husband."

Mellody sighed. She sat back and started from the beginning.

"It doesn't matter, Dr. Douglas," the patient said, "I know the truth."

Mellody remained sitting, trying to think of another way to approach the situation.

"I would like to go home now," the patient said, tears streaming down her face.

Mellody took her hand in hers, hoping to ignite her sole support system on how to console this woman.

"I want to see you tomorrow morning, okay? I've set an appointment for you."

The woman nodded, forcing a smile.

"I am sorry," Mellody expressed her sympathy again, squeezing the woman's hand and smiling. She tried her best to meet the patient's eyes and said, "I will see you tomorrow morning."

She told Thorpe to staff with someone else while she was out for lunch, and then walked out of the room hoping she'd dealt with the situation compassionately. Her job was dealing with problems of people, saints or sinners, who had nowhere else to go. She peeked at her watch, it read two o'clock. Mellody hurried to her office where Gia had been waiting nearly an hour.

"Hey," Mellody greeted Gia with a quick kiss. She tried to muster a smile for her but failed pretty miserably. "You don't look okay."

"Does it show?" Gia asked.

"Well, I've noticed you haven't been your boisterous self lately. You've been spending most of the morning sitting on the porch, alone. You can't be feeling depressed and lonesome when RJ is always a footstep behind you. What's going on?"

The ease with which Gia had adapted to life in Liberia didn't particularly surprise Mellody. It was the fact the senator's trial and conviction was not shocking enough for her to reconsider a marriage into the family. It seemed Gia had not gotten a wrong impression; but neither RJ, Katharine nor Mellody knew what her parents thought about the whole thing. Mellody wasn't sure if her parents knew the details. They had been given a chance to come to grips with the fact that their daughter was engaged to an African man, they loved RJ, but they would have to deal with the criminal conviction of their in-law for the rest of their lives. She wondered if RJ even thought about that.

"Do your parents know about Daddy?" Mellody ventured. "I couldn't imagine RJ living the rest of his life without you."

Gia looked at her and asked, "What?"

"I was just wondering how they felt? I must admit, I worry about that sometimes."

"Mel, you can't be serious."

"I can," Mellody said. "How can I not, with a convicted criminal for a father-in-law. Not unless you and RJ aren't planning on having children."

"You mean, having a father-in-law who was wrongfully convicted and murdered?" Gia asked. "Marriage first, then children," she corrected. "Don't give us kids yet."

Mellody squeezed Gia's arm, as if satisfied. "You'll make my brother a wonderful wife," she said. "You two will be fine. Now, how about me doing a quick check-up to see what's making you feel yucky."

Mellody decided she'd do nothing more extraordinary than take vital signs, but when Gia complained about feeling dizzy and light-headed, as if she had the flu, she decided to also do some basic blood work. She set out all the tubes she needed, got the tourniquet and alcohol swabs. Gia rolled up her sleeve. Mellody prepped the chosen location, placed the tourniquet on Gia's upper arm and tightened it enough the vein bulged. She patted the vein gently, got a good angle and inserted the needle, drawing not only blood, but a quick gasp from Gia.

"Sorry," Mellody apologized, pushing the vacutainer into the holder.

"How long have you planned on staying?" Gia asked. "Would Roger Williams Medical Center still hold your position?"

"I'm not worrying about Roger Williams Medical Center," Mellody answered. "Promise you won't say anything to RJ or Mom. I haven't actually considered it yet."

"What, exactly, are you considering?"

"Working for the WHO," she whispered.

"The World Health Organization, that's great Mel!"

"Hush! I'm trying to listen to your heart," she said, placing the stethoscope over Gia's chest. "You can't say anything yet… you have to promise."

"Is it because of Dr. Cho? I didn't think it was that serious," Gia teased.

Mellody rolled her eyes.

"Actually, it's Dr. Lennard Klause. If I do decide, I'll be working with him."

Mellody took Gia's temperature, measured her pulse, respiratory rate and blood pressure. She looked into her eyes and ears, tested her reflexes and looked at the color of her lips and nail beds.

"Your pressure is a little high, but nothing to worry over. We've all been stressed out over this thing. Maybe we all need to stay away from Ma Teete's palm oil dishes," she joked.

"What about Shakari?" Gia asked.

"What about her?"

"She is way too 'Californian' to live in Africa," Gia pointed out.

"Well, I'm African," Mellody said, flashing a quick grin. "She's been bugging me to come to Liberia, why would she mind?"

"Come see me and come stay with me, are two different things," Gia recited the African parable proudly, and then added, "Mama Teete taught me that one."

Mellody chuckled and looked up at her.

"I can't see Shakari leaving behind a chance at morning television and life in Rhode Island to move to Africa, in a village that is nothing more than a glitch on the map," Gia said, candidly. "She rarely misses Good Morning America and you know she is used to stuff… lots of it too."

As Gia had implied, there really wasn't a lot about Shakari she didn't know. The point was, as much as Shakari loved Mellody, she loved her make-believe celebrity lifestyle too, maybe more.

"She doesn't have to move to Africa," Mellody said. "I'll have more time dedicated to my work."

"That's exactly what I was thinking," Gia shrugged.

Mellody resumed the examination.

"Has your period been regular?"

"Same time every month, same three to four days," Gia said. "I haven't missed and I'm on the pills."

"I'm sure you took some anti-malaria medication before coming," Mellody said, placing her stethoscope around her neck. "And, I hope you took all of your required shots too."

"I did. RJ would have killed me if I hadn't. Dr. Braxton prescribed some Primaquine for me to take, which I did take."

"Do you need anything?" Mellody said and reached over and patted Gia's shoulder, indicating the examination was over.

"No," Gia shook her head. "Not really... just concerned about this light-headedness."

"Well, I'll just wait for the result on the blood work." She leaned in and whispered, "And, don't tell RJ just yet."

"Promise," Gia said, crossing her fingers.

Mellody looked at her wristwatch. She made a mental note to pick up a handful of charts Thorpe had put on the desk.

"You want to hang around here for a few, or you've got plans?"

"I promised Mom that I would go to the DOC meeting at the church tonight. And, guess what? I'm the guest speaker."

Mellody chuckled. "I'm sure Mrs. Vinton, over there, is just dying to introduce you to those poor women, if it is the Lord's will," she joked.

The two roared with laughter.

"It's a good cause though," Mellody said, seriously. "Women in this country need all the help they can get. They work hard for everybody else except for themselves. Be ready to meet the most incredible women on earth."

Chapter Forty-five

RJ gawked in amazement at the sheer number of women stuffed in the hall. Some were sitting on the floor, trying to make room for more women still. Some were sitting in groups, talking in low tones. Every square inch along the walls was covered with people sitting with their backs to the wall. Small children cried and played as their mothers tried to keep them close.

The DOC organization had their annual meeting planned ahead of time, as suggested by Lynnette Vinton, and had invited Gia to uplift, encourage, and inspire. Gia, not only wanted to be absolutely awesome, she wanted to entertain the audience with real anecdotes and real tales of life experience to inspire them to take responsibility for their own lives, and encourage women to go after their goals.

While waiting for the meeting to start, an elderly woman tugged at RJ's sleeve and said, "Tell me about your wife."

RJ looked down and smiled. Her eyes were big and round. He'd recognized her from the New Year's Eve watch meeting at Words of Christ Church.

"Her name is, Gia," he said, "and she has a big heart."

The woman gave him a gentle smile.

"She is very smart," RJ continued, "but she would never use her abilities or her education to belittle someone else, or make herself seem superior."

"Is she the white lady?" the woman asked, pointing toward the front.

"She's Italian-Mexican," he said, as if it would have made a difference.

"She's very pretty," the old woman said. "I saw her at JFK today. Just wanted to make sure it was the same woman."

"Today?" RJ asked. That explained why she'd asked Mr. Tom to drive her, he thought.

RJ and the old woman turned toward the front as the women started a joyous chorus to begin the program.

Violence against women and girls represented a global human rights problem and every day at work Gia heard stories from women in crisis, but the ones told by her new African women friends would, no doubt, be more compelling than anything she'd ever heard. Rarely had she heard about women and war and how they managed to survive the war terrain. The wartime stories were just as terrifying as the prewar stories. The stories tonight were mostly about rape and pedophilia and told with heart-wrenching simplicity and tact.

A few women started with tales of men who have a fondness for preadolescent girls and how economically disadvantage parents willingly offered their young daughters with hope of some financial benefits. It was even alleged that futile attempts were made to lower the age of consent from sixteen to twelve by lawmakers. One woman touched her stomach unconsciously and drifted out of the meeting and into her memory before she resumed and finished her tragic story.

Gia learned of the unfortunate reality of young women in need of jobs to earn money for their livelihood and who are forced to use their bodies, their most valued treasure, offering sex in exchange for work. Sexual exploitation had become common and respect for women, diminished.

Some victims finally gave voice to sexual molestation. The account of incest was never discussed openly, as victims never came forward. Most times an adult family member knew, but the child would be ostracized and told to remain in silence, to protect the image of the perpetrators and family name. The fear of disgrace had guarded their secrets.

Despite the shame and stigma, through their own strength and ambition, these brave women had built up courage to protest the rape culture in their society, demanding dignity. The sermon of rape being a crime was preached vehemently after the war. New laws were on the books now, if you rape, you could spend the rest of your life in jail. Change had come to Liberia.

A small celebration erupted when Lynnette Vinton introduced Gia. RJ stared ahead to catch her eyes, he did; then he nodded showing his support. She smiled and looked extremely relaxed.

"I am touched by the stories each of your lives have told," Gia said, looking at the audience. Most of the youthful faces staring at her were showing the strain of life on them. "Your words hugged my heart, and I feel connected to you. What is special about each of you is, your courage took you to the dark places and you never gave up. In spite of everything, you still believed in hope."

Her message was short and thorough. It began with the point that they were all heroes; they had gone through a considerate degree of hell and had made it. When they learn to heal the past, forgive and let go, their hearts will become wiser.

A story followed, one in which Gia told with brutal honesty. A man had impregnated his two stepdaughters, fourteen and sixteen, and their mother would not believe that they were actually raped, in the interest of saving her marriage to a well-known preacher. The girls were underage and were unable to get the pregnancy terminated on their own. What happened next was worst; they'd both been infected with AIDS. All this happened in America, she emphasized, these things don't just happen in third world countries.

Gia wanted to touch them in a way; she did. A woman in the audience asked if the girls were still living. They are, she told them, but with a life sentence of pain and suffering. Their babies were also infected. Another woman wanted to know what happened to the man. The audience was pleased to know that a Women's Rights group filed a lawsuit against him for attempted murder, using sex as a weapon. Some remembered too well how such weapon was used against them; old women, pregnant women, adolescent girls and even babies were raped during the war.

"Rape and sexual exploitation is not love," Gia said. "Love comes from a good place," she pointed to her heart.

The rest of the message was about rediscovering the passion for the things they love and to take action towards their goals. Gaining clarity about life's purpose and practicing self-respect, loving yourself just the way you are.

"Peel away the mask that you have been conditioned to wear and identify," she stressed. "You are rich inside your soul, therefore grab hold of every opportunity and put it to use. It's good to see that you are all moving your lives forward. Just like Albert Einstein told his son, 'Life is like riding a bicycle. To keep your balance you must keep moving.'"

Gia then ended with the words of Eleanor Roosevelt:

'*You learn by living; you gain strength, courage and confidence by every experience in which you really stop to look fear in the face. You are able to say to yourself, "If I lived through this horror, I can take the next thing that comes along." You must do the thing you think you cannot do*'.

After the meeting, the kitchen was bustling with action as sandwiches were prepared and served. Katharine and Lynnette poured she-punch (non-alcoholic beverage) into paper cups, talking constantly about the new programs they were starting. People were handed a paper plate and a napkin. As they shuffled along, a sandwich was placed on the plate, a cookie was added and a cup of punch was waiting at the end of the line.

Another line waited patiently at the sign-up tables, as many women added their names to join the movement and attempt training programs the DOC would be offering. Gia had donated five thousand dollars to start an adult literacy program. RJ and Pastor Peabody helped work the line until it was momentarily short and RJ needed the break to call Mellody. He excused himself and dialed Mel's number as he walked out of the hall. She picked up on the second ring.

"I didn't know Gia was at the hospital today," RJ said, concerned.

"Yes, she was. She didn't tell you?"

"No."

"She felt light-headed, so she called me. She didn't faint nor had a seizure… just felt light-headed. All her signs were normal. Gia told me she was feeling better by the time she was ready to leave. How did the meeting go?"

"Great," RJ said, now studying the crowd from the doorway. "These are remarkable people, Mel. Most born without a prayer or a chance, yet they survived. They trip and fall, but they get up and keep trying."

"Yep," Mellody said, "that's what I told Gia today.

Chapter Forty-six

YASSAH had warned Grace, "Don't you ever see yourself as RJ's girlfriend... it's too dangerous."

Unfortunately, she had been right, not jealous. There was no need to wonder what was going to happen between RJ and Grace, nothing.

The persistent knocking on her room door forced Grace to get out of bed. She struggled to sit up, and then got her balance to move toward the door. It seemed a mile away. With all the strength she could muster, she turned the lock and opened the door.

Yassah was standing before her, dressed as if she was on her way to church.

"You missed a good meeting at the church. What the hell is wrong with you?" Yassah said, looking at Grace standing in wrinkled clothes, with rumpled hair, red and swollen eyes. She smelled like liquor too, as if she'd taken a bath in beer.

"Nothing, I'm just tired," Grace slurred out a few words. Her eyes revealed her heartbreak.

"You've been drinking? Or, crying?"

"A little of both," she chuckled. "C'mon inside, I don't want Uncle Moses seeing me like this."

"It's RJ, isn't it?" Yassah said, with a tone of accusation.

"No," Grace lied. She looked ashamed.

"Okay, you don't have to admit it," Yassah said. "But, stop disgracing yourself like this. You're too good for that."

The truth hurt. Suddenly, Grace broke down crying and Yassah let her.

Yassah and Grace had been like sisters since they met at the Johnston's home. They had each other's back during the war, while at the refugee camp in Ghana and during the period of resettling as returnees. Yassah was feeling awful about what had happened to her friend, even after her strong warning. They were the best counselors for each other, compassionate most of the time, but tough enough to insist on the truth, whether it hurt or not.

"Men like RJ don't fall in love with us," Yassah said. "He's not like the ones here, but still."

Grace frowned. "He's different," she said, shaking her head. "He'll be a good father, a good husband, that's how I see him. Unlike most men, RJ liked hearing me talk about my dream of becoming a lawyer."

"I see all that stuff too," Yassah admitted, "but I see the dark side, also."

"What dark side?"

"Like I said, Grace, those men don't fall for us. You've done well for yourself, you have a good job, a boss who doesn't feel he has to sleep with you."

"He tried," Grace corrected, stoned face.

"Diallo tried to get in your pants too?"

"Don't they all? Of course he tried, but I told him, no. I had too much respect for his wife to do that to her. I told him, he could keep his job if he wanted to. I knew he depended on me for too many things. He couldn't run that office without me. I am his eyes, ears, feet, and hands…everything."

"I can't believe it," Yassah said with a chuckle. "But then again, men are dogs."

"Diallo is not so bad after all, though," Grace said. "He apologized to me and has never tried since."

Yassah thought it was the perfect opportunity to say the honest truth, what was on her mind. Besides, once she gets something in her head, it tends to stick.

"Are you still hiding your belly?" Yassah asked. "I can barely tell you're pregnant."

"I know, but people will soon begin to suspect," Grace said, "especially Irene Zarway."

"I think she already knows," Yassah said.

"Puh-lease. How would she know? Did she say anything to you or Uncle Moses?"

"No. But women can tell when other women are pregnant. I knew you were pregnant before you said anything to me."

"I'm a grown woman, Yassah, and I don't need the lecture or stress from them."

This was true, Yassah admitted to herself. While Grace was living under their roof, she was paying for her lodging. However, the facts still remained. It was Alex Massaquoi, not RJ, who should matter most now.

"Of course," Yassah said, and then added, "You will have to get over RJ. It's not like you're going to see him every day. He's going back to the States. You still have Alex."

"I know," she nodded. "But I'm going to miss RJ anyway."

It was then that Yassah felt her sister's heartbreak.

"Yeah," she said and paused, as if trying to decide how best to comfort. "It will be hard, but life moves fast. Who'd have thought we would be standing here like this? Could you have imagined it? I couldn't. I have my own house."

Grace began to cry, hugging her arms like an abandoned child. Yassah looked at her and felt a knot form in her chest. She inched closer.

"No, don't cry no more," Yassah said, slipping her arms around Grace's neck. "I'm not letting you kill yourself over this man. I know in my heart what he means to you. You have your baby to think about now. Grace, you will make it through this. We've made it through a lot more than this. Maybe you should come and stay at my place for a few days. Okay?"

Grace drew in a long breath. "Okay," she said and swiped at her tears.

Chapter Forty-seven

Two mornings in a row Katharine had slept late, getting up around noon. She wasn't sick, Mellody had already checked her sugar and blood pressure, and everything was normal. Just suddenly she looked awfully sad and tired. And out of concern, RJ went to her room to check on her. He found her sitting in the senator's favorite chair, a La-Z-Boy recliner he had shipped to him one Father's Day. When he walked into the room, the first thing he noticed was a pile of used tissues in her lap.

"What are you up to, Mom," he said. "You okay?"

Katharine looked at him, yet trying her best to hide her sad, tired eyes. "I'm fine," she said and offered a faint smile.

"You look tired, Mom. You've been sleeping late these few days too. Sure you're okay?"

"I just needed a little extra sleep, RJ, that's all it was. Unlike Mel, I listen to my body. She'd work until she drops."

RJ smiled.

"I'm proud of you, Mom," he said, staring at her eyes. "You've really held up well. These few months have been hell, to say the least. I couldn't imagine how you feel."

He sat on the bed, close to the La-Z-Boy, taking Katharine's hands in his. She smiled softly, and returned his affection with a slight squeeze of his hand. RJ leaned closer and took a deep breath.

"Why don't you come live with me and Gia, in the States?" he said, exhaling.

"Oh, RJ… I don't know," Katharine said, looking away, her voice faint. "I haven't had time to think things over."

Katharine could not adequately hide the intensity of what she was feeling; anger, sadness, hope and fear, all whirling together. It was mostly sadness crossing her features.

"Gia and I would like you to come," he insisted.

"I'll be okay, RJ… really."

"I know, Mom. We just want to be sure."

Katharine lifted her hand and stroked his cheek. "My baby boy," she whispered. "Don't worry about me, I'll be fine."

"Will you do something for me, then?"

Katharine smiled and waited.

"Would you?"

"Yes, I would," she whispered."

"Please, Mom, don't hide anything from me, intending to protect me or Mel. I want to take care of you the way Dad would."

Katharine sighed, and then she smiled. She nodded her head as if agreeing.

"Maybe, you can come when Mel's coming, okay? Just for a little while," he said, cautiously.

"I'll think about it," Katharine promised. "No need to worry, okay?"

"Okay, Mom," he said and got up.

Knowing she could use the rest, RJ kissed Katharine gently on the cheek and walked out of her room.

Katharine knew just the thing to do when RJ walked out; read Robert's note, the one he'd given his lawyer to give to her. She grabbed her Bible off the night stand and opened it to I Corinthians 13, just where she had put the letter. She held the letter close to her heart, feeling the emptiness of not having her husband around, and then she sniffed at it to see if she could smell him. Part of her wanted to cry, instead she pried the top of the envelope with her finger, where it was sealed, and ripped it open. And then, she slowly unfolded the page, peering closely at his handwriting. The letters looked precious on the page, this is what it said:

My Darling Kattie,

It is very important for me to express to you how much you really mean to me. I wish I could do this while holding you in my arms and gazing into your eyes. I've always cherished every thought of you, prized every memory of you that rises from the depths of my mind. I've truly loved you in the years that have passed, and I will truly love you always.

I was empty without you Kattie. I told you, it's true, and now I'm telling you while weeping. Thank you for being my wife, and thank you so much for my children. Thank you for all the wonderful things you made happened in my life.

Sorry that I have made it so difficult for you, and it will test your inner strength, as it has for me. I wish I had not put this cloud of sorrow in your heart. I am sorry. I'm truly sorry, Kattie, please forgive me.

This is not goodbye, because even in silence, you will be in my heart. My love be with you, Kattie. I'll always love you.

Robert J.

The last paragraph was the jolt of fortitude that Katharine so desperately needed. She had chosen I Corinthians 13 because her feeling for her husband was the truest essence of that very description, love; always patient and kind, never jealous, never boastful or conceited, never rude or selfish. It does not take offense and is not resentful, takes no pleasure in other people's sins, but delights in the truth. It is always trusting, ready to excuse, to hope, and to endure whatever comes.

Katharine read the note once more. Twice, actually; then she folded it and placed it where she had put it before. Holding the Bible in her hand, she closed her eyes and for a moment, pictured the senator's smile, and his touch, remembering it would be thirty-eight years in three days, when in front of God and everyone else, he had promised his love and devotion, in sickness and in health, for better and for worst. She began to cry. It was then that she set the Bible on the table and got back into bed.

Chapter Forty-eight

EARLY Friday morning, Mellody was sitting at the kitchen table alone drinking steaming hot coffee and eating cornbread when Katharine walked in the kitchen.

"I thought Ma Teete was off today?" Katharine said, knowing Mellody couldn't boil water, much more make cornbread.

"She is," Mellody answered. "If I can deliver a baby out of the mother's body... don't you think I can make coffee?"

Katharine laughed.

"Actually, Gia made breakfast," Mellody said. "Ma Teete gave her the recipe. If I may say so, it tastes like Ma Teete made this cornbread. I cannot tell the difference."

"You know, Gia cooks pretty well," Katharine said. "I love her cooking. Where is she, by the way?"

"Mr. Tom took her shopping."

"What about RJ?"

"He's at Razaq's soccer game... we've all been so busy that nobody realized Saint Patrick's had made it to the semi-finals. Either way, I know you'd not have known."

"You might be right, dear," Katharine said and opened the fridge. She was pouring out a glass of orange juice when Mellody's phone started ringing. "Don't tell me it's the hospital, you just got home."

"It's not the hospital, it's Shakari," Mellody said, smiling.

Mellody left the kitchen and went to her room.

Thirty minutes later, after airing things out with Shakari about her extended stay in Liberia, she returned and found Katharine still in the kitchen, sipping on the same glass of orange juice. Katharine glanced at her as she took a seat on the chair next to her.

"Mom, why are you looking at me like that?" Mellody asked curiously, with a little chuckle.

"I'd rather not say," Katharine mumbled and sighed.

"Why not, you can tell me anything," Mellody said, and then added, "As if you don't always speak your mind. Of course, you do."

At that, Katharine's mind raced for the right words. Because this was her little girl and they had had many girl-talks on the important things so easily, like experiencing her first period. Because she'd read in the Bible that homosexuality was wrong and she was very concerned about Mellody's spiritual relationship with the Lord. She hoped the entire family would get to spend eternal life together. Because she'd seen how harsh people were against gay people and she wanted to protect her children as best as she could. Because Mellody was her baby and she had no reason, ever, not to love her. Because....

"Well," Katharine said finally, "If you would just listen to me, please. This is hard for me to tell you, or anyone else."

That was the thing about life, Mellody knew. There was a time for everything and her coming out time was now. As she grasped this confrontation of her homosexuality with her mother, without the mind games, she realized that it was something Katharine always knew, sort of a silent understanding with herself, as life went on. She'd never made it a big issue, though she knew Mellody was different from other little girls at an early age. Then again, who knows what is normal anyway? Every creature is uniquely formed.

"I'm listening, Mom," Mellody said. "Go ahead, lay it on me."

There was a deep sigh before Katharine began speaking.

"I've always known you were different," Katharine confessed, "Since you were a little girl. You always preferred being around RJ and his friends."

"That's because hanging out with them was much cooler than

hanging out with dumb girls who only cared about what the boys thought anyway."

"And, the boys liked you, you know what I mean."

"I know, Mom. But when the teenage years struck, RJ's friends began to be interested in me; not friend interested, but girlfriend interested."

"What's wrong with that? What about Gary Tolbert? I thought you liked him."

"Yeah," Mellody chuckled. "Gary was smart, handsome, and would do anything for me. But I always thought of him as a best friend. When he asked to go steady with me, I even tried, but there was a startling result."

"What do you mean?"

"While he was looking at me for companionship, I was always looking for something I suppose would never be there."

"I liked Gary," Katharine said, cutting her eyes. "He's the ambassador, you know… to China."

"I know and I'm very proud of him."

"How did you know? You, two, still keep in touch?"

"Yes, as a matter of fact, we do. I talked to him three weeks ago."

"Mel, I wish…."

"No, Mom," Mellody interrupted. "I'm tired of you wishing for something that's not there. You and everybody else… y'all suspected me of being a lesbian because I've never had a boyfriend around. You were in denial and especially your friend, Lynnette Vinton, and her church members; they wanted to know about my sexual orientation and not me."

"I hate that word," Katharine snarled."

"What word, 'lesbian'?"

"That's the word, couldn't you use another word?"

"Gay?"

"I don't know if I like that one either."

Mellody sighed.

"Mom, why couldn't you be like Daddy?"

"What do you mean, dear? You told your father and not me?" Katharine stared in disbelief. "I can't believe it."

"He accepted it, you know, with a little skepticism. I guess because he always thought that everything about me was perfect."

"That's because you are just like him," Katharine mumbled.

Mellody ignored the remarks.

"I told Daddy that I didn't see my sexuality as a curse, and that if he wanted to think everything around my life was still perfect, then he could."

"What did he say?"

"Unlike you, Mom, he had no clue, but he accepted me. He was not just waiting for me to pull the rabbit out of the hat."

Katharine was still doubtful. After rolling her eyes, she asked, "When was this?"

"Right out of medical school, when I finally admitted to myself that I was gay... I mean a lesbian."

Katharine scowled.

"Sorry, I forgot you hate the word. I don't know any other words to use."

"You told Robert and you couldn't tell me?"

"Part of me thought you knew," Mellody said, sensing a touch of jealousy in Katharine's voice. "And, you really didn't want to admit it. Maybe because of your church, I thought. I, not telling you, was easier than hurting you. I knew the right time would come, like now... and hopefully I would be in a better place to make you understand. So, I kept it to myself."

"You didn't exactly hide anything, so to speak. That Chinese doctor...."

"Cho?"

"Yes, Dr. Cho and Shakari, you were not hiding them," Katharine pointed out. "Anyone could tell those women are more than 'friends.'"

"Mom, I am who I am," Mellody chuckled. "And that's enough for me."

"Do you know what the Bible says about being like that?"

"Yes, Mom, I know," Mellody said. "Believe it or not, I read the Bible. In fact, I get Our Daily Bread every month. I've subscribed for years. Remember the woman Jesus told to go and sin no more?"

Katharine nodded.

"Well, did she? We don't know. In the fate of mankind, I believe

God truly exists, but how people are going to be judged when it comes to being admitted to heaven, only God knows."

Katharine looked dumbfounded, to say the least.

"Surprise, Mom?" Mellody chuckled. And then, she put her hand on Katharine's back and began rubbing her back as if consoling her. "I'm not going to tell you that my homosexuality is right, Mom, but I will never tell you that it is wrong."

Katharine said nothing. She didn't have to. Mellody knew Katharine understood that her lifestyle had nothing to do with her. She sat without moving, as if trying to absorb her daughter's existence in the hope of loving her and accepting her, just the way she was.

Chapter Forty-nine

SAINT Patrick's High school soccer team had their big semi-final game and RJ had promised Razaq he would be there cheering. This was the first time RJ would be watching him play and Razaq was eager. His new Adidas would add a little extra spice to the show-down. Razaq was as smooth a midfielder as some college players, even at fifteen.

The game promised to be tense and exciting, the winner was to play B. W. Harris for the championship. Razaq and his teammates took to the pitch for the first half and on the opposing side, Tubman High lined-up their best players. Tubman High Cardinals were yet to put a wrong foot in their quest, winning all eight of their matches and boasting an impressive record of a perfect season. They were gunning a repeat.

The Cardinals had shown something more valuable to their game plan when first half was coming to a close, creating plays out of nothing, but Saint Patrick's would hold them to a scoreless half. Razaq wanted to hear RJ's opinion of his play. He'd tried so hard to score with the new pair of Adidas F30 Dante had sent him, but saw both chances go over the bar. The fast handling and incredible agility of the shoe made it the perfect shoe for the fifteen-year-old. It had given Razaq a dose of confidence too.

"You were a champ out there," RJ told him at half time. "You had a real good game."

Razaq grinned, even though he tried to hold it back. RJ's pep talk sparked a brighter fire of desire for him to score in the second half. He saw his face, heard his voice and had longed for his smile of approval. He gave RJ a thumb's up and then took off to join his team.

Second half was as spectacular as the first. The fulcrum of team Tubman High, sixteen-year-old Malik Snorton, completed an incredible thirty passes, offering a master class in consistency and accuracy in the game. He placed the ball to his teammates making darting and penetrating runs to the left, right and center. Snorton's ball-winning skills had allowed his team an eye on the final. Before the game, he had ensured the coach and his teammates their school name would indeed be engraved on the trophy at the end of the season. At full strength, the Cardinals stars were truly expressing themselves.

However, Saint Patrick's was not without its talents either. Their impenetrable defense proved a hurdle too far for the Cardinals. Besides, Razaq Douglas had the ability to help his team out of tight situations, which he had done time and again over the season. With a moment's inspiration, he would once more.

In the game final moments, the Cardinals pressed and pressed, but Saint Patrick's defense held on. Then Saint Patrick's resorted to their game plan, route one, with a purpose; a long ball to Douglas. Although shouldered off the ball, Razaq struggled mightily in the box and finally got it over to an uncovered teammate, standing alone. The ball was shot beneath the rushing goalkeeper and found its way into the back of the net.

Goooooooaaaaalll! A thunderous wave of applause engulfed Samuel K Doe Stadium as spectators cheered. Saint Patrick's was now leading Tubman High one to zero. The Cheerleaders went into their routine, bouncing, chanting, short skirts, tights, and firm legs. Several people stood, clapping and fans rose to their feet, waving miniature green and white flags.

The Cardinals fought to the final seconds, but Saint Patrick's held on to win. After the final whistle, some Saint Patrick's players celebrated by kissing the ground and some bowed in prayers, while Malik Snorton lie prostrated in grief with some of his teammates.

Soon Saint Patrick's team heaped in a circle at the center of the field, cheering their coach and star players to a game well played. RJ continued to lead the fans in celebration at the sideline. A little later, Razaq expanded his celebration by leaving the team and running to his brother. Soaked with sweat, they hugged.

"That was an awesome game, Razaq," RJ shouted, as he released him. "I am proud of you."

"I wanted to score, but I had to make the pass," Razaq said, beaming with pride.

"You did the right thing champ, you assisted," RJ high-fived him. "You setup the goal! You set it up, buddy."

Razaq was about to return to his teammates when RJ stopped him.

"Wait," he said, pulling a bag from behind his back. "I have something for you."

Razaq looked at the bag, wondering what special thing could be in a wrinkled paper bag.

"You keep working hard on your game," RJ said and handed him the bag.

Razaq quickly reached into the bag and pulled out the shirt, a Barcelona 2010-2011 home jersey. He immediately recognized the classic red and blue Barcelona colors that ensure the team's iconic place in soccer, being one of the biggest clubs in the world. He held it to his chest for a second or so and then turned the back of the jersey toward him, trying to guess whose name was on the back. With widen eyes he read aloud the name, RICCIOLA, handsomely printed above number seven.

"For me," Razaq sighed and offered a big smile. "Thank you, RJ," he screamed, and then hugged him with the warmest hug.

"It's all yours little brother," RJ said, struck by the feeling there was a real connection between them.

Razaq quickly took off his sweaty jersey. He pulled the new Barcelona home jersey over his head, tugging it here and there, until it was properly in place. Then, he turned to face his teammates.

"Coach! Coach, look what I got!" he shouted.

Coach Payne noticed the jersey and covered his mouth, being instantly hysterical. He and the rest of the players, from both teams, ran to Razaq. Their faces were dripping with both admiration and envy. Razaq paused so they, and he, could enjoy the moment. A thought came to mind, and RJ snapped a picture with his cell phone. Coach Payne applauded, and so did everyone else standing around. Razaq hugged his brother again.

Chapter Fifty

RJ dropped Razaq home and drove aimlessly for a while, before heading to Moses Zarway's house to find Grace. As he drove, he kept veering from remorse to acceptance and back to remorse. He found himself reliving the night he took her home after their hang-out at Sugar Shack, which only made it worst. Why had he really slept with her? Why could he not stop thinking about that night? He said a short prayer, one of pity and forgiveness, and said to himself, *don't let it ever happen again.*

RJ got to the house and Uncle Moses told him Grace was not at home, he had not seen her all day. On a hunch, he went to Yassah's place, but not until he'd driven by a couple of times before it finally registered to him where exactly it was. It was late the night he'd dropped her off after the Sugar Shack hangout.

Grace was sitting on the front porch, alone, with her face downcast and it was only when he got close that he realized she was crying. He didn't quite know what to do. Before he could decide what to do, Grace saw him and hurriedly swiped at her swollen eyes.

"Are you okay?" RJ asked when he reached her.

"No," she answered.

His heart clenched.

"Do you want to be alone?"

Grace considered it for a brief moment.

"I don't know," she said at last.

RJ stood where he was, not sure what to do. He slipped his hand in his pockets. "Would you rather be alone?" he asked again.

"You can stay," she said, and gave a downhearted laugh.

He could hear the sorrow in it. He took a seat.

For a while, they sat without saying anything. Grace inhaled slowly, and her breathing became steadier. She swiped at the tears that continued to slide down her cheeks.

"I brought you something," he mumbled.

Grace tried to rally with a shaky grin but didn't quite succeed. "You came to say good-bye," she said, gently turning her face to RJ. When he tried to meet her eyes, she turned away.

"This is from Gia and me," RJ said. "It's just a thank you card. We appreciate your help."

"I was only doing my job," Grace said, eyes downcast. "I just wanted to be able to make a difference."

"You did," he said and handed her the envelope.

Grace took the card, hesitantly, then turned away and swiped at a tear.

"Thanks," she said, her voice was almost inaudible.

"Do you mind if I sit?" RJ asked.

She nodded 'sit' and forced a smile.

RJ sat on the edge of the chair, leaning forward with his right palm resting on his knees.

"I want to talk to you about law school," he said.

Grace looked up, almost instantly.

"Gia and I would like to help out, if you let us. And just so you know, it was her idea," he went on.

Her gaze was steady now, digesting the offer. RJ rose, and she knew their conversation was nearing the end. Her heart melted, but she suddenly found her voice.

"I don't know what to say," she said. "Nobody has ever done something like this for me before."

"Well, you deserve it. You deserve the best there is... and I mean it. I know you will make a good lawyer. Anyway, our contact information is in the envelope... e-mail addresses, phone numbers... let us know when the tuition is due. Whatever you need, please...

don't hesitate. We'll make sure you get it… it's a full scholarship we're offering."

Grace looked dumbfounded.

"Thank you," she said, and then added, "Tell Gia that I say thanks. I appreciate this…you know that," she sniffled.

"I know," he said, feeling her heartbreaking gratitude. This was the least he could have done for her.

"So, you're leaving for the States on Sunday?"

"Yes," he said. "And, I'll be back to work in a week."

"What time is your flight?"

"Early in the evening," he said. "We'll probably be at the airport by four-thirty."

Grace rose from her chair.

"Good-bye RJ," she said, extending her hand. "In Liberian English, we say, 'go good.'"

RJ stared at her, froze for a moment. And then, without giving it any thought, he pulled her into an embrace.

"Take care of yourself, sweetie," he whispered, squeezing tightly. Then he released her and walked away, not looking back.

RJ walked to the car knowing he'd been right about his feelings for her. Taking the long way home, after a couple of hours, he tried forcing the feelings away.

The rest of the afternoon was spent on the porch, in the hammock, absorbing the nightmare the family had been through.

Chapter Fifty-one

DOWNTOWN Monrovia had the typical tourist venues—souvenir stores and tailor shops, packed with colored tie-dyed and embroidered cloth, which they made up immediately into African or European styles. There were a couple of places specializing in Liberian handicrafts; carvings in sapwood, camwood, ebony and mahogany, stone items, soapstone carvings, ritual masks, metal figurines and reed dolls. There were a few upscale restaurants, internet cafes, jeweler shops, and elegant boutiques and drugstores. The one thing missing was a coffee shop, a place for drifting poets and folksingers. But the streets were busy; people scurried by, some with money to buy wonderful things and others, cursing at hardship for derailing their lives.

Gia was impressed with the old-fashioned mom and pop groceries stores which competed with the modern air-conditioned supermarkets. She wore a satisfied expression as she stepped inside them, taking to the place. One reminded her of a tienda (Spanish for shop) in Mexico, near her grandmother's village. There were no shopping carts or baskets. And, there were no aisles, as all the goods were stocked behind the counter.

Throughout the afternoon she'd shopped for things for her parents, Paola and a few paintings for Dante to add to his collection of African Arts. She'd heard about an artist sculpting art from bullet casings and wanted to buy a few pieces. It was there they met, after she'd purchased the pieces she liked; a map of Africa, a palm tree and one with a woman carrying her baby on her back.

Gia recognized his potbelly and the receding hairline at the sides of his forehead. Only the sides and back of his head had hair, leaving a horseshoe shape. She hoped he did not recognize her. He, however, did. News and rumors are like mosquitoes in Monrovia, Ma Teete had expressed often enough, to know that he had been told who she was.

"Excuse me, Madam," Judge Tweh said politely. "I've been told that you are the senator's daughter-in-law. I'm sorry about your family loss."

Gia could not bring herself to say "Thank you" to him, it simply was stuck in her throat. She knew how much he adored Dante and was tempted to shout at him, I am Dante Ricciola's sister and I could even bring him to your house! She couldn't either. All she did was give the judge the most uncomfortable stare.

"In spite of the situation, I wish you have a pleasant stay in Liberia," Judge Tweh said, trying his best to make their encounter as normal as possible.

Gia managed to mumble a weak "Thank you" as her stomach tightened.

"I was wondering…." He said and stopped.

"Yes," she fumed, but held her fire. She bit her lip and waited for him to finish.

"I would like to buy you lunch," Judge Tweh offered, politely.

No way, she thought, he had the audacity.

"Thanks, but I'm meeting my husband later for lunch," Gia lied, offering a phony laugh.

She'd referred to RJ as her husband, she mused to herself.

"Maybe next time," Judge Tweh said, struggling with what he really wanted to say. Then, he did. "You are Dante Ricciola's sister, I've been told," he said, visibly delighted.

"Yes," Gia said, welcoming the opportunity to break his heart.

Such pleasant discovery made Judge Tweh smile. This was the closest he'd come to meeting Dante Ricciola. Gia, however, was not smiling. She wanted him to feel how painful a broken heart can be.

"Dante Ricciola is…."

"If you will excuse me, Sir," Gia deliberately cut him off. "I have to finish here so I can meet my husband."

She'd said husband again, and was suddenly filled with pride.

Judge Tweh cocked his head to one side as if he'd been misunderstood. His face turned into a smirk. The smirk said; I, Judge Tweh, am your brother's biggest fan.

"I've never missed a single game that Dante has played in," he managed to grunt.

And, Gia shot him a look that said, who cares!

Judge Tweh struggled for a short, painful pause, and then said slowly, "It's my pleasure meeting you, Mrs. Douglas… good-bye, Madam."

As Gia walked away, one step in front of Mr. Tom, she took a deep breath and told herself not to stop until they reach the SUV. There were quick glances and awkward stares, but she didn't stop until she got to the car.

"Please, Mr. Tom, we can go home now… I suddenly don't feel so well."

They drove quietly to the house, passing the few places Gia remembered. She pointed out City Hall, LU campus, JFK and Sinkor Circle. Mr. Tom was proud of her, that she'd remember those places in such a short time.

When Mr. Tom pulled into the driveway, RJ walked off the porch and was there to meet the SUV. Gia got out, walked toward him and slipped her arms around his neck.

"How did it go with Grace?" she asked, wearing a curious expression.

"She said, 'thanks,'" RJ said. "And, thank you for being who you are."

Gia wrinkled her brow, and he kissed her forehead.

Chapter Fifty-two

MA Teete had prepared the last supper with a beautiful spread--white cotton cloth, white napkins, colorful flowers in a vase, a large pitcher of iced tea, and at least six covered dishes. It seemed there was enough food for an army. RJ sat across from Katharine, where the senator usually sat. Gia and Ma Teete sat on one side while Mellody and Razaq sat on the other side. Katharine took Razaq's hand and the rest followed, joining their hands around the table. Every head was soon lowered and Katharine began to pray.

It was a lengthy prayer, as she thanked the Lord for everything, including her husband's death. Gia peeked at Katharine as she was talking to her Lord, her face was perfectly content. After about ten minutes, she finally ended her prayer with a flourish, a long burst in which she appealed for the forgiveness of her sins and everybody else's. After everybody said 'Amen', she released the hands she was holding.

Ma Teete politely asked those sitting with the main dishes before them, to remove the lids from the bowls. One bowl contained a pile of lamb chops smothered in a sauce that included, among many ingredients, onions and peppers. In another, there was a mound of jollof rice still hot from the stove. There was okra sauce in one bowl, which she explained as she had prepared it with cholesterol-free palm oil because Mellody had preached to her, long enough, about certain types of oil in her diet. There was a platter of rice bread and another large pan, still covered, in the center of the table. Ma Teete pulled the napkin off, revealing at least three pounds of hot sweet cornbread. She removed a huge wedge right away and placed it in the center of RJ's plate. "I made this just for you," she said, with the biggest smile ever.

"Thank you, Ma Teete," RJ smiled, "I'll sure miss this."

"I've taught Gia to make it," Ma Teete said, "because I know how much you like it. I've never met a white woman who makes Liberian cornbread better than the Liberian women," she joked.

Everybody laughed and the feast began.

"Ma Teete, this looks delicious," Gia said as she speared a piece of lamb with her fork.

Gia always took a little more than she would finish because RJ had fallen into the habit of honing in on her plate after cleaning his.

"You going to eat that?" he asked, soon after wiping his plate clean.

Ma Teete offered him more food because she liked the idea that Gia had piled her plate and that RJ didn't have to bother hers.

"No Mama Teete, it's okay" Gia said. "He loves to eat off my plate, so I always put a little more than I can finish."

Gia swapped plates with RJ and got a clean plate for her dessert. After a few minutes, he'd cleaned the second one too.

"Someone will have a lot of calories to burn off," Gia teased.

Katharine looked at RJ and everybody laughed.

It hit him. He retired his fork for a moment, sipped some water and gazed at Gia. Yes, indeed, it was true.

"A little dessert wouldn't hurt, though," she winked. "After all, I don't know how soon we'll be eating Mama Teete's cooking again."

Ma Teete looked dumbfounded, to say the least.

"Guess who I met today?" Gia said, her eyes shining with mischief.

"Actually, who do you know in Liberia?" Mellody asked instead.

"Who was it, honey," RJ asked.

Everyone was eager to know.

"Judge Tweh," Gia announced.

Everyone froze.

"Oh?" RJ asked. "Did he know who you were?"

"Well, yes," Gia said and went into the entire account of their meeting. When she finished everyone was roaring with laughter.

Nearly two hours later, after most of the food had been eaten and their last supper was winding down, Ma Teete, fixing her eyes on RJ and Gia, asked for everyone's attention. Then she spoke of love and commitment, of patience and honesty, and of the importance of keeping God in their lives. She told them that life wouldn't always be easy, but that if they kept their faith in God and each other, they would always find a way to overcome anything. It was as if she was speaking at a wedding. She spoke with her usual eloquence, and like a teacher who had long ago earned the respect of her students, wished them a happy life in America.

"Thank you, Mama Teete," Gia said, her voice soft. "I'll never forget how well you've treated me."

"You're my white daughter, yah," Ma Teete said, accepting Gia's compliment.

"I like that," Gia said, looking at RJ. "I really do."

He smiled and winked.

Suddenly Gia's phone rang.

"Hello," she answered, looking at Razaq and smiling, aware of the caller. "It's for you, Razaq," she said and handed him her phone.

"Hello," Razaq said, surprised.

"Hello, champ," the voice on the other end, said. "This is Dante."

Razaq bolted out of his chair. His mouth fell open, as wide as anyone had ever seen it. He was surprised, and then he was not. Surprised to hear Dante's voice and had trouble picturing him talking to a soccer super star.

"Dante Ricciola," Razaq whispered; his eyes wide and harsh. Then he listened. Then he repeated, "Dante Ricciola." More listening, then, at full volume, he forced the words out, "I nearly score today… just like you." Then, pause. "Yes, Dante, I like it." Pause. "I think it was the reason that I nearly scored." Pause. "Okay." Pause. "Yes." Pause. "Thank you." Pause. "Here she is," Razaq said and handed the phone back to Gia. He took a deep breath and sat back down.

"So, what did he say?" Mellody asked.

"Uhm…. he said that he heard I am a good player," Razaq said, almost boasting.

"Aren't you glad I didn't tell him that George Weah is your favorite player and not him?" RJ teased.

Razaq gave RJ a look that said, YOU BETTER NOT.

After dinner, RJ and Razaq cleaned up while the women chatted in the living room. Mr. Tom drove Ma Teete home and kept the car overnight because RJ seemed too worn out to drive him home.

Razaq went to bed soon after. Katharine, Mellody, RJ and Gia remained in the living room and they talked until nearly midnight, but Gia was now quieter than usual. She wandered to the bedroom and when she didn't return, RJ went to find her. She was sitting on the bed.

"You okay, honey?" he asked.

She drew in a long breath. "Yeah," she said, exhaling.

"Why don't you get ready for bed, you look tired."

She nodded as if she had considered it. RJ went back to the living room to say good-night to Katharine and Mellody. When he got back, Gia had already taken a shower and was under the covers. He took a quick shower, went to the other side of the bed and crawled in beside her. She shuffled the covers before turning out the light, and then lay on her back, staring toward the ceiling.

RJ turned on his side facing her. "Good night, honey," he whispered.

"Good night."

He couldn't sleep, not for a while, anyway. But he didn't want to toss and turn, in case she could.

Then Gia whispered, "Hey."

"Yes?"

She rolled over to face him.

"You know, I expected you to pick up the phone when I called, especially after midnight," she said unexpectedly.

His head bobbed up, his eyes lifted, as he looked at her. An apologetic, almost sad expression formed on his face. Then, after an extended guilty pause, he looked away, pondering as to when had she called and he not picked up. It was the night when he had gone to Sugar Shack with Grace, he remembered. Then, he looked back at her.

"And, why didn't you? You didn't think I would have noticed?" Her eyes were pinned on him.

RJ felt his heart in his throat.

"It must have been the day I worked late with Diallo…at his office," he lied, right to her face.

One mistake in judgment and now his life could be wrecked. Guilt rattled through him. And fear. For weeks, he'd tortured himself, imagining life without his Gia, a rare species indeed. Night after night, he'd envisioned himself wallowing in pain that only a spouse who realizes they've been caught cheating feels, pathetic. This is what happens when you cheat, a voice whispered in his ear.

For a moment, he felt the huge weight of guilt and the idea of owning up hover over him like a waiting avalanche. All he needed to do was ask Gia to listen and spill his guts. Yes, I cheated on you. Yes, I made love to another woman, and now we—yes, we—have to deal with the terrible consequences of what I've done. Tell her everything; commence the end of his life, as he knew it.

But he just couldn't make the words come out. 'Oh God,' he thought, 'I wish I could take that entire night back, every second of it.'

Gia brushed his arm. "I'm just glad this nightmare is over," she whispered, her voice soft, her thumb moving slowly over his skin.

"Me too, honey," RJ said, and wrapped his arm around her.

RJ felt terrible that he had held back the truth from her. They had always shared everything, good and bad. He also felt the overwhelming need to pray, to talk to God. God would still hear him, even in his partial belief in Him. He was sure that he wasn't agnostic and he would be eternally grateful if God could get him out of this.

He began to gently stroke her hair, which he habitually did when he needed her to listen. Every time he moved, every twitch of his finger, reminded Gia how much he needed her, how he had since the first time they heard about the senator's arrest. He had gone through an overwhelming amount of grief dealing with his father's trial, painful execution and now, the need to clear his name.

They lay quietly for hours before falling asleep in each other's arms.

Chapter Fifty-three

THE unseasonable sun began its rise from the Atlantic on Sunday morning, what would be a glaringly sunny day. RJ sat up on the bed while Gia stayed sleeping. Her half-Italian, half-Mexican genes were proving quite conducive to tanning in Liberia, she was several shades darker. But her face was lit with the glow of dawn, as her hair fanned out over the pillow. She had one arm across her chest and another above her head. All RJ could think was how lucky he'd be to spend every morning for the rest of his life waking up beside her.

Ma Teete was off, as she had already bid them godspeed with the festive Liberian spread the night before. Katharine made breakfast, something she had not done in a while. They were out of coffee so she made iced tea, which was unsweetened, with big chunks of lemon in it. It was actually delicious. She put Razaq's favorite cereal, Honey Nut Cheerios, on the table, with some fruits. Then she made scrambled eggs; overdoing it a little. Razaq sat quiet and reserved, barely lifting his spoon.

"You okay, honey?" Katharine asked him.

"Yes, Mom," Razaq mumbled.

"Are you positive you're okay?"

"Yes… but I was just thinking."

"I know," Katharine said, "I'm going to miss him too."

Then a voice cut in, "What are you up to, Razaq?"

Razaq turned and saw RJ standing in the doorway, hands balled into two fists, ready for battle or whatever. He crackled. RJ liked the sound of it so much that he crackled also, lowering his hands.

"I wish you weren't leaving, RJ," Razaq said, a sad smile crossing his face. "I wish you would stay." His eyes never left RJ's eyes as he finally said what he was burdened with, "What's going to happen when the soldiers come again?"

His concern was dramatic enough to give anyone goosebumps. RJ looked at Katharine, and then at Razaq. He sat down. He had a thought, here we go again, Gia would be perfect for this. But something inside told him not even the greatest Psychologist would make a frightened boy understand how quickly he'd have to face his fears. It was his big brother's job.

"Razaq, I want you to listen to me, okay?"

"Uh huh," Razaq said, shaking his head.

"You are an American, Mom is an American, no one, I mean no one, can just come in here and arrest you and haul you to jail. Do you understand?"

Razaq looked at Katharine, then back at RJ.

"I want you to believe that, because that's what it is," RJ insisted. "Right, Mom?"

"It's the truth Razaq," Katharine said. "What happened to Daddy isn't going to happen to us. I've already told you that."

"You don't have to be afraid, Razaq," RJ said. "You have my numbers, you have Mel's numbers, and you have Gia's numbers. And, I know you can take care of Mom," he said, staring at Razaq's eyes, "I just know it."

Razaq listened until RJ was finished, then the conversation slowly drifted to him and how well he was going to deal with it all.

He looked up and asked, "You sure I can take care of Mom?"

"How about we take care of each other," Katharine said, "just the way we always have."

Just then, Gia tapped lightly on the door and poked her head in first.

"Come in, dear" Katharine said. "Have some breakfast, if you can call it that. Sorry, we're out of coffee."

"That's okay, Mom, I'll just have some orange juice."

"We're out of that too," Katharine said.

"What are you drinking? I'll have some of that."

"Iced tea, scrambled eggs…."

"Iced tea will do, Mom, thank you," Gia said and sat down.

Katharine poured a glass full and handed it to Gia.

Gia took a sip of her iced tea, put the glass down and reached across the table to take Razaq's hand. "Do you remember the story about David… in the Bible?"

"Uh huh," Razaq answered.

"He must have been about your age, maybe a little older… or younger, but when he killed the giant, he was young like you. And every time he was afraid, or was faced with something he couldn't do, he wrote a song or a poem."

She got up, walked over to Razaq's chair and put her arm around his shoulder.

"I know this is hard for you, honey," she murmured, "but there's something you can do."

Razaq's eyes brimmed over. "Really?" he asked.

Gia smiled. "Really," she said. "Every time you're afraid, get your Bible and read Psalms. That's where all of David's poems and songs are. Or, you can write your own, as if you're writing little notes to God."

Razaq thought about her idea for a moment. "I will do that," he said, a little twinkle in his eyes. "I can do that."

Gia looked at Katharine. Her face had lit up. Razaq suddenly regained his appetite and ravaged his Cheerios.

After breakfast, Gia finished up the packing.

Later she and RJ shared a bowl of soup before he and Mr. Tom loaded the suitcases and bags in the car. Mellody was still at the hospital and Razaq went to soccer practice, before the final game. Just Katharine would go with Mr. Tom while he drove them to the airport.

The airport was packed with travelers, most of them standing because the small number of chairs available had long since been taken. There seemed to be hundreds of people waiting for the Delta flight to Ghana, then to the States. It was Sunday, the only day of the week for Delta flights. As they bumped and got pushed toward the gate, many wondered when Delta would add more flight days, though that idea was irrelevant at the moment.

RJ, Gia and Katharine walked into the terminal, and when they saw the crowd, stopped along the edge of the line and began their wait. The crying was over, at least for RJ and Gia.

Katharine clutched RJ's hand and tried to be strong. "I'll miss you, RJ," she whispered. "I love you."

"I love you too, Mom," he said and hugged her. "Stay strong, okay?" he added, pulling back. "I want to hear from you every day… email me; I've shown you how."

She nodded.

Then Katharine and Gia got entwined in a tender embrace.

"I love you, dear," Katharine said, fighting back tears. "Thanks for being so wonderful… if it is God's will, next Christmas will be better. And, y'all need to set a date," she added.

Gia smiled. "We will, Mom," she said. "And, I'm looking forward to next Christmas." She kissed Katharine's cheek and released her.

The first announcement was made, asking those who needed extra time and those in first-class to come forward. Pushing and shoving rose to another level. The three hugged again, Katharine fought back tears.

"Call me as soon as you get in Atlanta," Katharine said.

"We will," RJ and Gia answered.

Then, Gia and RJ joined a long line that quietly inched away. As RJ handed over his boarding pass, he turned, caught Katharine's stare and waved.

"She'll be fine, honey," Gia whispered.

Afterward, RJ and Gia disappeared into the plane. Katharine turned and fell in with the foot traffic out of the building. Mr. Tom was right at the door to meet her.

On the plane, Gia sat holding her phone in one hand and RJ's hand with the other. She waited until they had lifted off from the runway and then she turned her phone on. She had missed two calls in the noisy house as they were packing up and making sure everything was loaded in the car. Mellody had left a message and Dante had also left a message. She dialed her phone to retrieve them.

"Gia, relax, don't worry. The tests came back, and everything is okay. You're perfectly fine," Mellody said. "In fact, you're better than that. I hope you're sitting down. You're not sick, you're… pregnant."

Beyond the window, Gia blinked through her tears, as if trying to figure out how to break the news to RJ. She could see a layer of clouds spread beneath the plane, but had no idea where they were. She turned to him. Feeling her stare, RJ turned, met her eyes and smiled.

"You heard Mom," Gia whispered. "We need to set a date."

RJ took her hand.

"Soon, I hope," he said, softly, "I can hardly wait."

About the Author

Photo by Portia Langley

OPHELIA S. Lewis is a poet, essayist, and creative writer. Heart Men is her first novel, and seventh book. She is the author of My Dear Liberia, which retells the enjoyable days in Liberia before the civil war. Her work appears in Diamonds & Pearls, a collection of poems published by the National Library of Poetry.

Especially interested in women and children's services, Lewis wrote two children's books in 2009; A is for Africa, a book where beginning readers learn about things in an African village as each letter is featured in a word on its own page with a photograph and The Good Manners Alphabet Book, which teaches young children good manners using the alphabets.

Follow Ophelia Lewis on
twitter: @ophie2020
website: www.ophelialewis.com
facebook: facebook.com/ophelia.lewis

Read All The Heart Men Books

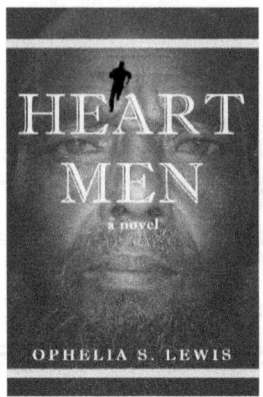

Heart Men (a novel)
Paperback / 244 Pages / 2011
ISBN 13: 9780975360965
eBook ISBN: 9780975360996

Dead Gods (HM2)
Paperback / 396 Pages / 2014
ISBN 13: 9780978362522
eBook ISBN: 9780978362539

Readers Reviews

"I am REALLY ENJOYING Heart Men..."—*Richelle Howell*

"Overall, HEART MEN is an INTERESTING read...I ENJOYED RJ's PASSION for life, his LOVE for his family, and his tenacious search for the TRUTH...I certainly enjoyed his story. It held my interest from beginning to end."—Damali Griffin (Imani Literary Group Book Club Member)

"This is a story that has NEVER BEEN TOLD...I was pleasantly surprised to find out it is a LOVE STORY more than anything..."—Manseen Logan (Bella Beau Marketing & Publicity)

"I just finished reading HEART MEN here in Ghana on my Kindle...I LIKED IT A LOT...It seems that there are so many TABOO SUBJECTS in a society, and this is one not just in Liberia but everywhere...—Tim Nevin

Read on for an excerpt from Dead Gods (HM2)
By Ophelia S. Lewis

Print and eBook
Available from Amazon.com and other retail outlets
Available on Kindle and other devices

1
❧⟋❧

THE world connects at lightning speed, but things were still as if it was 1986 in Liberia. After 15 years of civil war and six years of an elected presidency, progress was painfully slow. Although the cellular phone was booming and substantially more widespread than fixed line telephonic transmission, technology was otherwise, creeping out of the Stone Age in Monrovia—a city police department without computers on every detective's desk, and a wish list of working fax machines and photocopiers needed for critical documents. Forget quick access to DNA technology. Some would admit fingerprint was still being matched by human eye. All this is hard to gasp in today's CSI effect, but it is what it is.

His pay is not the biggest pay, his job is not the easiest, but Officer Lonos is a man who would rather die for his principals than live without one. He accepted the occupation as an officer knowing the responsibilities and hazards involved. As far as he was concerned, hell was not large enough for heart-men. Based on the most recent crime scene, it was evident the heart-men had struck again.

Behavior science never changes, so criminal profiling is still a quick thinker's investigative tool. For the detective in such environment, criminal profiling is always brought to the forefront of law enforcement. For one thing, such crime involves co-conspirators who could keep secrets. Secondly, logistics, the means of transportation. Getting from point A to point B increases having to be neat and discreet. Then, lodging the victim. They had to put their victim where extraction is done without drawing attention. Disposal was the final and easier step, Liberia's shorelines, the beaches.

As far as Lonos was concerned, Aaron Dolo had only done enough for his conscience to feel as if he had done something. The police chief had not done nearly enough because CeRue Manor, the mastermind behind most of the mishap in Monrovia, was still a loose thread.

It was no wonder that some consider victims of the heart-man unlucky. Murdering for human parts is a peculiar wicked deed, but a heart-man does his job and not cares about his soul. Keep in mind: heart-men are serial killers. Everyone takes part in a crime and everyone knows it's a crime except for the mastermind. As immoral as it is, CeRue Manor saw it as a business and made sure to keep it that way, buying and selling human parts as commodities. Lonos had yet to prove it.

The Good Book teaches: 'For the love of money is a root of all kinds of evils'. It is through this craving that some wander away from their conscience and does not experience anything close to a sharp pang of guilt. They push God completely out of their life, and set their hope on the uncertainty of riches. These kinds of people always want more because greed strengthens their hands. Lonos saw Manor as someone insatiable.

CeRue Manor had the sixth sense to foresee the rich future. Now that Liberia was about to dip her foot in oil, he vowed to play a key role in it too. He was doing well, more than well. His wheeling and dealing concealed some of the biggest unlicensed business operations in Africa that made millions—the smuggling of diamonds, underage girls, and human organs. Since kickbacks and corruption turn a blind eye to regulations, smuggling paid exuberantly well, along with illegitimate private clubs.

If there was a place where people could meet with reasonable confidence that their deeds would not be exposed even in their world of ultra sophisticated matters of illegal, or even murderous, it was Manor's exclusive club, Le'Toit, (English translation-The Rooftop), a facility not for public. No one set foot in some areas and it was Manor who prescribed limits for his establishment. Even his trusted acquaintances went so far, and not further. Le'Toit was surrounded by hidden security cameras, and only Manor knew their locations.

'A fool's paradise', that's what Lynnette Vinton, aka Salvation Lady, calls the club, but services were premium all the way. "Satan is in the walls of that place," she often said.

Activities at Le'Toit was not limited to just a place where rich men met and drank, organized prostitution soared. Underage girls, barely teenage, were shipped in from neighboring counties to entertain these men. They had not come on their own, most being kidnapped. His assistant, an Ivorian native, handled all Manor's commodities, directing the routes of his precious freights—girls, human organs, drugs, diamonds, and weapons.

Inside the naughty housing of Le'Toit, amid the drinking, gambling and businessmen chatting their wheeling and dealing, the winding hall led to a place where a darker side of Manor's financial bloom lies, the top floor. Young girls are kept here to satisfy the men's lusts. The girls are forced to have sex with men for long hours, and are denied contact with anyone, family or others. Some were put into an international placement agency for mail-order brides. Human trafficking by unregulated placement agencies for maids, rather than prostitutes, was also a part of Manor's business. Demand for maids was increasing because in America and Europe, people would pay far less for what they would normally pay legal agencies for people to cook, clean, and look after their children.

Manor did not employ stupid people either, and his employees were compensated very well. Over half of his staff were imported into Liberia and they all had one thing in common; convicted criminal. He made sure all his well qualified employees had salaries bumped way higher than their counterparts, paying them far more than they'd earned any place else. His medical team was structured with an Asian doctor, an Indian surgeon, a Jamaican bartender, and a head waitress named Peaches.

Peaches had worked Las Vegas five years before coming to work for Manor. Wild as hell, she had spent more time in the backseat of cars than she did in the classroom, could drink any man under the table, and always had a purse full of pills. Other than her legal documents, passport or driver license, Peaches didn't need a last name.

Cheah Boatswain, a Monrovia city police officer, ran Manor's personal security force. Once a war lord, Boatswain was one of those who tried to make a holocaust out of Liberia all at once, fueling the senseless civil war with acts of violence beyond wordy description. Most remembered the mad killer, a short man with a shaven head and bushy beard. Though Boatswain had grown his hair and shaved his beard, people remembered him.

A civil war had been ignited because a few Liberian men turned war lords, set their minds on reversing peaceful living to war time so they could take ownership of things they did not want to work for. To rule you must serve, but their mixed-up instincts, and sneaking urge to power, permitted them to rule and get fancy cars and big houses they did not pay for. They turned from being family guards to become gun smugglers' customers who turned them into dogs. They sold drugs along with the country resources, like timbers and diamonds. They put guns and drugs into the hands of their sons and taught them to be rapists and murderers. The assaults on women were inconceivable, as if these men had never clinched to breasts that nourished them.

Today, lawless killings were in the past. But like every place in the world, crime still soared in Liberia.